ON HIGH AT RED TIDE

A NOVEL

GABRIEL HART

PIG ROAST PUBLISHING

Pig Roast Publishing
PO Box 41214
Providence, RI 02940
pigroastpublishing@gmail.com
www.pigroastpublishing.com

FIRST EDITION

Cover art by Corinne Halbert

ISBN 979-8-9891470-3-8

grow, out of control: a "harmful algal bloom." Only in this hell to where I return could growth be high risk to all who surround its blossoming. Since this red tide answers only to the moon, I'm propelled to the edge of the world—the coast, a seaside town where desperate acts occurred. To put on a show, repetitive, on a loop, conducted by violence of each new wave. Where before, I saw myself insignificant, a destructive curse, just for existing. Now, reflected back through their eyes, I can finally see myself. Once as the glow of fireflies, darting evasively, chased by those vowing to capture me, and when caught, my light died.

But tonight, I am Luciferin: bringer of light to Mother Ocean of submerged and clandestine decay. With every crash of every wave, I discharge nocturnal emission of deep blue flash in the curl when the circle completes to white foam. The only way I can communicate from beyond my early grave, refracted in their oculars, above their sighs of surprise. The young and dumb, on the shore like sitting ducks, though I'm no longer here to harm; rather, to dazzle, the eroding last-ditch effort to atone for my oversight. My blue flashing: I'm still watching you. I only wanted to make you sigh, groan ecstatic, and smile. Right now, I'm nearly satisfied, the way you can't believe your eyes. Her gaze so persistent, so vast that I'm trapped. Imprisoned; in the name of liberation, I am stealing her vision, reversing the susceptible into vacant haunted vessels enabling the dead to return to zero. Paralyzed in hindsight. The curve of the earth behind me, the rotating film reel in which we're confined to every frame, you can't see it moving until you start running away. To all those with a death grip on disbelief, long after the show has concluded, who claim phytoplankton is not a sentient being, please consider, compare, and contrast: when I was a person living, up until my final moment, I was never thinking.

Ceasing to exist without our memory, I kept a third eye: the camera's perversity. Opting to capture what's already on display, where with your own God-given eyes, you can look, admire, and move on to the next vision of beauty. The image already burned into your mind; all the work done by the divine.

Yet it's insufficient for a beautiful beach town to be left alone. Its likeness must be stolen, then sold back to its admirers reduced to two-dimensions, minus the energy. Postcards, the town's most lucrative export after enduring the threat of methamphetamine. Our life could not be still, when our eyelids defied the sunsets, remaining wide enough to swallow all shadow.

There on the cliff, I see shutterbugs compete for the vantage, opening their tripods faster than the next benign shooter, arguing who owns the better angle with sharper equipment, who will get away faster to print the facsimile. The facsimile of the subject who did not ask to be photographed, the living things who did not give their consent.

You may have captured the coast; the crowded Blackout Beach boardwalk, the deep blue whale mural sensationally mimicking what is living only a block away, the lifeguard tower whose tanned and chivalrous saviors turn their oiled backs to children drowning in the streets behind them. You cannot zoom in on every life that gives that photograph a soul you assume you're stealing. And you think you are being sneaky, expedient, and crafty, but those who are floating away have a perfect view of what you are doing.

ONE

The Vigil

1

There is Mikey, walking down PCH as the ocean ingests the sun, the horizon blasting a tapestry of pink and fire-orange solar/aquatic psychedelia. It's easy to take the glaring beauty of your town for granted when you think the cops are after you for something you haven't even done yet.

Nervously, he keeps pulling his Wolverine t-shirt over his exposed rotund belly, uneasy about the older kids taking over his garage. Like a Janus scale of injustice, those two just showed up stumbling drunk, carrying: one sack of St. Ides 40s which they have since pissed out all over his invasive weed-riddled garden; another bag full of change they stole from the soda machine at Hotel Laguna. Heavy and cumbersome, it held more money than he'd ever seen. Forty-six dollars and eighty-five cents, they told him.

They just invaded; one in a flannel has a black eye and a puffy scabbing lip, the other sweating profusely in a leather jacket, saying: we heard it's cool to drink here and if it's not we're doing it anyway. But as Mikey marches down PCH propelled with purpose from their urgent command, he doesn't exactly want them to leave. They're older by a two-year eternity; punk rockers, so he nearly feels honored. Even after their ridicule, when he told them to shut up or they'd wake his drunk mom; they just kept laughing, telling him: go pimp us more 40s. He was all *I don't think I know how* and they were all *you don't think, you just fucking do it.*

Approaching the Circle K, its night lights ignite, illuminating two girls loitering, one root-exposed bleached blonde in striped sweater and overalls, the other blue-black mohawk in a ghostly white slip (designating her black ones for bad days, the mean times). He sees they're whispering, pointing inside, then to the parking lot; toe-tapping tense, planning something.

When they see him, they freeze, then s'up him with their chins.

"I'm about to pimp beer—you two wanna go in on it with me? I got all this money," he says, flexing the change bag, bulging. "My place is cool to drink."

For a second they're suspicious of his benevolence, but he's even more unkempt than them and too young to be a narc.

"Jasmine has a fake ID but she's too afraid to use it. Oh, and hi, I'm Katrina," the blonde says, curtsying. "I'm trying to convince her how easy it'll be since she's wearing so much foundation and eyeliner. She looks, like, way older than she is."

"Let me see the ID?"

Jasmine hands it to Mikey. It looks nothing like her beyond the heavy make-up on the woman's photo who's at least fifty pounds heavier in the face.

"You got more of that make-up you're wearing?"

Jasmine nods dutifully.

"Sorry, she doesn't really talk," says Katrina. "She's shy of her teeth. But she like, lives for makeup," she explains. Wearing that ghastly amount of foundation, tourists often applaud her, assuming she's a mime when she's standing alone, staring into the ocean.

"Good. It's going on me—I'll go in to get the beer," Mikey says, thumbing his chest, doubling-down on the daring errand, establishing himself in charge. Snickering anxiously in miniature language, the girls lead Mikey scurrying to the dumpster, finding the last rays of sun to light up their back-alley vanity.

Onto his chubby, stubbly, acne-erupted face, they cake on foundation, too much rouge, eyeliner heavy, already dripping, applying green eyeshadow like the hideous ID woman is wearing. When they finish, he looks like Tammy Faye trick or treating.

"Perfect," says Katrina. Jasmine smiles, unclasping her compact mirror.

"Nah, if I see my reflection I'll lose my nerve," he says. "See you in five minutes."

Entering the store with freakish confidence, he heads to the back coolers. Recalling his mom saying Molson Ice gets you more fucked up than other beers, he grabs a twelver, then passes a huge display of ZIMA—they're new, look sophisticated—he grabs three to impress the gang. Arms overloaded, he bangs his bounty down, grabbing three smokes from the tub of loosies.

"Three single cigarettes?" the clerk asks. "That's 75 cents—a pack of Quality Smokes are only a buck fifty."

"Ah... yeah. Trying to quit, honey."

"Suit yourself. $18.95."

Drag Mikey waits until his jackpot gets bagged, says keep the change, swinging the sack of coins onto the counter, exiting before the clerk changes his mind. Seeing his partners peering over the wall giddy for his return, they bolt, then slow down, playing it cool and coy at the crosswalk, then take off running again, laughing victoriously. "The guy didn't even ask for ID," he says. "Pretty sure he was just terrified and wanted to get rid of me." He distributes the smokes, saving the first cigarette of his young life for himself.

2

Shuffling down the driveway toward the garage. Mikey swings up the garage door extra hard, a victorious entrance.

Guilty: two red-faced devils covered in their own crimson life juice roaring with fugitive laughter. Tristan and Hackman first met earlier today after Hackman beat him up at school; then, after tearing off Tristan's red flannel like a bullfighter as he lay bleeding, he saw a Black Flag shirt underneath—a simpatico punk rocker, so all was forgiven. In complex pardon for the wounds he inflicted on Tristan, Hackman began cutting himself with a razor blade, a fresh one. Mikey's stomach twists, understanding the other two have bonded in blood, hollering like barking coyotes tearing apart the midnight prey of their own tender hide.

"Rad, you brought chicks?" says Hackman. "Wait, look at me—you *are* a chick? Fucking ugly bitch too, wow."

Mikey wipes the neck of his t-shirt across his face, smearing his makeup into bruise-colored blue. "Least I'm not pouring blood. And what the fuck happened to you guys?"

"Sorry, Mikey. We're drinking, we didn't know how much we'd be bleedin.' Didn't wanna get it on your floor, so we just started smearing warpaint on our faces."

"Fuck, I barely even know you guys," Mikey grumbles, peering at the house, praying his mom won't stir from the racket. "Please, just be quiet."

But her bedroom door creaks open, ricocheting down the hallway, out the back door Mikey foolishly left ajar, reverberating through his ear into full body shudder. Grabbing the arms and shoulders of the girls, pushing the backs Tristan and Hackman, Mikey shoves them in the garage. Shutting the door, he eye-pierces the gang, over his mouth one finger, the other pulling on a tiny chain hanging from the exposed bulb on the rafter.

A voice cuts through the yard like a blown-out speaker on ten. *Michael Lawrence you get the fuck out here right now!* To hide at home: impossible. Mikey must take another one for the team. Shrugging his shoulders, his head downcast, he exits the side door to face his solitary parent.

Upright fetal in the darkness, the others crack the side door to spy.

Holding the doorjamb, repeatedly losing grip, her other hand points at Mikey. She whispers mean streaks at his nodding head. The others fool themselves, assuming its shadow obscuring her reveal, but the moon's illumination leaves nothing to faith. Her eyes: sullen and sunken. Her face emaciated, a reminder they're all just skulls underneath, that precariously thin layer of flesh separating their shared environment from the inevitable Face of Death inside them all. Her legs tremble, so thin and bony they're clearing the hems of her cuffed Daisey Dukes, avoiding contact with the denim. Severe, exaggerated, a communal hallucination. A mothball potpourri: vodka and Virginia Slims anchoring a woman otherworldly, a decayed totem of too much reality. Street people akin to this image go neglected, if not hospital patients on hopeful mend, but this is Hell Comes to Your House; The Cautionary Tale Come to Life. A Mac & Cheese Mommy Dearest. They're enmeshed at first sight. A premonitory head-on glance imparting a preview: the Ghost of Boozer's Future. Stricken with terror, the shock settles into a wash of sympathy, then of duty, to the adopted matriarch of their hive, The Queen Bee.

Coughing roughly, she spits on the ground, stumbling back down the hallway.

3

It's not a question of: *"It's 10pm, do you know where your children are?"*

Laguna is lackadaisical, its flagrant hippie-hangover of neo-Liberalism run rampant, the question framed more for the children:

"It's been twenty-four hours—do you remember who your parents are?"

After seeing Mikey's Mom, they stopped returning home, exchanging absolute freedom for the burden of proof, the dark gravity of her ABV, shuddering at the thought of losing her hospitality. If a child is going to drink, they're going to drink; safer to get wasted with the chaperone than running from pigs on the beach's nightmare sand.

Yet even in the comfort of Mikey's home, drinking remains a race—every child anxiety-riddled, every gulp another sprint forward to feeling normal. Once everyone is seeing double, Mikey facilitates show and tell: to acquaint himself with these strays, why each one was refusing to return home. "I live here so obviously I ain't going fucking nowhere. Hackman?"

"Shit, I was living with my mom in Moreno Valley, one of the only white kids in an all-black high school, so I stuck out, got picked on hard, the shit kicked of me daily. Found out all the hits on me were being ordered by this guy Bron Todney, big-ass football player, until him and I started brawling every day after school. I always lost but I'm addicted to that adrenaline, the big fucking crowd. It kept escalating until I called him the n-word. Wait—am I allowed to say nig—?"

"*—Don't* fucking say it," warns Tristan.

"Whatever. Anyway, I got kicked out. My mom thought I was gonna get killed if I went back to school, so she sent me here to live with my dad, who told me this morning that I can't come back home until I get a job, but instead of filling out applications, I beat the shit out of Tristan and, uh, now I'm here," Hackman says, guffawing.

Tristan nods stoically but can't keep his eyes off Katrina, her freckled cheeks, her dripping eyeliner and platinum locks, all features popping, a forever afterimage. "What about you?" he says, s'upping her with his chin.

"Oh man…" she says, "Dude, okay… my mom's like, a total slut or something. There are always different guys over. She always wants me to leave, so Jasmine and I just, you know, make friends. Sleep on couches or wherever, some dude's beds…" She laughs. "And Jasmine's story is… You wanna talk, sweetie?"

Startled, Jasmine's monotone burst gains audible spike, then nose-dives into mumbles, back to silence. Her head returns downcast, ashamed how quickly she loses her nerve.

"She's a little sensitive, been through a lot," says Katrina. "I kinda take care of her now, isn't that right ya pretty little skank?"

"Katreeenuh…" she slurs, sick of her best friend embarrassing her into being social. Katrina assumes verbal abuse her will train her—a rogue therapy work-in-progress.

Mikey regains control of the show and tell. "Tristan?"

"Honestly, everything is cool at my house," says Tristan, shameful. "Almost too cool. My parents are hippies, never really snapped out the '60s. But I'm into horror and punk and nonfiction books, *facts,* just like, real fucking life, you know? So, I lie to them so they can stay blissed out. Long as I keep lying, I can do whatever I want."

He pauses.

"I guess I crave a sort of discipline? Not parents, but a gang type situation, with rules. Rules, but no rules, if that makes sense?"

The gang concurs, synchronizing their gulps to normalcy.

"I feel like we're a gang now, right?" Tristan doesn't so much ask as he insists. "And the thing is—we're all going to be the leader." Too young to understand human behavior betrays idealism, he adds, "And you know, since we're cutting tonight, we should just become blood brothers."

"But we're girls, we can't all be brothers?" says Katrina, Jasmine perking up with concern.

"You can be sisters," says Tristan. "Two friends just cut themselves then push the wounds together, so you're sharing the same blood. Like you're the same person now."

"Fuck that," says Katrina. "You don't know where any of us have been, who we've been with—"

"… or where we're going, either," says Tristan, "but from now on we're going together. You in, Mikey?" Hackman and Tristan have semi-fresh wounds they hard scratch to interrupt the congealing, globules of ruby juice again flowing freely. Hackman hands Tristan his razorblade. Tristan cuts Mikey's forearm. *Ziiiiiiip.* Too easy. "The newer the blade, the sharper they are, the less they hurt," says Tristan. Pressing their arms together, applying mutual pressure on their openings.

"Sounds like a song," says Hackman, repeating: The newer the blade, the sharper they are, the less they hurt. Mikey can't help joining their chant: The newer the blade, the sharper they are, the less they hurt.

The girls wince, refusing to cut, allowing the boys to believe they're the same person now: one giant bleeding organism.

Beach town fashion panders to day-glo tropical patterns, every child a default billboard for surf-culture branding. But Tristan, Hackman, Mikey, Katrina, and Jasmine lean to black clothing; not to stand out, but to become silhouettes. Living so fast they're accelerating a self-negating prophecy. Black attracting heat, they're more active at night. Disappearing, integrating into the shroud of evening where they can get away with more, even when stumbling, sniffing inquisitively. Like Patterdale terriers, bold beyond their capabilities, alternating strays seduced by strange odors, abandoned by the other mutts who can't stop running.

Mikey can't hold his bladder any longer. He relieves himself on the shadow side of a palm tree's trunk already smelling of piss. His fresh piss moistens the crusts of recent piss, year-old piss, trickling into ancient hippy piss ingrained in the fibers that no rains can wash away. Now, all the same piss. He hears laughter, the rest running toward him. They too, must piss. Giggling at the perfect way the streetlight hits his naughty stunt, pissing on paradise, whipping out their modest teenage cocks, adding to the bubbling stream frothing, over-soaking the dirt around its decayed exposed roots, forming jagged pitchfork ammonia rivers down the sidewalk, steam swirling into the briny air. The girls press their bare asses against the grain of the trunk for more discrete, orderly streams falling in line like divine gravity, cascading down its ridges. For the first time, everyone sees each other's privates, so from now on, nothing will be private.

Jasmine lights two menthols, hands one to Katrina, prompting the rest to light up behind her. Outstretching her lighter to the lowest frond, Jasmine flicks the flint on the drooping skeleleafs. It goes up, spreads like red ink spilling, flames climbing to its combustible head. Now a palm tree crackles before them, a monumental torch. A makeshift lighthouse for their hazardous coastline. The season of red tide imminent, a beacon to attract attention.

4

To its congregants, Main Beach becomes Blackout Beach at sunset. Since Big Jim sabotaged the fuse box, recutting the wires every time the city attempts to rewire the electrical; when the beach goes dark, it remains dark. Only the moon lights a path ever thinning, shimmering like shattered glass until the ocean lines the sky. Concealed by shadow, a panoramic view for police flashlights slicing up their all-night ragers.

Tristan teaches Mikey, Katrina, and Jasmine how to pour cups of ocean into the soda machines, malfunctioning the circuitry to spit out beer money. "It only works with saltwater, who knows what's in the ocean these days," he says. Counting their loot under the banyon tree, they see Big Jim waddling forth. Stuffing the coins back in the trash bag, they know how he is: he'll say the pop machines are his territory.

But it looks like he has even worse news.

"You hear Hackman got busted?"

Tristan wipes his bangs from his eyes, realizing Hackman isn't with them.

"So, check it out," says Big Jim. "Hackman and Dirty Anna were picking the locks under the parking garage while we kept watch. They were taking too fucking long, probably getting greedy, I know Hackman was getting beer money for you guys tonight, he was saying today's his 18th birthday."

"Wow, double bummer," says Katrina.

"And then Dirty Anna has her $200 a day habit. Next thing: cop pulls into the other side of the garage through the alley, caught 'em with their hands in the cookie jar. Cuffed 'em both right away, drew a huge crowd, fuck."

To process, the gang fidget and pace, looking right-left while their stomachs knot, the whole world suddenly out to get them.

Obscenities punctuate fists hitting palms, Docs kicking up grass in clumps.

Big Jim laments gravely. "And the really bad news is that it was Sawyer who got 'em."

"Who is Sawyer?" asks Mikey.

"Officer Sawyer, to us here on the beach, is Public Enemy #1," says Big Jim. "Only he's a cop, which of course makes him unstoppable. Make matters worse, he's been at it since the '60s. Ever heard of Altamont? The Brotherhood of Eternal Love set that off. We made Orange Sunshine, best acid of all time. Everyone from Leary to Manson came down here to score. Got so big we did deliveries, smuggling Sunshine and hashish over borders, on planes, insane."

Taking a sip of the Miller 32 between his legs, he belches.

"Anyway, Altamont.... Brought it to the concert to evangelize, ended up dosing the Angels to chill 'em out, only they freaked out. Heads rolled, blood spilled—bam, there's your end of peace and love. Who cares, we were making money—until Sawyer busted the Brotherhood, most still doing hard time, it's just me and one other guy left on the outside. Sawyer is always looking for the next subculture to smash, so be careful out there. We got way out, man."

The gang wear varying degrees of smirk listening to Big Jim's history lesson. They've found their first enemy, Sawyer—no opponent for a turf war, just one to avoid entirely. Staring at one another, they project the torch being passed down to them from the psychonauts who killed utopia. The gang's identity tempering in the cyclic bonfire of the sun extinguishing into the ocean.

But no sunset can subdue them. They snap, smoke, pace, and curse, their restless energy early onset DTs: alcohol withdrawals aren't just for bums and Mikey's mom anymore. Mikey the most brittle, nerves like glass, whiplash from the buzzing on his belt, grabbing his side like appendicitis.

"You have a pager, Mikey? You dealing drugs?" Tristan says, giggling.

"Nah, it's just so my mom can get a hold of me when she needs something. It's kind of like caretaking a terminally ill patient." The gang follow Mikey to the payphone.

"Surprise, surprise—Mom needs booze, can't get outta bed today. She said Reef Liquor just started doing delivery, they get paid on the porch. She must be in a good mood, said whatever we want is on her, the girls can come over too, maybe we can actually hang out in the living room."

5

Hackman sulks on a bench in Laguna Beach Police Department's processing room, his feet tapping, nervous energy never-ending. Wiping fingerprint ink on his black leather jacket, biting fingernails off the other hand. Head down in shame, eyes a thousand miles through the ground.

Footsteps echo down the hall, getting closer.

Sawyer, Laguna Beach Chief of Police.

"Hackman, follow me."

Trailing Sawyer into a small white concrete room containing one table, two chairs. "Have a seat," he says. "You ready to get fucked in the ass by little niggers in juvie?"

Choked to respond; any answer will be the wrong one. Staring at the wall, catatonic like Gary Oldman in *Sid and Nancy*.

"If you're too much of a pussy to speak to me, you won't last a fucking second in juvie. They're fucking piranhas, you're a fucking guppy. So, let's make a deal—you're *my* bitch, now."

He looks up at Sawyer. "Fuck. You."

Sawyer grabs the papers, whips them across Hackman's face, wishing it were a baseball bat. "Fuck me? No, *you're* fucked, and you'll fuck everyone on the beach 'cause you're working for us now, narc."

He assumes these pigs want the Blackout Beach scum he aligns with and knows for sure his dad can't find out about any of this or he'll be whacked back to Moreno Valley like a volleyball.

"I'll do the narc thing to the best of my ability if you don't tell my dad about any of this," looking Sawyer dead in the eyes, down the barrel of his own finger, pointing at Sawyer, still pointing at Hackman.

"You're uh…" Sawyer points to the paper. "Eighteen today? Well, happy birthday, Daddy's Boy. We don't have to tell him shit now. All we gotta do now is get your signature here basically saying we can bust you again if you fuck this up. Big boy jail."

Sawyer pauses, cloying sentimental. "Listen, you're a good lookin' kid underneath all that punk bullshit. Only reason you're not going to jail today is *because* you're a good-lookin' kid…"

Hackman snaps. "What the fuck is that supposed to mean? And you're calling *me* faggot?"

"What I mean is that you're on the right side of white, okay? That's big currency in this town, especially when you're in trouble. Pay extra special attention to guys like Carlos, Black Freddy, all those exotic scumbags. We're not just busting petty crime—we're keeping this town white as fucking possible. And don't waste your time telling a fucking soul I said that—no one will believe you."

Hackman wants to unzip himself from his Caucasian skin right there, walk out of that Nazi Cop Lion's Den, straight into the ocean and never look back. A numbness submerges him instead. Sawyer expects Hackman to do some *Twenty-One Jump Street* shit as well, logging any suspicious activity at school, report to the station, *then* hang out at the Beach and do it all over again.

An overnight Hitler Youth cop.

Jail might be a better option. With Dirty Anna in there, at least he'd have the street cred she carried and fuck it if he doesn't have a place to stay when he gets out—there's always underneath the boardwalk, where all you need is your shades to shield your eyes from falling sand.

Or, Hackman thinks, *I could just be the worst narc in history.*

Yeah.

6

A man rings the doorbell with his elbow, holding a cardboard box of assorted beer, a pint of Kesler, a fifth of Popov. Cracking the door with a shitty grin, Mikey hands him a twenty and a five, careful not to reveal Mom behind him; the mere sight of her could prompt a report to a social worker.

Distributing the beer to the gang, Mikey works his way to Mom's corner, sitting stately on her La-Z Boy throne; the only place she inhabits besides her bed. Nerve damage from lifelong dipsomania has hit her legs, now challenged to walk anywhere beyond the two rooms.

Mikey unveils her fifth of Popov.

"Why, thank you, handsome," she says. "Oh, and the orange juice for my vitamin C?"

"Fuck, I'm sorry, looks like we forgot the OJ, ma."

She's already uncapped the vodka, bottoms-up. An ungodly swig that would faint a frat house, her throat undulating wildly to ease it down. The gang's eyes widen— the first they've seen hard booze gusto from a lady. Speechless; their own bottles shoved in their mouths.

"So, what'd you all do today?" Disarmingly polite now, engaged attention to all her children.

"Hackman got busted, cops took him and Dirty Anna—" says Mikey.

"God-fucking-damnitt," she says, shaking her head. "That's what he gets for hanging out with that Anna. Anastasia, Anesthesia, Steez, Skeez whatever they're calling her this week. You all know Anna's not allowed here anymore, right? Fucking junkie doesn't appreciate booze." Eyes bulging, she takes another liberal swig. "Don't tell me it was Sawyer who busted 'em?"

Heads nod dreadful.

"Ah nuts, that's a slippery slope for all of you then."

Their stomachs drop in sync.

"I mean, look at the cops these days," she says. She points to the TV, a news broadcast— grainy camcorder footage of a black man being bludgeoned half to death by the LAPD. "You're not careful, you'll end up like that poor guy."

The room goes silent. They gaze at the screen—the first broadcast of the Rodney King beating, something they assumed happened out there, but not to this degree of corrupt bloodlust. Captured on video, right place, right time; the veil finally coming down on the LAPD, igniting their own small-town paranoia. Hypnotized by the brash display, they want to do something, anything besides just staring.

Tristan thinks it's like The Two Minutes Hate from Orwell's *1984*, a novel he's convinced is nonfiction. Rather than projecting this analogy out loud, his mind returns to the real life they're sharing.

"Big Jim gave us the whole rundown on Sawyer," says Tristan. "He told us all kinds of shit like the Brotherhood of Love…"

"Oh, yup. Brotherhood of Eternal Love, the Hippie Mafia," says Mom, animated by memory. "Those guys were so crazy, and Jim was a big part of it, uh huh! They made the crazy stuff, Orange Sunshine. That stuff brought everyone down here. You know who used fucking come down here and score that stuff from 'em? You'll never guess—I'll tell you— fucking Manson. Little Charlie and his whole crew, all those pretty girls and weird guys would come down here to get that stuff, just to hang. They loved it here."

Unbuttoning his camouflage army jacket, Tristan grins, revealing his *Charlie Don't Surf* Manson portrait t-shirt.

"No way—on a shirt? Far out!" she says. "I fucking knew that guy. You know how I say 'gig' all the time, like 'that's your gig, this is my gig?' That's the guy I got that from. It's the little things that stick with ya, I guess."

Tristan and Mikey side-eye each other, telepathic by giggling. A centrifugal force pulling the gang into the undertow of a dark, nihilistic river flowing from the '60s shitshow, the next of counter-culture kin. A flood of elation, a psychic weight raising goosebump warmth. Arm hairs erect, they pass the Kesler around, the plummeting napalm falling sweet down their throats with each competitive sip. Erratic popcorn-rhythms of half-whispered comedic hate dreams litter the living room. Now even Mom is laughing, slapping her protruding kneecap, her Popov now half-way past the label. Everyone huddled up, shoulders smooshing, heads bonking, a meeting of the minds. Thirsty mouths like baby birds squealing for regurgitated nourishment from their Momma, never enough to go around when the thirst is this deep, their wells so dark you can't see the bottom, it just goes and goes, bottomless until the hungry ghosts make their presence known, rising, rising, slowly closing in on the margins of endurance and mercy, up, up past the lump in the throat.

"Get the fuck out of my house, all of you!!!"

Her finger like a pistol, Mom lunges it toward each kid like a sniper, picking them off one by one to anchor her sudden 180 mood swing. The victor: her rancor; the losers: the younger, gasped to silence over pummeled stomachs.

"This here is my gig! The garage—that's your gig!!!"

Their heads whip, then descend. Stumbling onto their feet, their drunkenness hitting quick, crashing into walls out the back of the sinking ship. Mikey stays behind to fight a fight he'll never win, a stalemate personified in her thinning skin.

In the garage, their time out: Tristan and Mikey bookend the boombox on the cold concrete. Above, Katrina and Jasmine lay on the top bunk, chins on fists. A unified yet somber awareness: a false sense of freedom in their condemned orphanage.

A harsh authoritative knock on the garage door breaks malaise. Their heads whip one way, eyes the other.

"This is the police, open up!"

Fuck, can this night get any worse? thinks Mikey. Sounds like the butt of a rifle slamming against the garage door. Jumping up, he crouches back down, slowly lifting the door, a curtain revealing their fate.

Hackman.

They keel, pantomime hair pulling.

"Man, we were convinced you were the fucking cops."

"Well, what really sucks—I actually *am* the fucking cops."

"What?"

"They fucking got me. Gotta narc my way out of this mess. Good news, long as you're all in on this, we'll all be okay." Sticking the barrel of his BB gun in his mouth, he pretends to pull the trigger, theatrically jolting his head backwards.

"But seriously, trust me—we'll be okay." He stares at the ground, another spastic giggle masking his lingering doubt.

"How can you be so sure?" says Tristan. "This is the fucking cops we're talking about. You're reporting to Sawyer now."

"I've got a plan. I'm not gonna fuck you guys over, or anyone we know on the beach." Hackman pauses. "I'm gonna go after tourists, man. Clean that trash off our shores."

"How long you have to do this for?" says Mikey.

"They didn't say, exactly. Tristan, can I ask what you're whispering to Mikey?"

"Don't worry about it," says Tristan. "No reason to worry, right Officer? Just doing your job, right Officer?"

Slamming the door behind him, Hackman walks outside, trapped in the great wide open.

7

Tristan, Mikey, Katrina, and Jasmine orchestrate havoc as duty, their after-school extracurricular activity. Emboldened by their impromptu palm tree arson reported in the police blotter, it's a rush of anonymous notoriety, the satisfaction of jolting a complacent town, a warped righteousness in every petty crime.

Craving more, it escalates into an insular contest every time one of them make the paper. They've all been featured in the blotter: vandalism, mail theft, trespassing; just skirting any major offense. The last thing they want be is Dirty Anna in jail or God forbid, Hackman the fucking cop.

From back alleys to sewer tunnel rogue arteries, the four become subterranean crime rats, drawing crude maps of its circuitry into their muscle memory.

Their stunts comprise 90% of Laguna's small-town blotter. They take pride in their little corner of the local media; local antiheroes finally making something of themselves. They clip out their news ink and stick it on the fridge, edging out Mikey's Al-Anon documents off display. The blotter clippings so abundant they run out of magnets, before switching to scotch tape, finally graduating to Elmer's glue for semi-permanence, their petty crimes like outlaw paper mâché.

Suburban shadow terrorism can only fill so much void: Tristan feels personally betrayed by Hackman, a sentimentality disproportionate after only a two-day friendship. Bloodshed evaded pleasantries and crammed in eternity; forming, Tristan assumed, an iconic duo. Instead of emoting, Tristan insists Mikey's place be rechristened The All the Way House (rebloomed from Mom's withered tales of alcoholic halfway houses), forcing the others to construct walls of distrust to protect their debauched bunker.

"Don't *ever* let that fucking guy back here, Mikey," he whispered, one eye assuring Hackman was hoofing it back to the pigs where he belongs. Tristan realizes he must take Mikey under his wing since he's a whole year younger, teach him everything he knows whether he likes it or not.

Tristan isn't humble about the way he devours nonfiction. "'Cause it's real, it's real fucking life." When he gives Mikey shit for still reading comics, he grandstands about the "real" books he's read: Chomsky, Guevara, Mandala, X, Hoffman, Leary; all the essential revolutionaries whose faces adorn capitalist T-shirts Laguna baby boomers buy their children. Tristan feels gifted with an elevated intellect of systematic oppression and "struggle," convinced it's giving him a substantial backbone for the current guttersnipe chapter he's living in.

Since some revolutionaries are essentially egomaniacs empowering masses to rise up and kill in their name, Tristan spends far too much time thinking about murder, death in general.

"You know what else is real life? Serial killers," he says, handing Mikey the new copy of *Answer Me!* containing the *Night of a Hundred Mass Murdering/Serial Killing Stars* proto-listicle profiling the most notorious psycho killers of all time who are 99.9% American, framing them as outlaw rock stars, with stats like baseball cards, dripping with the blackest humor.

"And look, this one does the same thing with people who totally offed themselves," he says, handing Mikey issue three with cartoon Hitler on the cover, featuring the article *Killing Me Softly, Roughly, and Just About Every Other Fucking Way Imaginable: 100 Spectacular Suicides*.

"See, they don't teach you any of this stuff in school. Like, I want to know about the Charles Starkweathers *and* the Black

Panthers. What do you think they're trying to keep from us, Mikey? No wonder why people kill themselves."

Since Mikey also loves horror movies, he's wide eyed consuming this new reading material.

"Dude, your two favorite movies are *Texas Chainsaw Massacre* and *Henry: Portrait of A Serial Killer*—two flicks based on real life. This shit is *real*, Mikey." Tristan turns him on to *Badlands* and *Bonnie and Clyde* to further encourage his graduation from benign ghost stories to works based on true crime.

Since he's the most well-read, Tristan feels entitled to reign in the gang. He calls a meeting in the garage, where Katrina and Jasmine are now living, unbeknownst to Mom who rarely leaves her confines just twenty feet away. In the top bunk, Katrina writes vague love letters to Tristan she ends up crumpling while Jasmine reads back issues of *Propaganda* she stole from the record store. Staying up all night like conspiring vampires, they sleep the day away in staggered two-hour comas, slurring loopy and squinting in harsh beams of dust mite infested sunlight.

Tristan holds court at the front of the garage door. Mikey pulls up a chair beneath Katrina and Jasmine, their arms hanging over their bunk, already bored.

"Okay, so I don't want to be some kind of fucking cop, but we've got to set some rules here," says Tristan. "When kids form a gang, it's because their blood families failed them. So, a kid goes looking for another family, one that suits his or her identity, one that gives initiations into adulthood so they can grow up to actually be a real fucking man or woman."

The three nod in solemn solidarity; Tristan's message loud, clear, and empowering.

"So, the question I'm asking here is: what's our identity? Besides being notorious. I think Mikey would agree—any more notoriety and this whole house is gonna get busted. It could ruin our lives and we don't want to see Mom go away, do we?"

They shake their heads.

"So, let's get some things straight and I'll shut up from now on—I don't want to be the leader any more than you want one."

They brace themselves.

"One. We are anti-racist, anti-homophobic, anti-bigot, anti-establishment, and oh yeah, anti-fucking-cop. We can't have guys like Hackman blur those lines for us now that he's a pig, right?"

"Right," they say.

"Okay, number two—no hard drugs. That's why Dirty Anna's locked up and now Hackman is a fucking pig because of Anna. You see what I'm getting at here? It's poison. You can't be revolutionary and be on fucking drugs."

They're like, *yeah, totally.*

"Okay, now we need a name—a strong identity that can account for anything we do."

"I've been thinking about this," says Mikey. "What about The Vigil? Like we're mourning a dead world. Like, shining a light to expose the darkness, but also, we *are* the darkness—a way of showing what society has done to youth by being their worst fucking nightmare."

An abbreviation of vigilantes, The Vigil agrees it hits the spot.

"Now that you've ditched your comics, it's time you realize heavy metal is fucking lame too," says Tristan. He chucks Mikey's *"... And Justice for All!"* cassette against his bedroom wall. "What punk bands are you into?"

He winces. "I'm not sure?"

Tristan throws his hands up, signaling a lost cause.

"Wait, like The Misfits? Are The Misfits punk?"

"Yeah, Misfits were good, only now Danzig is doing, like, Halloween cock-rock, so fuck them."

"Oh," Mikey ponders. "Then who are your favorite punk bands?"

"That's easy—The Sex Pistols, and Fang."

"Oh, cool. I've heard of the Sex Pistols, but not Fang. Got any of their tapes?"

"Yeah, we'll get to that but it's not really their music I love them so much for."

"Oh, then why do you like them?"

Tristan smiles. "Okay, this is your test—you have to figure out what those two bands have in common. Many claim the Pistols were manufactured, like a punk rock boy band or whatever, but they share something with Fang that makes them both legitimate outlaws. They each had a notorious member who did something very specific that in my mind renders most punk bands like The Misfits total posers."

"Okay. Is it something they sang about, like in their lyrics?"

"No man, it's something they did in real fucking life."

8

Opting to keep his distance from The All-The-Way House until this whole narc thing expires, Hackman's spit-shines his routine into covert science without tarnishing his street honor. Convincing the beach crowd that it's only temporary, he tells them he's a "good cop," deflecting the heat off them and onto tourists, adding further spectacle to their discordant circus.

When school lets out, he narcs at the beach past sundown, partying his brains out with Big Jim and the whole crowd; requiring liquid courage for pay phone calls to Sawyer, reporting innocent suspects for impending stings.

He can spot his victims from a mile away: the naive tourist kids in town with their parents for the weekend, wearing mall-bought Bob Marley or Grateful Dead shirts on the wander to score weed. Squares among the curveballs, their trepidatious vibe eclipses their bold claim to counterculture. They look more like narcs than Hackman does.

Since Big Jim monopolizes the Main Beach weed game, all he must do is take their money, hand over the grass after Hackman seduces and middle-mans the dubious transactions.

"Hey, you guys looking for weed?" he asks.

Their puppy eyes light up and they nod their heads, afraid to say more until prompted further.

"Okay, my man Big Jim here is only selling eighths for just $60 or halvers for $120. The kind. How much money you got?" Hackman prods, overcharging; he steamrolls them, overstimulating the conversation so they can't second-guess.

These kids carry large bills—their weekend allowance from affluent parents—so Big Jim and Hackman carry a stack of smaller bills for a quick exchange. Once a safe distance down the boardwalk, Hackman runs to the payphone by the antique toy shop.

"Hey, Sawyer? Yeah, I'm alone. I see two young teenagers—one with red hair, the other with brown hippie braids, shaved sides, both wearing shades, board shorts, Birkenstocks. They've got an eighth on them they're trying to sell to young kids on the beach in five pinches, about ten feet from the playground right now, heading toward Hotel Laguna."

Running back to the banyan tree to observe the setups, Hackman giggles with Big Jim; their weekend entertainment and party money sorted.

It's sunset, golden hour where eyes struggle to adjust— Hackman fails to notice The Vigil at the movie theater across the street, waiting in line to see *Silence of the Lambs*; another flick Tristan tells them is *real fucking life*, inspired by Mexican serial killer Alfredo Balli Trevino. Abandoning the plan to pour their pint of Kesler discretely into a concession stand soda, the four pass the bottle back and forth, gulping heartily in the opening night queue. Jasmine passes it to Mikey, who's staring at a Mexican youth behind them in bleached splattered jeans, Ox-Blood Docs and red suspenders over a Specials t-shirt.

"Hey, want a sip?" he says, grabbing it from Jasmine.

"Nah, man. I don't drink, that's cool you guys know about Trevino though." He'd been listening to *everything they've been saying the last twenty minutes, sorry couldn't help it.*

"If you don't drink, what are you hiding under your flight jacket?" asks Tristan.

"This shit," he says, handing him a rolled up *Muerte* magazine. "Name's Rudy. I actually seen you guys at school today, but I just moved here and didn't want to be all up in your shit."

"Go ahead, get up in this shit," says Tristan, motioning him to join them, and the line begins moving—to admission, to concession, and into darkness.

9

Freedom is ignorance, Tristan thinks. Only a hippy town's high school would be dumb enough to open campus for lunch. The Vigil stash beers in the bushes on Short Street, the de facto off-campus smoking section. Crack a cold one, light a hot one. Just because they must go to school by law doesn't mean they can't make themselves at home when no one is looking, returning to fifth period feeling just a little nicer than they left fourth.

Yet Katrina's running to Short Street, panicking.

"They just, like, assaulted Jasmine."

"Who did?"

"The jocks. Like, four of them took turns slapping her ass, pulling up her slip, a big crowd egging them on."

"Where are they now?"

"Probably still hanging on the quad. A couple teachers walked by like they didn't want to get involved."

"Where is she now?"

"I took her to the bathroom, she was crying."

Mikey and Tristan spring up from the wall. Hoofing it to the quad, they make a quick pit stop to find that new guy, Rudy—he's a year older, a sophomore, from a rougher neighborhood in the outskirts of L.A. Unaware of how many guys they're about to brawl, they'll need all the help they can get.

Approaching a group of suspender clad toughs blasting '60s reggae from a boombox, they spot Rudy—his stony gaze of experience locks with theirs. When they parted ways from the movies, he told The Vigil to holler if they ever needed anything, especially if it involved chingasos.

Exchanging casual salutes, they point to the school, pounding their fists. Rudy nods, requiring no details. A sore thumb Chicano on the receiving end of beaner catcalls, he's been waiting for his chance to get these privileged jocks in one dead end spot. Positioning himself to the front of the gang, he leads them into the maelstrom.

Still in the quad, the jocks cackle in high pitch mock, basking in the afterglow of slapping The Vigil's girl.

"You late-bloomer pendejos gone through puberty yet or what? You like hitting girls?"

The sportboys freeze, caught in crosshairs. The Vigil creep in arrowhead, unraveling.

Rudy throws the first punch, uppercutting the first one to stand up from the bench and fall backwards into another, pinning him underneath. Tristan pounds a nose feebly shielded by forearms. Mikey squares off with another. Getting every first hit in, disorienting their opponents into bewilderment, the jocks lose momentum before they can gather any. Tristan pauses—his punch made a loud *crack* in a boy's forearm, a bone break. He's terrified yet satisfied. It's like a great horror movie, only this is real life. Adrenaline surging, he's now the main character. He looks to Rudy, bloodying another face beyond recognition, his single fist pummeling, a jackhammer forming a splattered blood-bib around the neck of the kid's shirt. Tristan runs over to Rudy, pulling him away, signaling Mikey to run with them before any faculty catches wind. It all lasts thirty seconds, and unlike most school fights where the illegal assembly cheers, this is eerily silent. The audience is in utter shock from the underdog's uprising.

Jasmine emerges from the bathroom at the last shot of carnage. Rudy takes her by the arm, eerily soft, gentle. "We took care of it, let's go."

Tristan yanks Katrina's arm like it's not attached to the rest of her, nearly dislocating it; she curses as they accelerate.

They won, but they run. Forgetting the consequences of raining justice, that they'd go to fifth period vulnerable to expulsion, they keep running, shortcutting through the empty football field, stomping rapid into the backstreets.

10

Mom is passed out, oblivious they're out of school early. Calming their adrenaline, they all crack beers except Rudy, who looks despondent, like he's somewhere else entirely.

"What's up, man? You okay? Here, have a beer," says Mikey. "You fucking annihilated that guy."

"Ah, no its cool. I don't drink, man. Not anymore. I'm okay, but I shouldn't have done that, man."

"What do you mean?" Katrina says. "You're like, a fucking hero. Right, Jasmine?"

Jasmine nods, her eyes smiling brightly at Rudy.

"Man, it's complicated. So, like, I came here to Laguna to live with my uncle, lay low…. I got into some shit."

"What kind of shit?"

"I don't know if I can trust you guys."

"Dude, we just spilled blood together. What more do you want?" says Mikey. "Anything goes at this house, but nothing leaves, promise."

"Do we need to do the thing first?" says Tristan to Mikey.

"What's the fucking thing?" says Rudy.

"We're blood brothers," says Tristan. "Bonded. Should we chop you up?"

"Ah, okay, okay," says Rudy, nodding his head. "Like some white boy *Blood In, Blood Out* shit? I like it."

Mikey grabs the razors, repeating: *the newer the blade, the sharper they are, the less they hurt*, assuming Tristan will chant along. But he's gawking at Rudy—already cutting a good slash in his own forearm with a stiletto switchblade catching a piercing mid-afternoon glare from the window.

Rudy gives Mikey a *no man, I got this* smile, twirling his stiletto, motioning the others to receive their cuts with *his* blade.

Tristan and Mikey stare at the knife; how much deeper shit they'd been in if he pulled it out in the fight. Sharper than a razor out of its cardboard cover; just a pressured twist from the tip and they're gushing. They alternate pressing their gore into Rudy's wound.

"Seriously, man... what happened to you?" Tristan says.

"I mean, it's not what happened to me," he says, scanning a grave look into everyone's eyes. "It's what happened to him."

Rudy is the first person they've met who has killed a human being.

Located between Los Angeles and Orange County, his hometown of Whitter is precariously placed off the 72, a straight shot up the 39 where Huntington Beach Nazi skinheads could crash Mexican backyard punk shows to antagonize them into imbalanced brawls. Since Nazis know they're outnumbered in L.A., Whittier is one of the last frontiers where they can stir shit up, still be feared.

"So, my cousin was having a party in his yard, four bands playing, keg, you know? Next thing we know these boneheads show up, barge their way into the pit, bashing the heads of younger kids. Luckily my cousin's friends are like, security for the parties, you know? So, they were packing—showed the boneheads their piece, so they get the message, bailed quick. But the main guy's wallet gets left behind, must have fallen out in the pit, so we go through it and there's like, a couple hundred bucks, so we fucking laughed.

"But one of the kids who got bashed was my nephew, Ernie. A big gash in his forehead. We take him to the hospital. They hook him up to a bed and all that—turns out his brain was bleeding, you know, like internally. He goes into a coma. We get scared, then we get fucking maaaad, you know? Like he wasn't going to wake up.

"So we hop in my cousin's truck and hit the 39 down to Huntington. We have the fucker's address, find his pad, pay him a visit. We wait outside, for like, a whiiiiile.

"Eventually he comes out, alone, gets into this car, and we just follow his ass. We throw a rock at his windshield to get his attention. Makes him real mad. He sees us dip out so then *he* is following *us*.

"We lead him to a park, pull over. He gets out thinking he's just gonna take on my cousin, but I get out with my little friend here"—he twirls his knife again—"and I fucking stabbed that fool, right in the chest, over and over, right in the fucking heart, man. I fucking killed the guy."

Rudy says it like he still can't believe it.

"And the thing is, my nephew ends up making it out of the coma the very next day. How's that for revenge? Now I'm the fucking dick. Wiped a guy right off the Earth like I'm God or some shit.... And you know what part hurts the most, what keeps me up at night?"

His speech devolves to a croaking whisper. "Like, what if being a Nazi is like being in a coma too, you know? I made it so that guy would never wake up from his nightmare.... Like, you can't teach someone a lesson when they're dead, you know?"

Rudy's head droops, heavy with burden.

"So yeah, this shit hurts. I had to leave everything behind, so I'm kinda hiding out here at my uncle's until it's safe to go back. My uncle was all gangster back in the day, so he gets it, this problem, this feeling. It seems like we got away clean, but man, I feel fucking dirty."

Rudy sort of hugs himself, rubbing his biceps, freezing from his past. 'Every day... like I can't think straight anymore."

His eyes well up, knowing he may never rise from the sinking. Scooting closer to him, Jasmine hugs his leg. Katrina rubs his shoulder to stop his clawing at himself.

"I hate to ask this, Rudy," Mikey whispers. "But what did you do with the body?"

"Ah, well... I mean, we took care of it, you know? Made it disappear. My cousin has friends, you know? That's all I'm saying though. I'm done."

Examining their wounds, Tristan and Mikey are fully tripping. They've been cut with a murder weapon.

By the murderer.

It feels fucking cool.

Tristan and Mikey erupt with laughter; triggering side eyes from Katrina and Jasmine, whispering "gross" as they exit the living room.

11

Next day: No Rudy. Like they just plucked the bean from the cabbage patch.

Concerned by his absence from school, Tristan and Mikey flank the payphone at Blackout Beach. "Hey, yeah... is Rudy there?"

"You mean Rudolpho? Listen, this is his uncle, Jorge. I can't really let him talk right now. He was suspended from school today. Who is this?"

"Ah, just tell him that his friends from school called, I guess. Mikey, what's your pager number?" Tristan says, cupping the phone, repeating the digits. "Thank you, sir."

"Motherfuckers," he says, slamming down the hook.

Walking back to The All The Way House, Tristan devises a plan: They'll set the school on fire.

They enter the garage, startling Katrina; she's crumbling paper. Jasmine pretends to be asleep. "Wake her up, please? I need everyone's ears," says Tristan.

"Okay, girls—tomorrow, we need you to take your nail polish remover, splash it on top of the paper towel dispensers in both girls' bathrooms. Make sure no one is in there. Wait until after the bell rings for first period. Make sure it splashes up the wall and hits the ceiling a bit. Sync your watches. At fifth period go into the bathrooms, pull out a bunch of paper towel, make sure it's still connected to the roll, light it on fire. Do it fast, leave immediately. Have someone watch the door, tell 'em some chick did something unladylike in there or something. You wouldn't be lying." Hyperventilating with coercion, he continues. "Ok, then me, Mikey—first, I mean, just look how much this school is just asking for this—they've got those dwarf palm trees just dangling over the trashcans in the quad, leaning right up against the history, math, and science room, then the bathrooms, which are already gonna be on fucking fire if we sync this up."

Tristan snatches the 32-ounce Big Gulp cup Mikey had been drinking whiskey and Coke from, lights a Marlboro Red, takes a couple puffs to get it going. "Follow me outside, I'm gonna teach you a lesson from *The Anarchist Cookbook*.

"The cig is gonna be the fuse. These Marlboros are full of chemicals, so they burn faster than, say, a Winston. Marlboros are gonna just keep on burning, even when no one's sucking."

He tapes a full matchbook to the straw, pinches the cig's filter, fitting it into the straw's end nice and tight, the other end smoking steady. He grabs two large pieces of newspaper, crumpling them inside the cup.

"Okay, now give it a sec. Watch."

Smoke billows from the top of the straw. Tristan comically waves his hands then *zaps* it like a magician, fire engulfing the cup.

The gang applauds. The cup collapses on itself like its taking a bow, reduced to ash and spiraling toxic fumes.

"So, we're gonna drink sodas instead of beers for lunch. We'll whip these up then book it back to class after we drop 'em into each of those trashcans."

12

Asses have been in seats for less than five minutes when the fire alarm erupts, echoing through the hallways. The history teacher screams—flames lick her window overlooking the quad. Audible panic from science and math. Glass breaks, classes bottleneck into the hallways. The whole school files out to the football field. Katrina and Jasmine, halos hanging, feigning surprise, converge with Tristan and Mikey. The four casually glance over their shoulders, admiring their pyre and giggling at vain attempts from security, spritzing it with tiny extinguishers.

On the quad, four trash cans torched and spreading up the palms, two more fires in each bathroom blackening ceilings, all threatening to reduce the school's whole horse-shoed nerve center to angst-ridden ash. Distant sirens sing a sour song, harmonizing with the campus alarm. Adolescents in the hundreds pour from every corner, consolidating to the field like dutiful ants, bubbling with fear, confusion, giddiness. Six plumes of billowing black smoke bundle into one large dark cloud over today's lessons. The siren's whistle ushers in two fire engines, parking with a pressurized screech. The yellow coats unravel never-ending hoses, charging through the main entrance. Black smoke fades to grey, then to white, then back to the boring blue sky. As the students cheer, the eyes of The Vigil lock in with each other, cheeks bulging to withhold their mania.

In their idyllic delinquent minds, setting the school aflame had more benefits besides quick revenge for Rudy's suspension: they assumed classes would be cancelled. But this school has magic money to make three portable prefab classrooms appear on the football field the next day.

"At least we brought down the property value," says Katrina.

"Yeah, shit… they look like trailer homes," says Tristan. He swings up his backpack to start walking. "Let 'em slum it a bit." Approaching the temporary classrooms, it really starts to hit him: *Fuck, we got away with it.* Picking a seat in the back, he's asked to stand back up again. "Tristan, you're wanted in the principal's office, first thing. Don't keep them waiting, please."

His stomach drops, though he's mastered the expression of mild shock.

"Oh? Crazy, okay."

Fearing the worst, he sees Mikey exiting the other classroom, catches his eye. They shake their heads, a signal to avoid walking in tandem. Exhaling heavily, internally freaking, they remain stoic.

It doesn't matter that they staggered their arrivals; there's a police officer, three sets of parents, and their three sons. One whose nose and teeth are broken, one who can't move his arm, and a third with an eye flaming black, red, and purple. A fourth, not present, lies in a hospital bed courtesy of Rudy, and astronomical bill for facial reconstruction already sent to Rudy's uncle. "We've called your parents. You're suspended until further notice," the principal intones.

No mention of the fire, their relief stillborn. Screwed, but not completely fucked. In lieu of juvenile hall, punishments are issued on a curve of physical harm committed. Rudy expelled, the others: a slap on the wrist with community service after school starting Monday.

"So much for staying out of trouble, cabron. Congratulations, you're a real wetback now," says his uncle, handing him his very own toolbelt. Rudy loops it through his jeans, silent and resigned.

Yet cringing from what Tristan said: *We did it for you, man. Revenge.*

You don't know shit about revenge, he thinks, but didn't have the heart to say it to their face when they were so pleased with themselves. Nor will they understand how relieved he is to be expelled. Now he only has to work. Accepting it as late penance for killing a man three months earlier, he relishes in the hard labor, the repetitive hammering of nails a focused meditation to finally process what he did back in the outskirts of Huntington. Every wall he constructs, his own cross to bear.

13

Jasmine is all eyes. Her evening wear is her daywear: a black lace slip, one strap perpetually off her shoulders, the rest of it draping her waifish frame, flowing hypnotic around her black Docs; an apparition forced into battle. A deflated blue-black mohawk parted in the middle, hanging over her shaved sides.

You can't not stare at Jasmine. Many assume she's a prostitute; her eyes a reluctant invitation, the lonely or arrogant presumptuous that she's somehow chosen them. Eyes so wide, they speak for her entire expression—both stunning and stunned. She doesn't talk much; instead, she hears everything strangers say behind her back: *she's too pretty to look so lost!* She could take full advantage of any tourist who stops to ask *are you okay?* but she doesn't really speak. She just walks off, finding another perch for reprieve until the inevitable invasion, someone trying to help her, or help themselves to her.

She is safest at the beach, where she can sit and stare long without bother, gazing far into nothing obstructing her view. And since she feels safest with Rudy, after sacrificing his education to avenge her; tonight, she's brought him here.

"So why you never talk, Jasmine?"

She answers the question with her lips, which must be pressed against his, a kiss, so to speak:

"I don't… talk… I just… do… instead."

Her tongue enters his lips to meet his, their saliva combining into truth serum. Jasmine pulls away, resuming her unbreakable duty of staring at the horizon.

"Why you keep staring out there?"

She relocks her lips with Rudy's to open them, oozing whispers:

"To make… sense out… of everything… that's happened… and everything… that might happen."

She pulls away, this time to ask the horizon: "Where do they all live?"

"Who?"

She shrugs. "Everyone who hurts us... Everyone we hurt... Everyone we will hurt."

"Shit, I don't know. Probably in the hills or some shit," says Rudy, barely awake.

Jasmine waits to gather driftwood until Rudy falls asleep, starting a fire to keep them warm. Every time it goes out, she licks her thumb to feel which way the wind is shifting, and she finds more things to burn.

14

The Vigil face the late afternoon sea glistening, legs dangling off the Blackout Beach boardwalk in playful sways. A rare moment of idle quiet, interrupted by Rudy's lapsing Catholicism.

"Why do I feel like they know more about space than they do the ocean?" he says. "Like, they've never taken a ship all the way to the bottom."

Tristan smirks, catches Rudy's eye from two heads down. "Pretty sure your heart explodes. Or your head. Whatever comes first." He pauses. "Whatever is weaker, I guess?"

"Damn. But think about it—when you die, you either go to heaven or you go to hell. So then what the fuck is the ocean?"

The four nod pensively. Taking long, crackling drags of their cigarettes, they smell a stronger, more woodsy scent.

What are you smoking? they joke. The sky beige-orange, the sun Hell-red, radiating a bright hazy sepia tone.

"We're on fire," one says.

"Yeah, we are," another replies.

"No, really, look. We're on fucking fire."

Tristan, Katrina, Mikey, and Rudy turn to the hills behind them, outlined in glowing red, popping from a veil of black blotting out half the blue. The whole beach stands, rubbernecks, gaping at nature devouring their town's upper tier. Some clumsily run—the wealthy homeowners in the hills—everyone else is awestruck. Others jump into the ocean. Within thirty seconds the flames are over the hills, the crackles audible, like a needle hitting a record, only music never comes.

Within an hour, Laguna is bumper to bumper, escaping in gridlock, evacuation mandatory. The fire is its own hyper-real army, the wind's fuel forming an arc of flame across the 133 freeway in the Canyon, beginning its climb up to the clusters of stilted mansions.

"Where the fuck is Jasmine?" they keep asking. Running back to The All the Way House, they find her in the garage, hiding beneath the covers.

It's not that Jasmine doesn't want to articulate her feelings about fire: that when it spreads, destroying everything in its path, it's not necessarily trying to devastate the landscape, its merely trying to exist to its fullest extent, eliminating all obstacles as fuel to simply survive. Much like The Vigil, fire will continue to conquer unless intervened by "containment," therefore it's nearly impossible to claim it's not a sentient, even selfish being.

It's just that she can't.

There are other ways to demonstrate your points besides talking, you know.

15

Giddy with excitement, The Vigil feed off the righteous pandemonium of class justice; the final arrival of the charred, post-apocalyptic landscapes they'd fetishized in their anti-war rhetoric. It galvanizes their mania, this backdrop more suitable to their punk rock Mad Max fantasies.

Tristan suggests looting, but with a class consciousness like the L.A. riots dominating every channel. "We'll just stick to the hills. Rifle through the remains of the richies, see what kind of loot we can get—they won't be back anytime soon."

They find a charcoaled foundation, a precarious deck on stilts singed to a black skeleton. Its winding driveway is a firewall, leaving the large storage garage intact. Tristan lifts it with ease, a couple burnt springs break from his force. Inside, flashes of blue and teal, exaggerated ocean scenes on canvas.

"Oh gross," says Tristan. "This must be the house of that guy who paints all those ridiculous whale murals all over town." Kicking a hole straight through the closest rendering, he falls over with his leg caught in the frame.

"Wow, you really hate that stuff, huh?" says Mikey, cracking up.

"Yeah, I do. Those murals are everywhere you look, when the goddamn ocean is right fucking there, zero imagination. Makes me feel like I'm drowning, the sick watery fuck."

Picking up a bottle to throw at another painting, its label gives him pause. "Oh, wow. Thallium?" he says. "I guess he is a sick fuck. You know what this stuff is?"

The gang shrug their shoulders.

"Poison. I recognize it from one of my mom's Agatha Christie novels. There's arsenic, and then there's this stuff. What do you think he's doing with it?"

"Well, the label says Fuji, it was with a bunch of photography equipment," says Rudy.

"Whatever, I'm taking it." says Tristan. "Let's get out of here before the cops show up."

TWO

Off-White Ashes

1

I can no longer be him; only recede, rise, and crash to define him.

He goes by Rico.

Just Rico.

Keeping his past airtight private, no one knows much about him other than he's just moved to Laguna from "somewhere in Mexico" to start over. Post-packrat, he's just opened his vintage clothing store *Blast from the Past* right there on PCH, a dream come true; even while living in its back storage room with no shower.

He tells them all to just call him Rico, "to keep it simple."

"Oh, like "Rico Suave?" everyone asks.

He laughs it off, a joke to himself when his favorite band is Jane's Addiction. He wears a red puffer vest, his signature cozy armor he removes only at bedtime along with the blue contacts he wears to look more American; a disarming, piercing gaze blurring lines between beautiful and sinister.

Selling cocaine in Mexico, Rico raised enough capital to move to the States, choosing Laguna not just for its beauty, but because he was sick of being called faggot everywhere in Mexico, where "fag-bashing" is encouraged and when committed, ignored. Notorious for its gay demographic and thriving nightlife located at Laguna's midsection: The Boom Boom Room, Main Street piano bar, West Street Beach; an isolated stretch of shore with a secret spot nestled between two descending cliffs, like a tuning fork half-submerged into the ocean, ideal for skinny dipping and moonlit hookups after bar cruising.

A week into establishing his vintage shop into trendy Laguna commerce, Rico is introduced to a new kind of kick.

The psychopharmaco's crystal ball: methamphetamine.

On the prowl for anonymous midnight cruise, Rico gets his introductory line at "The Boom" from this tan blonde in a tight muscle shirt, and Rico assumed it was only cocaine until his nose burned like lightning striking internally, cracking his brain into zero-gravity confetti.

"Different." he says. "I like this stuff. Actually, I think I'm in love with it. "

Blonde Boy tells Rico it's called *glass*—the purest, uncut version of meth. When Rico asks where he can score, Blonde Boy writes down a number for his guy—this sketchy-looking but basically trustworthy dude named Itchy, a tatted-up desert rat from the Nazi Lowriders. In the desert, meth has long fueled bikers and sunburnt feral youth. Now it's breaking out from its white trash ghettos into gay bars overlooking the beach.

Itchy comes to town only once a week, but Rico is in luck—tomorrow Itchy's coming through Laguna Beach for his South Orange County circuit. Blonde Boy explains how funny it is, the irony that this guy might queer bash them under different circumstances. "Itchy hates coming to this part of town, but it's too profitable—he can't ignore us."

Slightly trepidatious of just calling a drug dealer out of the blue, Rico convinces Blonde Boy to introduce him to Itchy over the payphone outside.

"Rico, here's Itchy."

GO!

"Hiya, this Itchy? I wanna make a deal with you Itchy. I buy two 8-balls from you tomorrow. You keep it coming every week. Drop 'em off at my store like you're a customer. I can save you the trouble of spending too much time with the other faggots up the street. I'll be Rico the Distro. Sound good?"

Itchy is relieved—he'll show up at Rico's shop a half hour after it opens, a quick drop off/cash grab, then hit San Clemente, check in with his brethren skins before hitting up the San Juan Crips/San Juan Punks, save half a day.

2

Opening the front door, Rico kicks the stopper down, an eager sunray illuminating the entrance. An unassuming storefront masking the multipurpose headquarters, he's hyped to deal again, still amped from that confetti-brain stuff that kept him up all night pacing, a hyper-private self-appointed coronation as the new neighborhood kingpin.

Catching his reflection in the mirror of the sunglass rack, he attempts self-admiration. Instead, he's jolted by his bloodshot eyes, jaundiced with pronounced red vessels taking on lives of their own paths. He runs into the bathroom retrieving his blue contacts, returning to the cash wrap—what was once ritual of acclimated vanity; now, to veil debauchery.

Out the window Rico spots a short, tatted-up white guy in Oakley wraparounds, cut-off Dickie shorts and a wifebeater waiting at the light across the street. At first glance, he appears to have tight cornrows until he approaches closer; his shaved head with H.R. Giger-esque serpentine tattoos over his dome. He double-checks Rico's address in the black book he's holding.

He enters the store in a kind of dipping Crip-walk a Peckerwood could only pick up from eclipsing gang styles in the O.C. jail system.

Pointing at Rico, he's grinning. His teeth so jaundiced, they're nearly translucent.

"Hey, hey. You must be Rico," he says, swinging his arm around for a handshake. "What's up, bro?"

"Hello and welcome to Blast from The Past, sir. Can I help you find anything?" Rico's eyes big, anxious; his azure shields hinting a faint purple from the varicosed white. He motions to the rack of blazers, signaling Itchy of the protocol they discussed over the phone.

"Uh, yeah. I'm looking for a cool blazer," Itchy says, winking. He puts his black book on the sunglasses rack and claps once to commence business.

"Well, you come to the right place, my friend. This green Edwardian Teddy Boy jacket is one of my favorite pieces. See the black piping on the pockets? From the fifties. Very rare."

Rico slips the blazer off the hanger, smoothing out the wrinkles, placing a banded wad of twenties totaling $300 into the inner pocket behind the lapel.

"Here, try it on. I insist."

"Oh yeah. I'm lovin' this," says Itchy, dropping a baggie of two bulging 8-balls into the breast pocket.

It could have been a perfect handoff, but then Rico scrapes a bit off the ball with a key; enough little crumbs for a sample snort to let him know he's gonna be the same kind of happy happy joy joy as last night.

Kinda defeats the purpose of this perfect handover in the jacket I'm about to put back on the rack for you, but I get it, thinks Itchy.

Salivating, Rico's tongue licks his lips. Laying a credit card flat over the crumbs, palming it full force to crush. Flipping the card vertical, he dabs it into a tidy line. Already with a bill rolled up, in one swift motion he sticks it up his left nostril, throws his head down and vacuums the shit up with such force it throws him off balance, his leg stomping to reground.

Instantly, he knows this shit is golden.

Thrusting his head back up, saucer-eyes swirling marble-ocean blue, his panorama electrifies: a cop car screeching to a halt in front of the shop.

"Oh fuck." Rico choke-whispers past the bitter dripping throat lump.

"Good shit, huh?"

"No, bad shit. Cops. Behind you."

"Coming in here?"

"Lookin' like it... Oh fuck, yup yup."

Itchy hops over Rico's counter like jumping a turnstile.

Rico just stands there, high and paralyzed, sweat beading from his pores, eyes frozen on cops. The backdoor slams—Itchy's away, clean.

With the green jacket.

Containing Rico's other eight ball.

In his thrashing, rocking pockets: Rico's money.

An expensive mistake that will put him a week in the red—$300 = five days earnings he was aiming to triple—fuck.

He spots Itchy's little black book on the jacket rack, grabs it, and gently pushes it under the register. He starts whistling "Ocean Size" as the cops enter, exaggerating his personal battle hymn.

"Hello, Officers. Welcome to Blast from The Past—How can I be of service?"

"Is there a gentleman in here with you? We saw him come in here." says Officer Sawyer.

"Ah, no sir, no Officer but I also just got out of the restroom. Yup, just me, slow morning," he says.

"What's back there? Mind if we take a look around?" says Sawyer, advancing towards the back room.

Rico offers his endearing giggle—which could read as insulting or confusing or suspicious or maybe trying to buy time. "Oh, sure, sure go right ahead but I am warning you my cleaning lady is off too-day," he says, a cloying sing-songy Mary Poppins.

Sawyer and his Deputy beeline to the back door, throwing it open. Standing on the wooden deck, a staircase descending into the alley—a guy wearing a loud green jacket running out the alley onto PCH. Sawyer hyper-trots down the stairs, alerting the deputy to fire up the car, flip a bitch, follow him south.

Itchy books it, full tilt panic. Looking back: pigs flying.
Itchy is a green streak—dipping one block down an alley to the next, gaining distance through every blind corner.

Catching his reflection in a store window, a pang of shame electrifies him in "such a gay-ass Leprechaun jacket." And "Fuuuuck I took the money *and* Rico's shit," he reminds himself, dreading a homo-mafia tailing him behind the cops. Slowing down to an awkward jog, he scrambles to tear off the jacket; comedic, like he's being attacked by the thing. Four miles in ten minutes, he's barely breathing at Dorothy's Thrift Shop, a pile of cardboard boxes full of clothes blocking the entrance where he discards the loaded coat. $300 in his shorts to re-up the shit he just tossed, the loss makes him die a little, cramping up inside. He keeps running, tracing a horseshoe across Broadway, through the alley toward Main Beach, where he knows he can blend in with the freaks, hide out until nightfall when the Beach goes dark.

Hackman sits on the wooden bench in front of the lifeguard tower when his beeper goes off. He ignores it at first—he's gossiping with Big Jim, convinced it was The Vigil who set the school on fire and likely burnt the hills down. They're cracking up, full knee-slapping pride. Hackman wishes their dynamic wasn't so weird now, that he could just go over to The All The Way House to congratulate them, but Sawyer's making him work Saturdays now—Sawyer, who's calling him on his PD-issued pager.

Sulking to the Toy Shop payphone, reporting for duty, shaking his head, wondering how long this fucking shit is gonna last.

"Yeah, Sawyer?"

"Hackman, you at the Beach?"

"Yeah, Toy Shop phone."

"We've got two cars in pursuit of this guy Itchy, we think he's gonna end up there. Tattooed, bald head. He's either wearing a bright green jacket or a white wifebeater. He's from the desert, Nazi Lowrider, big-time drug runner. And uh, he's wanted for homicide in Riverside County."

Hackman's eyes glare at the word *homicide*. Not scared, but excited; something actually worth his subservient time. He restrains himself from saying *Wow, bitchin'!* so Sawyer won't get the wrong idea.

"Got it, Sawyer. Sounds like he'll stick out. I'll be at the tower. If he shows, I'll chummy up and stall the guy."

Hustling back to the lifeguard tower, he scans the beach's adjacent grassy periphery. Bam—there he is, Itchy, jogging with purpose across PCH, past the basketball courts where stunned blacks scowl at his swazi tats. At the boardwalk, he puts his hands on his knees, leaning over like he's gonna hurl from overexertion.

Hackman accelerates with Itchy's pause, mouths to everyone at the Tower—*hey, have my back, some shit's about to go down.*

Two cop cars pull around the corner. Waving his hands, Hackman points toward Itchy as he runs toward him. He can't believe this guy thinks he's safe on the beach where sand will only slow him down. A light ignites in Hackman's mind: sand. He jumps off the boardwalk and grabs two handfuls.

Gaining confidence, Itchy strolls down the boardwalk, arms heavy pendulums, weaving through tourists statuesque in comparison.

Hackman keeps slightly off path, hanging a whiplash left onto the boardwalk, a slow-moving train awaiting collision. "Hey, Itchy!" he says, throwing both handfuls into his eyes. Itchy curses, throwing blind blows, Hackman already behind him, jamming his fingers into both sides of his mouth, pulling hard; straining his kisser into a grotesque Compranchico grin. His knees grounded, the only option is to scream with gravity against him.

The two cars jump the curb, pull up onto the grass, cops swing out their doors, guns out. *PUT YOUR HANDS IN THE*

AIR! Four cops rush it, tackle him in case he's armed, whispering sweet obscenities into his ears, cuffing his wrists, hauling him to Sawyer's car. The beach crowd is shocked until the cops speed off. Big Jim shakes his head, palming two eighths in his cargo shorts. *I don't like any of this, not one bit.*

3

With its proximity to the vastness of ocean, just three blocks from its tides eroding civilization, the high school is unable to properly discipline its students. For their luxurious punishment, Mikey and Tristan are allowed to choose where to work off their community service: Dorothy's Thrift Shop, a dusty goldmine from which they score their clothes, books, and records. Signing in after school from 3-5; with thirty hours to do, they plan to knock it out in three weeks.

They see the green suit jacket on the rack at the same time, like something Shane MacGowan or Johnny Rotten would wear. The kind of jacket they'll never see again. They argue: *I fucking saw it first—my hand was on it before you*, before deciding its owner is whoever it fits best.

Tristan wears it like a child who raided his dad's closet, his hands completely disappearing up the sleeves.

Mikey's turn. He's a perfectly tailored soldier, ready for battle or at least a sweet photo he could hustle a tourist for. "See, being a fat kid ain't so bad," he says.

Tristan accepts defeat. Mikey hasn't gotten a signature look yet, not like Tristan with his dyed black hair over his smeared eyeliner; hardcore punk meets glam, his red flannel top-buttoned faux-gangster. With this green jacket, Mikey's blossomed as a modern Teddy Boy—he's been growing sideburns flanking his long bangs like Eddie from Rocky Horror, so it's like fate.

After Dorothy fills out their timesheets, they leave— Tristan looks back, snickering at Mikey donning the green treasure without paying, real casual. Shoving his hands in the pockets, Mikey pulls the jacket taut, something pokes his chest inside the breast pocket. He reaches in, grabs the baggie, its contents off-white, a small globe of opaque crystal. He nearly throws it into the bushes, instead asking Tristan, *do you know what this is?* Tristan rubbernecks, slowing his stroll. The two boys inspect the orb, holding it to their nose:

"Smells like vinegar or something?"

"A weird color, you think it's a gem?"

"Damn, I wanna say its cocaine but it's got those little red spots."

"I bet Rudy will know what this is."

Rudy lives on the couch of his uncle's small one-bedroom bungalow dwarfed behind a newly constructed and extravagant two-story craftsman on Grace St. in central Laguna. Rudy is alone from Thursday to Saturday, accompanied only by a pressure to avoid trouble. Dividing their time between Rudy's and The All The Way House, the Vigil keep him company, letting Mom cool off when she's on a bad one.

When The Vigil arrive, Rudy's on his second beer.

"I thought you didn't drink?" says Tristan.

"My uncle said its cool for me to drink as long as I stay home, so he leaves me a twelver to get me through the week while he's gone."

He distributes the bottles. The boys have their beers uncapped before Rudy can take his hand away. "Damn Mikey, killer jacket," says Rudy.

"Right?" he says, flaring out the pockets. "Oh yeah, we wanted to ask, you know what this is? Found it in the pocket."

Rudy holds it up to the porch light. "Shit... can't be totally sure, but I think this is fucking speed, bro. Yeah, 'cause coke isn't this see-through. That's why you hear 'em call it crystal sometimes."

"Have you done it before?" asks Tristan.

"Nah, but my cousin was on this shit a while. Fucking vampire shit, man. I do know it's kinda blowing up right now. I don't know though, still can't be sure if that's what this is."

"Only one way to find out," says Mikey, rubbing his hands.

"But what if it's some fucked up chemical or something?" says Tristan.

Rudy laughs. "Dude, if it is speed, it's all kinds fucked-up chemical."

"Well, I used to play drug dealer when I was little, after seeing Mom's friends doing coke at the house," says Mikey. "I've snorted salt, pepper, sugar.... I'll be the guinea pig, fucking pussies." He pulls his nostrils back like the pig people in that one Twilight Zone he saw on Thanksgiving.

"All right, the fat kid speaks," says Rudy. "I ain't touchin' that shit. But Tristan, why don't you take one of your psycho razorblades I know you got in your secret pocket and shave off a little corner of that mystery nugget? Take this card, chop him up a line, man."

Tristan pulls a fresh blade from his jeans, surgically scratching into the mysterious sphere. Flecks of white dust float upward into the late afternoon breeze, only to softly flutter down into a growing pile. Sliding the card through, he shapes it into an elongated streak—tap, tap, tap.

Rudy rolls up a dollar bill, handing it to Mikey with a nod, a reminder this was Mikey's idea. Mikey's heart pounds, alerting him it's really happening. Shoving it in his nostril, he lets it hang there in jest. They giggle and his head drops into foreign matter. Swooping down the line—*sniiiiiiiiiif*—the sound in his head amplifies, a series of explosive crackles, like fireworks bursting from his brain.

The effect is immediate; he's shot out of a cannon, whizzing past the stratosphere, convinced by an all-knowing orphic instinct that he's now versed in everything beyond space and time.

They crack up—Mikey's eyes are big as golf balls. He feels his jaw drop, snap close, then drop again. He can't stop rubbing his burning nose; the confined violence of his palm repeatedly squishing his searing cavity is so good that it's bad that it's good again. Lips vibrating with motorcycle buzzing, he ricochets his whole body into high kicks off the wall. When they fall on their backs dying of laughter, Mikey gives them gay CPR to gross them out, until they're back on their feet doubling over, unable to breathe, astonished their best friend has become a human comet.

"That's gotta be speed," says Rudy.

"Dude, my heart feels like it's gonna burst out of my chest in a good way, the best way," says Mikey.

"Damn, looks like fat boy is in love."

"Tristan?" Mikey is already cutting him up a line.

"Well, there goes the no hard drugs rule," laughs Rudy. "Going, going—gone."

Tristan is frozen—time crawls, then slithers, devolving inside him. All eyes on him to man up, do the line or risk the sting of ridicule. Tristan: the one who said you can't be trusted if you go against whatever the gang does, no givebacks.

On his knees barely comprehending a word, Mikey's eyes level to the table.

"Do the fucking thing, the whole fucking thing. I'm watching you," says Mikey, a ventriloquist dummy; even when he's not speaking, his jaw twitches sideways. Tristan knows the only way to escape this nauseating apprehension is *you just fucking do it.*

He grabs the bill, jams it up his nostril, puts his head down, partly in shame.

Sniiiiiiiif!

A dam breaks, his consciousness floods: a euphoria unparalleled. Tristan's teenage brain ejaculates, oozing, overflowing with all the secrets in all shadows that veiled all the lies, truths, conspiracies—hidden knowledge he always knew was out there somewhere and inside him all along drip-dropping into his head by angels or demons no such thing as good or evil that's the first rule everyone's gotta learn then we can start all over in a new world created by a new youth YEAH MAN THE VIGIL HAS ARRIVED to fuck shit up, delivering us all to our maker— ourselves— 'cause now we're gonna live forever. Even if the cops bust us we'll criminally reincarnate in jail and what are jails anyway man always putting us in a box whether it's a car or a house or a school it's all jail come and get us catch us if you can but we've got you by the fucking balls by holding this fucking ball we see something you don't see me and my gang in our burnt-out city we're just like the projects now oh shit projects I can think of a billion projects we can work on pranks statements manifestos and this town no this country this whole fucking world will never be the same because of us you just watch wait you can't 'cause we're sly we're sneaky we only come out at night and we know every back alley every sewage tunnel and every trick in the book we are gonna take your corrupt society make it worse before we make it work by throwing it back in your face your worst nightmare your children now we are coming for your children too not in some molester way but to add to our ever growing army of latchkey delinquents who you either made obey too many rules or gave way too many freedoms to but only 'cause you didn't care if we lived or died we were a mistake or unplanned the almighty dollar is your true love go take holiday photos with your wallet now display it on the mantle and watch it fall into the fireplace we are here to shake shit up like an earthquake all your unnatural fault one you play hot potato with but you can never give it back so here we are to give it back so you know what it's like forever and ever your hippy dream was a coma from which you've never woken we're taking away your keys blind-driving over your spines all your children you're Cain-raising our shrieks are the horn your alarm your tolling bell your siren the expired emergency we are the new authority.

"Yo, you okay?" Rudy lifts Tristan's bangs. "Damn, your

nose is bleeding. Fucking high elevation or what?"

Wiping his nose, Tristan does a freakish double-joint dance with his knuckles, cracking them like castanets. "Very... very okay, okay, k-k-k-k-k."

Reborn in glowing phosphorescence, Tristan and Mikey's guilty, trepidatious expressions can't quite match the glorious and kaleidoscopic all-knowing sub-plots their new altered physiologies entertain.

Rudy opens the front door for them. "Good, 'cause you guys are being a scene and I gotta wake up early."

4

Speed gives Tristan and Mikey hastened strides, animated gesticulations. Dancing to absent music; reacting to every man or machine moving or suspicious of its stillness. Strutting defiant down PCH, their periphery a swirling hue of predestination and extreme alienation, hollering to fractal cellular minutia. Acquiring a shattered sixth sense, radiating shards every direction; static pieces returning high-pitched telepathy burrowing back into their skull-radar.

This is who they are now, who they've always been. A wind tunnel without entrance, erasing exit and dissolving initiation. Every second gained; a cognition lost. Every step they take is a thrilling misdeed being buried under the growing mound from the next crime's excavation. Like two incongruent dogs digging up the whole yard looking for the bone, repeating hold ons: *wait, do you have the speed?* Every time Mikey says, *yes, I've got it shut up.* Mikey asks Tristan twice, untrusting he has it after all, Tristan laughs, asks him if he has it—*yeah I got the stuff it's right where it came from in my bitchin' new jacket.* Tristan freezes: *I don't believe you, prove it.*

Acclimating to the drug's uncanny ability to turn earthly constructs of time into malleable, borderless vapor; a twenty-minute walk to The All the Way House becomes a two-hour ordeal, only to end up at Bluebird Park instead, where the night dissolves into accelerated, effervescent fragments of time-lapse.

It's 8PM when they reach the porch frothing at mouths from an epic six-block journey. Their jackhammering hearts nearly seize— a cacophonous party in full swing without them, yet it sounds like the two of them are in the house, despite having yet to enter. Their heads twitch—they duck, their ears at the foot of the door to surveil.

Discussing in whispers: okay that's not you that's someone else is that me no I'm right here fuck what is Mom laughing about whoever is in there they're for sure talking about us we'll collect every snippet of slander then in five minutes we'll swing open the door they'll have nowhere to hide red-handed no red-tongued shit do we need weapons? Ready? We're going in—

Bursting open the door, they put up their dukes, only to be greeted with cheers familiar and foreign: Katrina, and Jasmine huddling around Mom; across the room are two new kids anxiety-drinking, attempting to blend in... and Rudy, grinning?

"Man, where have you guys been?" he asks.

They ask Rudy: "How the fuck did *you* get here"

"Well, I walked here right when I got off work. You realize we've been trying to find you for the last 24 hours, right?"

Tristan and Mikey are convinced he's fucking with them, an elaborate joke to melt their brains. Slivers of memory struggle to return, of gesticulating, babbling, then eventually waking up at Bluebird Park at nightfall the next night: tonight. But whatever they think about, it's like it's actually happening; anyone can tell them anything and it materializes a suffocated, choked, or imaginary memory they may have sped past.

"Who the fuck is this, why are you in my house?" Mikey barks, pointing at the new kids. Tristan wild-eyed, adrenalized but nowhere to use it.

"You be polite, Mr. Michael!" says Mom, pseudo-secretarial. "Rudy and the girls met these guys at Main.. uh, excuse me, Blackout Beach," she says, mocking hipness with air quotes. "Their houses burnt in the fires, so we're taken 'em in. And Tristan—don't forget you were new here once and how fucking terrified *you* were!" Her body arches to laugh, throws a coughing fit instead; Rudy and the girls laugh for her.

The two speeders dagger-eye the new bloods sheepishly waving at them.

"How do we know you're not the fucking cops?" Tristan asks, poking one in the chest. "What's your fucking name—your real name?"

He picks up Tristan's finger like a dead rat, drops it. "Name's Jeremy," he says, sugary-sweet. "And I swear to God I'll break this bottle over your head if you ever poke me again."

"Okay, sounds like he ain't the cops," Tristan says, the big case solved.

Jeremy and Dylan are only in eighth grade, yet they've mirrored The Vigil's patterns, even surpassing the Vigil's orphan disposition—post-fires, they're legitimately homeless, sleeping under the boardwalk to avoid the stress of their displaced parents.

Mikey and Tristan maintain the Vigil's membrane has been pierced, a breach of security. Isolating in the kitchen, the two find their speech crawling though sand; their minds suddenly doom-laden, their tough confidence gone, terrified to face their mutated gang in the living room.

"Maybe we need another line?"

"Yeah, definitely. For sure. Definitely."

"I'll go into the bath… the bathroom," says Mikey. "I'll cut up two…TWO lines on the left side of the sink, left side. I'll do mine first then you go in, bam bam."

"We need a distraction."

"Grab the boxing gloves in the garage. When I see you come back with 'em, I'll go to the bathroom. Tell 'em we're gonna have a boxing match. A fucking boxing match. Jump the new guys in. Pair everyone up to height…weight…WAIT… it's nothing… one by one we'll go in the bathroom, get ready, go. Go. Go. Go."

Returning with the gloves, Tristan appraises the contestants, pairing by size and weight. The rest move furniture into a makeshift ring, all except for this new Dylan kid sitting too close to Katrina, holding her hand.

Tristan's face ensanguines, jealousy worming out his pores. His clenched mouth purging rabid words. "You're going with me."

"Oh?"

"Yeah, me. I'm gonna beat the fucking shit out of you—"

The gang jeers at Dylan. His eyes morph from sweety-boy eyes to deer-in-headlights as his gaze shifts from Katrina to Tristan. Mikey emerges from the bathroom punching his palm, lifting his eyebrow to Tristan, a signal his line awaits.

"—But first I gotta piss," says Tristan, locking the door. Dollar bill rolled and blazing, he eyes the toilet lid, focusing on the off-white line containing bits of green Comet residue or something worse, no time to deduce its purity. He sniffs the whole thing with great efficiency, every last bit, zigzagging like a Richter measuring imminent magnitude.

Scraping every last molecule, then checking on the ground if any spilled, Tristan's heart skips when the bathroom door bangs, convinced it's the cops until he hears Rudy's voice. *What the fuck are you doing in there?* he hollers, detecting conspiracy, his shoulder ramming belligerently. The rusted slide lock breaks off—the door flies open. Rudy pulls Tristan's head from the fast stuff; he's messing with his nose, mission accomplished right in time. Rudy laughs uproarious, hilarious how they're squirming. The girls peekaboo behind the door jamb, further punctuating the bust, their taunting squeals playground elementary.

"All right fuck it, you gonna share or what?" says Rudy.

"Yeah, share, share!" says Katrina, Jasmine smiling behind her.

Mikey hears the bathroom door slam, pats his pockets, realizes he left the 8-ball on the sink. He opens the door to find Rudy and the girls on their knees crowded around the toilet consuming their share. One by one, they stand up, reinvigorated, euphoric, bloodshot psychotic.

"Mom? Let's get you into your room, okay?" Mikey offers, panicking. No answer, she has passed out. Picking up all ninety pounds of her, he carries her to her room; into her musty potpourri of vodka, Virginia Slims, and other scents so familiar he can no longer identify: the odors of neglect, of decay.

"All right let's fucking do this," says Tristan, his teen-tosterone eye fingering Dylan.

"Hold up—new guys have to do a line. At least one line if they're gonna fight, it's only fair," says Rudy.

Reentering the room smiling, Mikey waves Jeremy and Dylan into the bathroom. Cutting the lines, tapping the school ID against the toilet seat like nervous knocks onto Hell's gateway, every nostril sniffing, allergic to reality.

Every palm punched by its counterpart fist. Tristan hits his so hard, he might break it like the kid's arm at school; he'd rather shatter this Dylan kid under Mikey's roof. Resuming his corner, he signals Dylan to do the same, cue Mikey's acapella bell. The rest assume their place in the sidelines, screaming insults at both boys, fuming like two bulls.

DING, DING! hollers Rudy.

Forgetting his gloves, Tristan runs toward Dylan, windmilling his arm in Popeye-spin to throw him off. Dylan is frozen—already hyperactive, he's had a more pharmaceutical reaction to meth: slowing his instincts, trapping him in his own head; antithetical to physical performance. Tristan's fist hammers Dylan's nose, followed by an anvil-heavy swing from the left. Dylan hits the floor.

Tristan could quit but there's bloodthirst embedded in his heart, sharpened quills pressing up from beneath every pore, the only way out is through his fists. He keeps pounding Dylan, who writhes defenseless.

Rudy runs over, pulls him off. "You're gonna kill him, man. He didn't even get a punch in, you fucking psycho."

But Tristan can't stop swinging. Rudy wallops Tristan

once: his veterano fist the most articulate five-letter word to end any argument. His head hits the wood floor, a nauseating thump of something hollowed, his brain a melon bruised and rot-ready, the impact displacing air wafting upward, tearing down the serene crucifixion print Katrina stuck on the wall with scotch tape weeks ago; though Jesus appears unaffected, his lips remaining indifferent to the crude dick she had drawn with Sharpie, squirting his cheek.

"Fuck, get some ice—you really fucked him up," says Katrina, tending to Dylan's swelling nose. Collecting himself off the floor, Tristan is scowling; after all that, her arms still around the new guy.

Tristan walks into the kitchen, crunches some ice into a paper towel, applies it to his face, then to Dylan's.

"Sorry. Guess you're jumped in now. I'll make it up to you one day. I've been beat up plenty of times. Inevitable, but no fun," says Tristan, his fuel evaporating.

On Mom's throne, Jeremy receives his own initiation—Mikey slicing up his arm, another blood brother exchange beginning.

"Waaaait, isn't this too soon? Maybe not too soon. But soon, maybe," says Tristan.

"Nah, we like this kid, both these kids, The House's kids now," says Mikey. "Hey Dylan, you're already bleedin'. Girls, cut him loose, let 'em over here so we all crush our blood together."

Dylan hobbles over. Feeling outnumbered, Tristan taps him on the shoulder.

"What? I've had enough, man," Dylan says, startled.

Tristan dips his finger into Dylan' gory nose, tongues the blood off, licking his lips into a smile.

"He's okay, I guess."

5

Passing idle hands and up the nose, speed swells each member's presence, exaggerating their character. After the Vigil's first evening in their war against sleep: Mikey is now the undisputed shot-caller of the house "after Mom passes out." Sufficiently respected, he's now even feared when he strips naked, standing on the coffee table reciting Crowley's *The Book of the Law* (Jeremy's ass-pocket copy); his rotund belly hanging over the pages veiling his manhood, his tongue a glitched worm licking his lips raw. Once happy-go-lucky, his eyes adopt a demented glare. He has a compulsive new habit: popping zits on his ever-cratering face, groaning erotically with every ooze. After harvesting this farm, he deflates, sense of purpose lost. Yet still propelled by unknown force, he marches to Jack n' the Box, buys another Jumbo Jack. Removing the beef patty, Mikey rubs its charbroiled grease on his cheeks, creating new pregnant boils of masochistic pleasure. Nourishment a non-priority, eventually he eats the burger purely out of boredom.

Tristan gives true birth to his inner poetic psychosis, observing symbolism and prophecy in everything; a schizo bard never improving at Mom's untuned acoustic guitar no matter how much he plays it, content enough to pluck the low-E string, just staring at everyone. He's grown out his dyed black bangs specifically so Katrina will continue pushing them to the side, asking him what he's doing, telling him he's got pretty eyes.

Jeremy, who The Vigil insisted on pronouncing as "Jermy," is now Jerm. Since one of them already has a nickname, no one refers to Jerm and Dylan as "new guys" anymore; their first night was such a tactile fast lane initiation, no one had to explain subtleties. The Vigil feel they add without taking away. Jerm introduces them all to Crowlian magik texts and Thee Psychick Bible; books offering philosophies just vague enough they can tailor to their own anti-moralities. The Vigil is increasingly cultish, and Jerm's minimalist tight black attire, shaved head and furrowed brow transcends leader and follower. A semblance of potential diplomacy, if only superficial.

Dylan is the runt, his disposition blurred from fear or meth-paralysis yet adorably elfin: a choppy-coiffed Brit Pop boyband cutout, one-dimensional save his deeply pronounced cheekbones. He's prettier than Tristan but even Tristan develops a soft spot for Dylan, primarily borne of guilt from breaking his face at their first encounter.

Rudy maintains his character and integrity, though speed amplifies his Chicano-machismo; spewing rapid fire about his old hood, assuring they don't forget he's been through more than they could ever imagine.

Meth fuses Katrina and Jasmine even tighter, hellaciously motormouthing, monitoring the boys with side-eyes, counting the seconds before they do something stupid, their behavior becoming more unhinged by the minute. Solemnly swearing they won't do anything else beyond compulsive shoplifting, Katrina morphs into matriarch, scamming pizzas for the house, the only thing they can eat besides 25 cent Home Run pudding pies.

6

The 8-ball disappearing rapidly, the collective is in denial about how soon they'll need more. Mikey says it resembles a crystalized Death Star after the Rebel troops annihilated the top quarter of its sphere.

"This isn't Star Wars, man. This is real fucking life, and we need money," says Tristan. "I mean really—let's figure out a way to make money happen."

"Like what, get jobs?" Katrina smiles facetiously, then turns slack-jawed with the best idea ever, whispering into Jasmine's ear, giggling. The boys get uneasy. Especially Tristan, wishing he could feel her breath in his ear canal, every canal.

Katrina stands, clapping her hands twice to command attention. "Mikey, remember when we dressed you in drag? Let's do that to all you guys—we can spare change in front of the Boom Boom Room. We won't dress you up like total chicks, we'll just give you subtle eyeliner, little lipstick, bit of blush, just a little more faggy than you look already."

Silent, the boys won't admit Katrina's idea is brilliant. Another challenge, an impulsive dare because someone had simply thought of it, like the idea of doing another line meant they were already cutting one up. But every time they consume, they panic; Mikey's Death Star is now half-gone.

Transforming the boys into jailbait, the girls tell the boys: Quit fucking moving, this will all be over soon.

For two frantic hours, the girls make up the boys, holding their compact mirror up to each one.

"We barely look any different," says Mikey.

"Well, for one thing you refuse to take off your green jacket," says Katrina. "Listen, we know what we're doing: accentuating your orphan vibes. It'll tug on their hearts, they'll give you money. Like sad little dolls, like junkie Nutcrackers."

"Fine, but if they want anything in return for their spare change, we're out of there," says Tristan.

"Yeah, or else we'll crack the nuts of those fruits," Rudy concurs.

This is the fucking pits, Jerm whispers to Dylan.

The girls cut the sleeves off the boy's button-up shirts, tearing random holes in the fabric and safety-pinning the flaps back together. Skinny ties sloppy at half-mast like they've been tossed around a little. Heavy on the eyeliner, smearing it out the corners, an irresistibly sympathetic appeal until they look you straight in the eyes: trouble.

Before they leave, Mikey puts the decaying 8-ball in a cigarette case, tucking it into a corner of the exposed wooden wall frame in the garage. For transparency's sake, he lets The Vigil know this is where it's kept, but only he's allowed to touch it.

The girls: maternal pimps of their experimental rent boys hustling the friendly, buzzed and unbeknownst for spare dollars, keep the change. Lining up to the side of the bar's entrance, the boys claim their own spotlight, a side-show on the avenue of bustling muscle. Meth like lightning through their veins, they fidget wildly, one foot on the wall, chain-smoking—their best sexually-ambiguous James Dean—but their nervous chemical energy won't let them hold the pose.

The Boom's clientele rubberneck, stay a while; loving the idea of giving a dollar to the little pleading gutter angels. Every patron marvel at how quirky the town has become, how the boys just get younger and younger.

The Vigil make $100 in one hour, just for existing. Frolicking on, they roll with every unpredictable encounter, showing off their charming boyhood antics and witty comebacks. Rudy flicks his switchblade playfully; others adopt inexplicable Italian accents. This new hustle way too easy until:

"Hey, where'd you get that fucking green jacket?"

A Mexican man in a red puffer vest is half-way in The Boom double-taking Mikey, pointing at him accusatory.

"What, who, me?" Mikey says in earnest.

"Do you see anyone else wearing a green jacket?" Rico snaps.

"No, I just see some asshole wearing a fucking life-preserver," says Mikey, pleased with his variation on the *Back to the Future* bit.

Rico grabs Mikey by his lapels. The Vigil hollers. Shit hitting fan, they step forward. It looks like Rico is sloppily adjusting Mikey's collar until his hand goes all the way down his back. Mikey fumbles, grabbing Rico's head from behind. Rico punches them off him with his free hand, then pulls up the tag, still attached.

"See—*Blast from the Past.* That's my store's tag, that's my jacket. Where'd you fucking get this?"

He frisks Mikey further like an overzealous cop, his hand diving into the inside pocket.

"Where the fuck did you get it? Was there anything in this pocket?"

Mikey's stomach drops: he knows.

"No idea what you're talking about."

Overboiling into shoving, Rico is outnumbered, surrounded by seven amped-up kids pounding on him, a nucleus of impacting fists.

"Okay, ok, ok, k,k—OFF!"

Realizing how bad this looks, they back away—the last thing they want is anyone thinking they'd actually fag bash a queer.

"I just want to know where you got that jacket. Something very precious was in the pocket."

"I got it at Dorothy's, man. Never even heard of your shop before."

Rico glares. "Okay, again—was there anything in the inside pocket?"

"No man, no… nothing."

Rico stares deep into Mikey's eyes again, then casts a mind-fuck gaze to the rest of them, his blue contacts impossible to ignore. The Vigil's dilated pupils familiar to Rico, he shoves each boy in the shoulder.

"You're all on the shit." Rico socks Mikey in the chest. "You're lying to me, gordo."

The Vigil know they're guilty at least for half of what he's accusing. Paranoia strikes; they double-down— Rudy gets in his face, cursing in Spanish. Once Rico hears his native tongue, the shouting match simmers to civil negotiations, punctuated with heavy breathing in the brisk air; a vaporous conjuring against the ocean's midnight horizon.

The two attempt an intricate handshake, their rhythms staggered out of sync, clumsiness inspiring a mutual chuckle. Arms crossed, Rico follows Rudy a stones-throw distance back to The Vigil.

"So, here's the deal," says Rudy. "That is definitely this guy Rico's jacket. Since it still has the tag from his shop, he considers it stolen property. But a little back and forth let him know it wasn't you who took it. I let him know you stole it fair and square from Dorothy's. He's just as confused as we are. He knows it was this guy Itchy he was doing a deal with, who ran out with it. Point is, we did Rico's speed. Simple. He's pissed but understands we didn't know any better and—"

"No, here's the deal," Rico interrupts. "Either you give me all the money in your pockets, since I am out $300 from that ball, or you give me the jacket back. We can start there."

The Vigil look at one another: fuck.

"Podemos tener una reunion para descutir?" Rudy asks Rico. He nods.

The rest turn their backs, circling into a huddle:

"What'd we make tonight so far?"

"120 bucks."

"Fuck, we can't just hand that over to him. It's like we're getting robbed."

"It's legit though, we wanna be ethical, right?"

"Ethical? We're all on fucking drugs."

"Yeah, we earned that money though."

"Yeah, but you know we were just gonna buy more of the shit with it. Fuck."

"Mikey, the jacket. We gotta give him your jacket. That jacket won't get us through the week. This $120 will."

"I'm not taking off this fucking jacket."

"Okay, we'll take it off you then."

Mikey throws blows at Rudy and Tristan while they grab the jacket sleeves, pulling Mikey to the concrete. They slip his pride off. Shirtless, a battered necktie above his large belly, Mikey's eyes moisten.

They hand it over to a smiling Rico. "You guys got off easy tonight. We are cool for now, but just know one day when you least expect it, I'm gonna take something of yours I won't be able to give back."

Trapping them into another mind-fuck stare of blue artifice, he scans their faces, finally resting at Dylan.

"What the fuck are you looking at?" Dylan snaps.

Rico steals a move from Prince—two fingers point to his own eyes, then to The Vigil's runt.

"What the fuck was that?" says Dylan.

"Ah, just some fucking gay psychic vampire shit. I wouldn't worry about it," says Rudy.

7

Hackman wanders the streets late Saturday night, no narc or party action at Blackout Beach. Semi-relieved, he's exhausted. Starting to feel like an actual pig, he's bound to the illusion of free-range, slaughter looming. Lying to himself and everybody else, just to blindly rage without true autonomy. He assumed he'd be praised for restraining Itchy, but Sawyer hasn't mentioned it. Fucking pigs. Ignoring their last three pages—for all he knows they may bust for him deserting. He searches for a reason to care, a reason why he's wandering.

Refusing to acknowledge he's walking to The All The Way House until he arrives, staring at the front windows like a stalker, he pines for that vague-family structure just beginning at his excommunication. He wonders if enough time has passed. Maybe it wouldn't be so hard to convince them how much he was done being a fake cop.

Approaching the garage, he imagines a booze-soaked reunion, trading war stories after their inevitable narc razzes. A slam perks his ears—hearing the side door close, he cracks the yard gate: who's exiting the garage?

Mom teeters, surprised. "Oh, uh... hi Hackman, You good?"

"Good enough. Where is everyone?"

"I was wondering that myself. I just went in to see if they were passed out, but the place is empty."

"Mind if I go inside really quick, write them a note?"

"Go right ahead. Have a good night, Hackman. Good to see you, please don't be a stranger over here."

"Thanks. I think I'm done with the whole cop thing. Hopefully see you soon."

Mom stumbles past him, holding onto the wooden fence for support. "You have a good night," she says.

The Vigil return to a dark house, relieved; a signal Mom and her DT ghosts are sleeping. Go straight into the garage, says Mikey. To make certain she's asleep, he risks it over squeaking warped floorboards, stumbling bare-chested into her hallway. Silence, but her light is still on. Mom? Rustling, objects moving, something drops. Mom! She's either ignoring him or too drunk to divide her dim attention, nothing out of the ordinary. He walks down the hall and through his room, into the backyard where Tristan is exiting the garage, visibly worried.

"Hey, Mikey? Please tell me you have the stuff?"

"What? No. It's not there?"

"Nope."

"No one has the stuff? Everyone, turn their pockets inside out."

"Relax, Mikey. We all barely sat down. Rudy was the only one over there."

Mikey grabs Rudy, spins him around, checks his back pockets.

"What the fuck?"

He spins him back around, digs into his flight jacket.

"Fuck! I don't have it—

"It's gone, Mikey."

"Dude, I put it right fucking there before we left."

"Girls, empty your purses!"

"Wait, check this out," Katrina says. Jasmine is holding up a torn piece of 12-pack, a message scrawled in the brown.

Hey, Hackman here. Was in the neighborhood so I thought I stop by to see if you were up. I really miss you all. I think I'm done narcing. I'm not answering their pages, we'll see what happens. Come find me before they do, please. A page from you means one less page from them.

"What is *that* supposed to mean?" says Tristan.

"What do you mean?" says Mikey.

"I mean, he clearly took the shit. How do I know? Because he left us a fucking riddle to decipher. Wait, I've already figured it out. Look at this part: 'I've really missed you guys.' He's straight up saying he took it. 'Missed' is like 'missing,' like something is no longer there. So when he's saying, 'I've really missed you guys.' he saying 'I've really taken something from you guys.' Which obviously means he stole something from us."

A collective eureka gasps the room.

"And he wants us to find him, like this is some kind of fucking game."

"Well, fuck me. Now I know how Rico feels," Rudy says, throwing up his arms.

"Right. Now we play the game by ending the game."

"Go to his house and beat it out of him?"

"Yes."

"But that's like beating up a police officer, right?"

"He's just a glorified rent-a-cop, doesn't even carry a fucking badge."

"We're going to his house. Girls, stay here, we got this."

The five sprint out the driveway, hanging a tight left, blasting off like Greyhounds out of a starting gate, each nose-inching, dry-mouthed for vengeance.

"Faster!" Rudy urges. "We wanna find him before he gets to his house, so this don't turn into a home invasion."

Two blocks ahead, a short blond in a leather jacket.

"There he is. Go, go, go. He's almost to his place."

They scream his name. He turns: surprised, then elated. With a nervous smile splitting his face, he reaches out to hug Tristan and Mikey.

"Nope. Where's our fucking shit, man?"

"Huh? What do you mean?"

"You know what we fucking mean."

"Uh, no, I don't, actually."

"Game over, fucking pig," says Jerm, overstepping, only heresy for reference.

"What? Who the fuck is that guy?"

"Doesn't matter," says Rudy. "Quit playing dumb and give us the shit."

"What... the fuck are you guys looking for?"

"You were just in the garage, right?" Mikey says.

"Yeah, I left you that note."

"You left the note, but what did you take?"

"I didn't take shit!"

"So the speed just fucking disappeared, huh?"

"You guys are doing speed?"

"Well, we were until you took it from us—you bringing it to the station as evidence?"

Surrounding him like sharks, they grab onto his leather, upturning the pockets.

"I swear I have no idea what you're talking about!"

He shoves them off. Rudy backhands him, increasing aggression.

"Fuck! I seriously don't know! All I know is your mom was coming out of the garage when I got there."

"So now you're blaming this on my mom who can barely walk, huh?"

Mikey throws the first punch, nailing Hackman in the cheek. Tristan and Rudy punch downward on his skull. Hackman crumbles to the pavement, imbalanced scales accepted. Jerm and Dylan jump into the beatdown and Hackman goes fetal, covering his face with his forearms, surrendering to the fist-hail. He counts the seconds, praying they don't become minutes.

Dust hovering, they leave him writhing, pulling up his leather jacket to muffle sobs smearing his bleeding face. Lucky for The Vigil he looks homeless—if anyone walks by, they'll pretend he's not there.

"I grabbed his wallet," says Jerm, counting stolen tourist cash. "Hundred and change in here."

"Okay, there we go," says Rudy. "Tomorrow, we pay Rico a visit, see if we can't make this money grow."

No one argues—they've run out of steam for the night, the pavement quicksand. The six-block walk to The All The Way House out of the question. Rudy's pad a block away, where they walk in, collapse, and crash: paralyzed into hypnogogia.

8

Peeling open one swollen lid, Hackman sees he's unsafe in bed, though can't recall how he got there. Propping himself up with clenched obscenities at every new ache—his head pounds a Morse code of cruel pulsations; his fists, chest, and asshole clench. It all comes back to him as he touches his blood-encrusted face. In the mirror: right eye swollen shut, the other burst-vessel red, his fat lip pouty. Some appear tougher when they're beat up; he just looks pathetic. Humiliated rage simmers to boil, nowhere to put it, no one to give it back to.

In multiple limbos: between dead and living, delinquent and cop, victim and perpetrator, crime and the law. He could storm The All The Way House, they'd just do it all over again, all those new guys who don't even know him. He wonders where the girls are, if they know and if so, how they feel about it?

He gets a page—Sawyer. Hyperventilating, he steals a deep breath, blowing it slowly. *I'll answer Sawyer with my resignation*, he thinks; his mangled face proof he's a liability, a face that goes without saying "don't fuck with me"—instant clout if he enters juvee.

He checks the house. Dad gone, thank God.

He dials Sawyer; let's get this over with.

"Hackman?"

"Yeah."

"Where the fuck have you been? We've paged you eight times in the last twenty-four hours."

"Listen, I'm sorry. Sawyer, I need to talk to you, I—"

"That's why we've been trying to get a hold of you. We want to talk to you first. Can you come down to the station immediately?"

"Sure. I'll start walking."

"Great. See you in twenty."

Entering the station, his shades hide most of the damage.
He's met with strange smirks; nothing smug, but a warmth so improbable it's foreign. Feeding his paranoia: *Why are they all fucking smiling at me?*

Reaching Sawyer's door, he pauses. A deep breath before opening.

"Hackman. Thanks for coming down, my boy."

My boy? Sawyer's never glad to see him, never a thanks for anything.

"Jesus Christ! What happened to your face?"

"Um, I don't wanna talk about it. It happened off duty, so I'd like to reserve that right, please."

"Fair enough. Get you ice or anything?"

"It's fine, I'm just a little humiliated."

Sawyer nods. "First, I'd like to officially thank you for risking your life and limb to restrain Itchy so we could pop him the other day. We'd been after that guy for weeks and if it wasn't for you, we might still be looking for him."

"Uh, thanks."

"We'd like to offer you a full-time paying job here as a junior police officer."

Hackman dry heaves at the proposition.

"Just think it over, don't lose your lunch. I'm not expecting an answer right away. But just so you know, you've shown more guts, met more quotas than most of the paid police officers here. Sure, it's been nice to have a ferocious upstart like you working for free to pay off your debt to society, but at this point, we can't afford to lose you."

"That's nice of you guys, Sawyer. But I, uh... I've been doing a lot of thinking and...."

Sawyer locks eyes with him as he speaks, different than the last time he was in this chair, when Sawyer was berating him into informing. The look of respect unsettles Hackman. He squirms out of his chair and to the door, apologizing, stuttering excuses. But the more he waffles, the harder it is to properly decline.

Touching his swollen face, his fists clench again. Every sentimental tie to The Vigil no more than a frayed moment in time, his thread simply curled its own way while the rest conformed into one impossible knot. And suddenly, his only job is to see their unraveling.

"You know what, Sawyer? I'll fucking do it. Sign me the fuck up."

9

Arriving to *Blast's* locked door Sunday morning, The Vigil peek through the vibrating glass window: the obscene volume of foundation-shattering bass under cascading sheets of wailing guitar are emanating from the backroom where they see Rico headbanging, gesticulating to no one.

"Is this fool dancing, or like, talking to himself?" whispers Rudy, banging on the window with his fist, but flesh on glass won't cut it. "Here, give me your beer bottle," he asks Jerm. Banging glass on glass, any harder and he'll smash it—Rico whips his head at the rattle, grabs a screwdriver, approaches the door.

Cracking it open, Rico fists his tool for a quick stab if necessary. "What can I do for you, or what are you going to do to me?"

"We just came to talk," Rudy says. "We wanted to apologize for all the static the other night, see if we can't join forces, maybe?"

A smile beams over Rico's sweating face. "Oh yeah?"

"You deal, right? We figured you wouldn't be talking multiple 8-balls if you weren't."

"How do I know you're not gonna narc me out?"

"Do we look like narcs?" Tristan points to Jerm and Dylan holding open beers in their hands at 11AM.

"Get out of the street with that shit. Come inside...."

The Vigil enter, eyes widening at the racks of colorful '60s and '70s apparel, the walls painted with cartoon characters, hippie-disco hybrids. Whether Rico, the artist, knows it or not, the overall aesthetic is psychedelic, but a bad trip. Every painted character laugh-crying or cry-laughing with sideways googly eyes. Radiating lines imply each character is grooving, strained expressions like they'll never stop dancing, far beyond recreation, like it's no longer a fun thing.

Dylan stops at the register, gazing at the wall behind the desk adorned with Polaroids of young neighborhood boys, some he recognizes. Creeped out by this display, he wonders if anyone else sees the way Rico has been staring at him.

The Vigil form a half-circle around Rico in the back room.

"So, what can I do for you boys?"

"We're wondering if we could get a whole 8-ball, maybe two?"

"All for yourself?"

"No, we wanted to talk to you about that."

"You wanna deal? Well, we need to talk territory then."

"Not competition, we wanna partner up."

Rico's eyes light up. After going direct to Itchy's source he found in the black book, he's sold to a couple skater boys. But every time they come back, his paranoia swells. Ever since the cops chased Itchy through his shop, he's sure they're watching him.

The high school would be a fucking goldmine.

"Aha, okay, then. Let me ask you boys—how old are you? High school?"

They nod.

"So, you would sell to high school kids, yes?"

"Yeah, but out of my house," says Mikey.

"Whatever way you wanna do it, but word will spread fast, you know. 'Cause you're kids and I know how much *you* like it." Rico's tone is repellently flirtatious. "One more thing. This makes me your boss. Now you listen to me no matter what. I was doing this for years in Mexico, I know what I'm doing, I never been caught for anything—for *anything*," he emphasizes. "Whatever I say goes all the time and any time. Understood?"

The Vigil nod solemnly in unison. Best to be submissive, auto-nod to whatever Rico says, kickstart flow of product.

"Sure, only thing is we only have $120," says Rudy.

"I just got product from my new Itchy—I'll front you two

eight-balls and you pay back the difference at the end of the week," says Rico, shaking hands with all five boys, all witnesses to the deal now sealed in secrecy. Dylan last, he feels Rico's hand linger and yanks it away.

Rico paces the crash course: "You're gonna give some of this away. I know that sounds crazy, but that's what gets 'em all coming back with money, honey."

Instructing them how to fold paper bindles into little squares and how much to put in, he holds a ball up. "About a quarter of this gonna go away for free. All you gotta do is wait for them to come back. Long as you're not an idiot, they're gonna come back—do *not* give any away for free the second time."

Approaching The All The Way House two 8-balls heavier, The Vigil swear they're hallucinating Mom hanging halfway out the front door, waving to them like June Cleaver.

"Hi there! You boys hungry? I can make some. Sandwiches if you'd like. I'm just. Cleaning the house. You know it really needed it and call me crazy. I haven't even had a drink all day 'cause there is just. Way too much to do!"

They stop, stare at each other. The only time Mom lifted a finger was tipping a bottle to her lips.

"But you're not allowed in the house until I'm done. The girls'r in the garage!"

Suspicion weighs on Mikey's brow. Entering the back door, he hears Mom talking to herself and answering back, cleaning the house maniacally, the force of the broom propelling her forward; knees trembling yet rejuvenated with purpose.

Mikey's stomach twists. Opening her bedroom door to investigate further, it's a miracle—all her bottles vanished, her dirty dishes stacked ready for the sink, her books organized not only alphabetically but by fucking color of binding and... what the fuck, her bed made? How could she make a bed she never left?

Hackman's words right before Mikey threw that first punch: *You know, your mom was coming out of the garage when I got there.* Rubbing his temples with one hand, he leans on the hallway with the other.

"Mom? Everything okay?" He's barely audible over the vacuum she's plugged in.

"Oh, me? Oh yes. Yes. Of course, honey. Just turned over a new leaf this morning, you know."

Meth don't come from a leaf, ma.

"Sorry, are you talking still? Gotta keep cleaning. You hungry? I can make you boys some sandwiches."

Mikey's surprised they're not shocked Mom stole their drugs and is playing it off shamefully ragged.

"Mikey, you don't get it," Tristan says. "That's great news if Mom is on the shit. That means we don't have to sneak around with it, right? You won't even have to call her out. She's in on the *conspiracy* now."

"We can just be real casual," says Rudy. "She's got a guilty conscience for swiping it so what's she gonna do? Ground you for dealing drugs out of your new clean-ass house?"

Mikey actually thinks: *what if speed was the best thing for her right now? It got her out of bed, acting like a mom.*

"We can gradually just cut her in," agrees Tristan. "The train is already rollin,' man. Don't get bent out. We got some planning to do. For school tomorrow. Gotta stay razor sharp...." Tristan smiles, his tongue darting out as he holds up a blade and then cuts into the ball.

10

Much like Big Jim's Brotherhood of Eternal Love with their Orange Sunshine LSD, Rico and The Vigil put meth on predestined high pedestal, turning the world on in a more dystopian fashion. Their collective zeal is becoming one voice, a tone of emergency, of duty, even enforcement: you can't be young and *not* do speed. You'll be left behind. Abandoned. You think you feel like a loser now? Wait until we're a thousand miles ahead of you.

Unlike the Brotherhood, however, The Vigil provide no broken promises of world peace through their drug—only endless initiation into borderless hedonism, igniting inner-spaces of debasement, constructing human-esque insectoid nests to protect our ultra-prophetic projects. "Who can blame us—we're society's fault; no one understands us." The riddles cellular, cancerous, xeroxing into oblivion and all the way back to day three—

—the third day of no sleep on speed: a portal into Hell on Earth. All veils drop, your bloodshot webs like his shades in *They Live*, everything decoded nefarious. Yet the more doubt one entertains, the more one must uphold the conspiracy. Submit to the cycling dynasty governed by demoniac entities peeking behind the corners of your periphery, an endless party where you'll never sleep again. The more you resist, the more the nightmare simulates. Paranoia cannibalizing itself mid-somersault. A carousel spinning so fast it will kill you to jump off. And the tighter you hold, the more your knuckles protrude. Bone made of ash from your future's burning fuse.

Monday comes quick.

Rudy takes five bindles to the construction site, offering some to his crew. He can already see how fast that house is going to build itself. His uncle will be pleased, so long as he doesn't find out about their new tool. *The faster the house goes up, the faster I can see Jasmine*, thinks Rudy, never questioning why she insists they only see each other at the beach, only at night.

School: the perfect petri dish for meth. Enhancing performance and absorption—finally, it's creating *enthusiasm*. Wide awake, salivating, a school spirit no other curriculum can achieve.

Exercising discretion with this younger, less predictable demographic, The Vigil limit their allowances to Jerm and Dylan with five bindles to their junior high. Their first target: the D&D kids, their games never-ending and their addictive, compulsive personalities pre-existing. Nocturnal by nature, they're fueled by Hostess treats, chips, and caffeine from two-liter bottles of Mountain Dew, arriving late to first period like they've been on a bender anyway. Speed provides them a "buff spell" to endure their savage night, and if they do a line before school, it guarantees real life "experience points." Skeptical at first, the D&D kids relent to temptation once Jerm explains how vastly it will connect them to unknown worlds of even more unfathomable distance.

"Cheerleaders are doing this stuff too, it will get you so laid," says Jerm.

"We'll take all five bindles," they say.

Carrying fifty bindles between them, ambitious methevangelists Tristan and Mikey throw out the first rule of drug dealing: Don't deal when you're high. Yeah, right. Flying on their own stash gives them unprecedented confidence, pirating social waters far outside of their comfort coves. Losing count of how many different hats they wear throughout the day: corrupter, peacemaker, ambassador, comedian, alchemist.

They must bite their own tongues with the jocks who assaulted Jasmine. In turn, the jocks are suspicious why The Vigil are suddenly all buddy-buddy. They each take a bindle anyway—just business, nothing personal anymore.

Bro, the jocks praise it—it's far cheaper than steroids and ensures legendary aggression to their competitive edge.

Oh my God, the cheerleaders love it—it puts pep in their step. Plus, everything is *so funny,* even when it isn't!

Dude, the surfers dig it—it gives them courage for monster waves they wouldn't have risked otherwise, and the psycho drug fits their sport's bad-boy reputation.

Uh, the AP kids take some convincing. Yet, once The Vigil explain how they'll stay up all night studying with their comprehension sharpened, they're the first to come back for more; their parent's cash kindling to burn.

After months ditching school just to whisper circles on the top bunk in Mikey's garage, Katrina and Jasmine now go to a portable classroom across the football field; their truancy is notorious. Misunderstood at-risk youth isolated from the rest of campus, their last chance, soon to be neglected. Even the teacher is over it, outside smoking while the outcasts ignore a film on pursuing trade tech. Taking over the class's attention, Katrina hands out free bindles, convincing them meth will give them a new renegade identity. *A head full of the greatest ideas ever, you'll finally know what to do with your life!* Her pitch sweetened by Jasmine's head nodding affirmative until she shakes it "no," seeing Hackman entering the classroom.

Immediately locking eyes with the girls in the far back row—their jaws drop, giggling silent, whispering. Panicking, Hackman defaults to the front row, where they stare at the back of his head, casting sinister insults.

Hackman stalls at the door after class, the first move for the upper hand.

"Hey, so yeah, this is weird," he says.

"Hey... yeah. So, like, where you been? How'd you end up here?"

"Got carried away on the beach. Figured since I was narcing I didn't need school anymore. The days just all blurred together, next thing I knew a year went by." He punctuates a nervous guffaw. "I missed too much school to graduate, so here I am."

"Are you still working with the cops?"

"You know what? Doesn't matter. Sure, we have to be in the same class, but we don't have to talk anymore. How about I stay up here in the front row, you girls in the back, and we can just do our best to ignore each other, cool?" He briskly walks away, the girls dumbfounded.

After school, Katrina and Jasmine stall at Blast until nightfall instead of going straight to The House since it's been overrun with kids buying bindles who they wouldn't be caught dead with.

"Puneta! What the fuck, you bitches tagging on my wall?" says Rico, entering the showroom.

Giggling, they hurry to finish their lipstick graffiti: *"Revolution Grrl Style Now!*, *Boys To The Back!*, and *Rape Gets The Guillotine!* The Vigil girls have adopted the fast-spreading rhetoric of Riot Grrl, the confrontational, transgressive form of third-wave feminism dispersing through punk underground.

"Sorry, we just saw all the paint on the walls, figured we were adding to the art," says Katrina. Then, like she's reciting verbatim something she read somewhere instead of actually expressing herself: "You know, female empowerment stuff, which also empowers the queer community since all of us are being crushed by straight white male corporate oppression."

Rico nods his head, thoughtfully caressing his goatee at their in-store vandalism; now, like an art gallery. "How's the quiet one today?"

"She's been seeing Rudy, like a lot," says Katrina.

"Oh, so you like the brown down there?" He grabs his crotch. "I know the feeling. Though I like 'em all colors, ages—I don't discriminate, you know?" He walks behind his register, admiring of the wall of Polaroids capturing the neighborhood boys modeling his clothes off the racks.

"Rico, I'm sorry but that's kind of creepy, honey. Don't you think you need some photos of chicks up there too?" Katrina says.

Rico gazes up at his wall. "You know, you are right. I'll dress up you girls today, but you have to earn it by adding one more piece of revolution to my wall."

Don't Let Jealousy Kill Girl Love, they write in red lipstick.

"The batch I sold you last week doing well?" says Rico.

"Oh, that's why we're here. The boys are overwhelmed. We came to get three more. It's like the whole fucking school is on the shit coming over to Mikey's, like, all the time now," says Katrina, rubbing her sore jaws from clenching her teeth.

"Wow, you made enough for three? That means you're disciplined with your own use, yes?" says Rico.

"Well. Not. Exactly," Katrina says, her flow of speech stop and go. "We're all. Kind of. Pitching in for the third. It's like. Insurance. For someone special, I guess? Yeah."

"Beautiful," says Rico. Sprinting into his clothes-littered bedroom, he pulls open his wardrobe, only used for business now. Returning to the show room, he places three 8-balls in a mink coat on the girl's rack. "Speaking of beautiful, would you like to try this on?" he says, grabbing his camera.

11

The blaze of a 4PM sun shines harsh through Mom's dust caked window, piercing the shield of her thirty-six-hour crash. Her mouth drifts open, straining to recollect when and how she finally slipped into a blurred sequence of hypnogogic comas. With booze, she'd black out, wake up erratic, unaware if it was 6AM or PM. Never had she slept for two days straight after being awake for... four?

She gasps: who cleaned my room? Someone's been in here. Her worst fear, for this fleeting second, is that social workers came unannounced. Her *worse* fear: they found the rock. Her frail body shakes: am I freezing or seizing? Voices drift into her mind; uncountable dialogue from her children, other tones piling onto overlapping cacophony of chatter, like a hundred televisions bursting out of her skull. Terrified to move: if she follows the voices, if she finds the voices, the voices will have found *her*. Propping herself up, her muscles and bones like cracked rubber held together with Elmer's glue. Her feet touch the ground—she collapses.

The volume increases, vague articulations eclipsing consonants, cackling, squealing. She looks up—her undying constant: the television. Palms on the hardwood floor, she crawls to her ageless babysitter. Trembling, she climbs up the console and turns it on. Channel eleven, always on the news, reassuring her someone else somewhere else has it worse than her and maybe tell her what day it is.

A live trial in session: After the orchestrated murder of their parents, The Menendez Brothers roll their eyes, pretending to listen to the judge. It's the highest rated show on television, edging out all major sitcoms and soap operas. *TV is for comfort, not extreme brutality*, she thinks, witnessing guilt moistening the twin's privileged eyes as they plead their case to the judge, raising the volume of voices inside her skull—no, the voices are coming from outside, the garage and its perimeter, where she delusions the Menendez Brothers are lurking, talking to her son and his friends. *How can they be live on the TV and outside in the garage at the same time?* Nervous to look out her window, knows she has to just fucking do it... lifting herself up, she gasps:

She sees Mikey, Tristan, Rudy, Jerm, and Dylan; then looks for the girls—there's Katrina and Jasmine, handing a bag to Mikey, surrounded by dozens of kids she's never seen before. Cheerleaders, jocks in absurd letterman jackets, ragamuffin surf rats, normal adolescents her son wouldn't be caught dead with. *I thought we had a deal—you wouldn't hang out with kids like that so I wouldn't look so bad,* she thinks, assuming she's talking to Mikey telepathically. When he doesn't respond, her blood boils. *Coming and going like our house is a goddamned fast-food joint,* she thinks.

She focuses on two blond jocks who look nothing alike. *The fucking Menendez Brothers teaching my own son how to kill me,* she whispers. She looks at the television, peeks out the window again. *They're in disguise,* she thinks. *I fucking gotcha.* Scooting herself along, she clutches the TV, grabs onto the door frame, and continues down the hallway. She scales the walls sideways, her feet shuffling carefully like a jumper on a high-rise. Entering the kitchen, she opens the drawer and seizes the largest knife. She points it toward the back door, approaching her opponents on the other side. Swinging open the door, Mom falls out, stumbling:

YOU! AND YOU! She points the knife at the Not-Menendez Brothers. *GET THE FUCK BACK TO COURT! YOU'RE GOING DOOOOOWN, MOTHERFUCKERS!*

Mikey freezes, then runs over.

"Mom! Mom! It's okay, we got you—"

"What do you mean 'you got me'? I know what you're planning on doing to me..."

"Mom, it's okay. We know. Do you need some more? We have plenty now. Everyone here is cool. You don't have to feel bad anymore."

Holding out his hand, a whole 8-ball.

"This. This can be. For you. Okay?"

The crowd snickers, internally shocked. To her son, Mom gazes kindly. Humbled, she's complete again. Taking it from his hand, Mom backs slowly away, closing the door gently behind her.

Speedwalking to the Boom to make his rounds, Rico is trapped in his head, unable to dissect Katrina's implications: *We're actually all kind of pitching in for the third. It's, uh... like, insurance for someone special, I guess?* He doesn't want to be paranoid, but one appears more paranoid the more they deny they're paranoid.

Attempting to evade paranoia by running from his own head inconveniently attached to his body, Rico gives up at The Boom. Handing the bouncer his bindle, he jumps into the phone booth, and dials Rudy's number; crouching down, upright fetal.

Hi Rudy, Rico here. Explaining that he's not paranoid, he demands to know who this someone special is, since he's not paranoid, he's just their boss.

Rudy turns to Mikey. "Hey man, think we can invite Rico over, just to keep things open and cool? He's kinda tripping, but nothing a visit won't help."

Crushing a fresh 8-ball down with all his weight, Mikey looks up from the mirror to Mom for permission.

"Too cool. I'll make sandwiches," she says.

12

Stumbling into the kitchen, surges of detached kinetics propel Mom's thighs, knees, and feet to function, a perpetual motion double-jointed wonder. With a mind of their own, her legs are finally able to traverse the living room without gripping the furniture, goosestepping into the future, a defective yet stubborn android.

With only four pieces of bread left, she counts on her fingers, losing track of how many children she has now. Slapping down the slices, a circle of ham, a square of American Government Cheese, she smashes bread on top. Instead of cutting, she *chop, chop, chops* the two into countless smeared unshapely chunks. "FUCK!" *Forgot the mustard.* She grabs the French's, squirting the pile like dressing. She jumps at the sound of a knock, rushes to the front door, precariously balancing the plate of unsightly appetizers, her other hand turning the knob.

"Look at this too cool handsome man. You must be Rico?"

Speechless, Rico curtsies instead.

"Have a seat," says Mikey. "Our house is your house from now on, anything you want, just let us know."

The Vigil gather single file, waving quick bashful hellos. Rico nestles into the couch, closest to Mom's throne, edging out the new guys to sit on the floor. Dylan mouths *what the fuck* to a shrugging Jerm.

"So Rico, this is Mom," says Rudy. "Mikey's mom, who we bought the extra ball for. It's sort of a unique house."

"So, you're the magic man," she says, brimming over with joy. "Too cool. That stuff has been an absolute. Godsend. Not a drink in about a week."

"Don't forget to drink water," says Rico.

"Ugh... water... makes me gag. Never did anything. For me. Point is... I actually do stuff now. Oh, which reminds me—I made you guys sandwiches."

She points to the plate of calamitous cuisine. No one's eaten anything today besides 25-cent Home Run Pies—those frosted ooey-gooey pastries are all The Vigil crave for the extra blood rush, convinced it's keeping their bodies circulated and anchored to earth while their heads hurtle through the stratosphere. Though "regular" food has become a foreign, even invasive object, they force an appetite for Mom's disaster sandwichlets since she's gone through the trouble. Digging in, it crumbles through the gang's struggling mustard-streaked fingers except for Mikey, who grabs a chunk, rolls it into a yellow-stained ball in his hand, and pops it in his mouth like a pro.

"Ah, yes," says Rico. Nervous, he's upholding an honorable, unphased front. Assuming he'd seen everything back in Mexico, he's awestruck. This house is its own sovereign Third World country. "I know what it's like to fall in love with this stuff, Miss. Can I offer you some?"

"Such a gentleman. Of course," says Mom, beaming.

Rico lays out lines for the house, chop, chop, chop. "Okay so now I understand—one big happy family, are we?" He offers the mirror to Mom; her hair falls, veiling her weathered face as she sniffs the line.

"So where are you from?" says Mom, wide-eyed, inquisitive—she must know everything about her new friend. "What brings you to Laguna?"

"Not far, Tijuana. Lots of poverty. But lots of freedom to do anything you want there. Unless you're fucking queer. They'll kill a cocksucker there, you know. I just wanted to move to south California. Where there's more guys like me but somewhere I knew there'd be, you know, no mayates."

"Maya what?"

Tristan and Rudy whisper to one another, condensing a hyper-commentary of this synchronicity: Rudy citing Rico's Mexican racial slur for blacks, how ominous for Mom to have only picked up on the *Maya* part, which in Hindu, Tristan adds, means the supernatural power wielded by gods and demons to create illusions, which in southern Brazil, Rudy shudders, means "mother."

Rico turns to Mikey, whispers: "My mom is part of my business too, in a way. I send her money every month, to support her. She cashes the check, but never asks where it came from. She thinks it's from the shop, but c'mon, we know better." He play-punches Mikey in the shoulder, still whispering. "That's why I get a little intense with this business. I think more of my mom's well-being than my own." He raises his voice to projects to the room. "By the way, one thing I'd like to ask—when I walked up, there were many kids in the driveway who I don't see now. Customers?"

"Yeah, customers," says Mikey, turning to Mom. "Ma, just so we are clear. We've been sharing this stuff. With kids at school. Okay, listen—we've been selling the shit to kids at school. But look at this." He pulls out a large wad of twenties.

"Too cool. You know, I sold pot in the '60s. This is right up my alley." She starts her whole I Knew Charles Manson thing until Rico cuts her off. "Okay, so all the kids in the driveway—that must stop. Immediately."

"You know what we can do?" Mom looks over to Tristan's John Wayne Gacy poster above the couch. "First, Tristan— take down that fucking clown balloon poster!"

"Wait. No. Why?"

"'Cause it gives me the fucking creeps and you put it over the door to the basement."

Pointing behind the couch, a threshold they assumed to be a broom closet no one used.

Mikey turns to Mom. "We have a fucking basement?"

"Yup. Everybody up. Let's move this couch," she says.

Rising from the couch, Rico, Mikey and Tristan shift it away from the wall. Jerm and Dylan scatter out of the way, returning when Mikey opens the door. Shrouded in must and shadow, a staircase into darkened void. A light switch at the first step illuminates its vastness. They descend, treading cautiously, excited—hidden passageways pure ecstasy for a tweaker's imagination.

Their attention travels to the corner, another staircase leading up to the backyard. "Wow. This is perfect," Tristan's mind expands with the house's true layout. Leading the gang up the steps, he pushes open the latch on the wooden door laying cellar diagonal, emerging into the overgrown garden where they piss out their 40 ouncers. The elation unanimous, the possibilities endless. Before they know it, they're remodeling their boundaries to stave off their mounting anxiety. Flying on their lines, spinning, touching every brick in case it holds more secrets, they're in awe of how meth makes everything seem predestined, perfect.

"Okay, back to business," says Mom. "Let's make this official, like a casino. You guys can deal, but thirty percent goes to the house—and by that, I mean me."

13

The Vigil never asked to be popular and now no one will leave them alone. They possess what everybody wants, what many even want to be—the undiluted version of pop culture's recent commodification of punk rock found in corporate magazines and MTV, what kids mimic rather than tapping into their own reservoirs of self-expression. Ahead of the cultural steamroll to ensure they're not parodies, Mikey and Tristan commit their increasing androgyny to campus, provoking only the most daring fiends to approach them in their eyeliner, rouge, and lipstick: if you're gonna deal with us, now you gotta earn it.

Conversely, The Vigil girls grow progressively un-ladylike, picking fights with guys whose only crime was a second look; the double-threat of pepper spray or their faggot-looking boyfriends beating them up. The Vigil no longer worry about getting jumped; now it's just annoying when a spoiled kid in a new pair of Docs and Offspring shirt latches on for street cred. *Like, where the fuck were you when I had to fight for my life*, they think, begrudgingly accepting another twenty for a bindle.

Wads of cash are growing so fast they're running out of places to hide it all. They could always buy more eight-balls to have on hand, but it's unwise holding too much in case they get busted; a paranoid conversation they never finish, keeping four balls at a time, replenishing every three days, sometimes every two on a party weekend when the tides are high. Too spun to consider a bank account, their profits buried in backyard mason jars in the weed tangles by the basement stairs where they walk up and dig a new hole like they're simply gardening.

Acquiring six 8-balls a week from Rico, they're considering expanding downtown to Blackout Beach, but they're terrified Hackman or Sawyer would be on them like a sunburn. Clocking out at 8PM every night, they barricade at The House, unwinding by winding themselves up, sampling their product to assure its desired virulence.

Regimenting their days: go to school, deal the shit, take after-class appointments, deal/package more shit at The House. Every waking moment is spent keeping the circuit bending or breaking when they're tripping, covering their bases to asphyxiate Tristan's looming fear that every star in the night sky is a suspended satellite eye of surveillance. He used to never worry, knowing a star is a self-contained celestial disaster that's already happened. "Then why am I seeing it and why is it still happening?" he says, citing the conspiracy of constellations. "Why does nobody but me care that all those lights are... grouping?"

Mikey has disassembled every clock in The House so Tristan and Katrina have no idea it's 4AM, blabbering in the driveway how glad they are to finally be alone, to finally get to know each other... to really, really know every memory in every cell in each other's soul... like everything about you I want to know, right now, every secret is safe with me, I promise.... Promise-promise? Promise-promise! Talking so fast they just keep repeating, over and over without getting to know anything, repelling any secrets away. They start making out to see if it helps, sloppy lips sucking, oozing—finally, the moment they've both been waiting for until:

"Wait, where's Rudy?" says Tristan.

Katrina pulls away. "Uhm, I don't know. Why are you fucking thinking about Rudy right now?"

"Well, I just want to know where he is, anything wrong with that?"

"Who fucking cares?"

"I care. What if he's... what if he's caught?"

"Caught what?"

"We gotta keep track of everyone. If they're not here they might have gotten caught... or they might be fucking cops... or... worse—when was the last you looked up, Katrina?"

"Looked up?"

Tristan screams for Mikey until he peeks out from The House, stuffing money in his pockets.

"Get out here, man... this is serious. I need to talk to you guys. We need to have a meeting... a serious meeting...."

The three standing in the driveway, hearts pounding their ribcages, vibrating. Tristan points up into the gargantuan oak tree overhanging.

"Do you see them?"

"What? Who?"

"The people, up there... right... there. Don't point."

"In the trees?"

"Yes, right there... in the trees," Tristan says, still pointing. "They can see everything we are doing."

"Can they hear us too?"

"Shhhh... yes. All of us, maybe except for Jasmine... she's smart enough to not talk... but they can listen to her thoughts."

"Can they listen to our thoughts too?"

"Yes. Can't you see them up there? They move with the branches. With the leaves. They're camouflage beings..."

"I can see them now."

"Moving with the wind... and when the leaves are rustling... that's them whispering... Can you hear what they're saying?"

"No... but I can hear what they're thinking."

"Are they thinking what I'm hearing them thinking?"

"If you're hearing them thinking they're just waiting for us to fall asleep so they can install cameras... into our bodies... yes."

"Okay we cannot fall asleep then."

"Okay."

"Wait, where is Jasmine, Katrina?"

"She'd better not be sleeping."

"Yes, because if she is sleeping… there's already… cameras inside of her… so she is listening to everything we are saying."

"Can she see what we're doing even though she is sleeping?"

"Yes, and she can hear what we are thinking."

Tristan imagines Jasmine: the girl so tight-lipped, the only time she ever opens her mouth is to chain-smoke cloves and menthols or to suck on candy or slurp her spoonsful of Duncan Hines chocolate frosting. What secrets does she hide in her mouth when it's not smoke and sugar? He imagines it, therefore it's happening: like her mouth is giving birth to a baby, her lips forcing open into a circular aperture, a camera lens protruding, elongating, focusing. He can't tell if she is in pain or an accomplice, or if she's orchestrating the whole thing.

The three tiptoe, every fallen leaf an alarm; if they crunch it, it will alert the beings. Landmine ballet all the way to the garage, where they can feel Jasmine sleeping. Tristan thumbs his razorblade, the one he used for bleeding. "Let me do this," he whispers, and turns on the lightening.

There she lies on the top bunk, peacefully. Tristan climbs the ladder while the other two keep watch, as decoys for the beings.

Jasmine stirs, lips unmoving, ventriloquizing, "Tristan… what are you doing?"

He pinches her lips into pucker. She tries her hardest to scream.

"I just need… to see… what they are doing…" Pulling her

110

lips apart, her teeth revealing. "Oh my God. Oh my fucking God, they got to you, sweetheart... hold still... still."

Tristan straddles her body to perform surgery, renegade dentistry, her decayed teeth so yellow they're nearly green, spotted with opaque and translucent cavities; or tiny black cameras, a tragedy. He got to her right in time, if she would just quit screaming, if Katrina would just stop running inside, quit pulling him off the bed, blabbering what the fuck is he doing, both girls might see everything has almost died but chivalry.

14

Rico has been up for a long time. Sleep requires surrender and Rico won't let anything go. Every time his eyes close, even to blink, he sees the same thing: a demon bleeding into his whole periphery. You can't turn your head away from what you're seeing with your eyes closed; you can only keep your eyes open. Only, lately Rico has started seeing this demon out of the corners of his eyes, and when he whips his head to catch it, it disappears into the other corner. He can't tell anyone, or they'll think he's crazy, and if they don't think he's crazy, they'll know he's racist once he tells them what it looks like: a large black face either laughing or angry; either way, it's going to devour him, or just never go away. They told him there'd be no black people here. Who is They, Rico? He cannot answer himself; he's too afraid They might find out there's one living in his mind, then they might kill him. *Anyways, I'm brown, I can't be racist*, he thinks.

The demon surrounds his consciousness, suffocating his will to leave his own apartment. I don't need to leave, he says out loud to no one. Anyone who wants it, they can all come to me.

To distract himself, he turns on his small television, every channel different angles of apocalypse: L.A. engulfed in flame, its inner-city citizens rioting to signal anyone who will listen; they've tried everything else. Panicking, he shuts off the television.

Sitting in the grass watching Katrina spare-change, Jasmine has taken so many aspirin her stomach is killing her almost as much as her bleeding mouth, the salty air stinging the exposed nerves. Her top left canine hangs by a thread where Tristan excavated with his razorblade, telling her to hold still, this will all be over in a second, just shut up or they'll hear you.

Katrina is sweating on the outside, boiling on the inside. Vowing to never speak to Tristan again after what he did to Jasmine. She's furious at herself for being so spun, to think she let it happen. She's put on extra eyeliner to lock in the sight of each passerby, yet she knows she looks too desperate. Overacting friendly to tourists she's begging for money, she can't stop looking back at Jasmine doubled over, holding her mouth, refusing to look up so no one will see she's crying.

A dishwater brunette in jeans, high heels, and a Ministry T-shirt approaches, lifting her Ray Bans. "Oh man, what's the matter with your friend?"

"She's like, in really bad pain. Her teeth."

"Oh, man." Dirty Anna sizes them up. "I got something I can share if you're cool with it. How much money do you have?"

15

Rico's just about to open Blast when the shop phone rings; a voice he doesn't know, but a voice who knows. *Yes, this is Rico. Who is this? Oh, okay, but what's your name, please? Donny? No? Oh, sorry, like Tod-Knee. Okay, hello Mr. Todney, what can I do. Oh? Uhm, okay. Well, I'm sorry to hear that, uh. Can I ask how you know them? Oh, I see. Well, again I'm sorry to hear about them but, uh, congratulations on your good fortune, and welcome to the club, I guess?*

Pause.

Oh, okay? There's no club?

A longer pause.

Okay, well I have the high school alread—Not anymore? Mr. Todney, I don't want to get on your wrong foot. How about we talk in person? No sir, I don't carry a gun. I am a passionate person, but everything is negotiable. Okay. Park in the alley and just come up my back stairs... uh, hello? Mr. Todney?"

Rico's trembling hands relock the front door, reversing the open sign to "closed." Four minutes and thirty-two seconds later, punctuated stomps resonate up his salt-decayed stairs. Rico freezes mid-pace in the shadow of a large black man in short shorts, flip-flops, and a white Stussy T-shirt draped over his gut; a figure leaving almost no space in the door frame.

"You Rico?"

Rico's arms shoot up in surrender. Panicking, his eyes blink rapidly, like he's trying to believe what... who, WHO! ... he's seeing: a black man at his doorstep. His worst fear; not quite what he saw in his head, but too close. "Mr. Todney?"

"Well, I ain't the fuckin' mailman but I've got a message for you," He sighs. "Listen, I don't wanna be a dick. I really don't. But you and I, we're not friends. Let's get that straight first."

Rico wonders how to shoehorn his charm in. Instead, he acts so polite its rude again. "Understood, Mr. Todney."

"Okay fuck it, you can call me Bron. This mister shit's starting to wig me out."

"I apologize, Bron."

"It's cool, it's cool. Mind if I have a seat?" He scans the room. "Is there anywhere to even fucking sit here?"

Embarrassed, Rico shows him his clothes-littered bed. "Sorry, I don't really sit."

"Fuck it, I'm standing. So, here's the deal. I'm from Moreno Valley, next town over from where Itchy's gang's whole operation is. I'm part of the new ownership."

"Wait—" Rico squints. "When you told me on the phone those guys are gone, are you saying you robbed 'em? What do you mean by gone?"

"Nah, nah. It's actually even more complicated than that..."

"Excuse me for asking, Bron, but how in the world did you get involved with guys like that?"

"Nazi Lowriders? Nah, it's a good question, actually. My cousin, some prison debts, basically. But like I said, we came up huge when they asked to us to take over The Bunker."

"The Bunker?"

"The Bunker where they make the shit. These Peckerwood motherfuckers stole a backhoe from the cemetery, dug a hole big enough to bury a shipping container in—it's virtually invisible other than a manhole over a ladder down. Since they got busted, my cousin and his whole gang are there picking up where they left off. Luckily, they didn't bust 'em there—those boneheads are fucking idiots, but smart enough to know Itchy would snitch to reduce his sentence, so they steered clear of The Bunker until they knew it was safe. They all got busted before they went back, all had the shit on them, couldn't stay out of the game while they were hiding out."

Rico unfurls, suddenly fascinated. "Wow. So, your cousin owed them a favor."

"Man, I'm not sure who owed who what, but right when they found out Itchy got pinched, they had to evacuate The Bunker. To keep the beakers burning, they came to my cousin's gang. Since my cousin knows the game, the boneheads knew it'd be advantageous to have the crack, coke, and weed dealer's contacts cross-pollinate with their new drug, feel me? So, they taught 'em how to cook. Both sides mainly stayed out of each other's way, but in terms of politics, this was, like, a big-time truce."

"And where do you fit into all of this?"

"I deal for my cousin. But I'm an anomaly, Rico. I do well in school and I'm a motherfucker on the field, which makes me the perfect dealer. They'd never really expect it 'cause I don't fly colors or anything. My mom's mom croaked, got some inheritance, and moved my ass down here to keep me out of trouble, so I won't hang with my cousin all the time. She knew what was going on. But man, bad timing... or good timing... 'cause that speed shit is selling like crazy. So I'm still in the game. With my cousin, slingin' from the beginning. He says I gotta to stay in it. As insurance. Especially now that this speed shit is exploding, and now that I've moved here now, we've expanded."

Rico's head drops, he knows what's coming next.

"So, I gotta ask you, Rico—who are these high school kids you're selling to? Since I'm the source, source gets priority. The school's my territory now."

Mikey keeps $300 on hand at all times in case they need to re-up. Since their supply got cleaned out late Sunday night, he stops by Rico's on the way to school Monday morning, knuckle raps extra hard to snap Rico out of his usual morning malfunction.

The door swings open wildly at the first knock. Rico stands there bolt upright, eyes bloodshot and jittery.

"What?"

"I need to re-up, man."

Rico just stares.

"Mikey, we gotta talk."

Mikey will be tardy to school, too late to hear the audible whispers. Black guy, black kid, *a fucking black dude!* comes from everyone's mouths except Bron Todney. He feels it the second he walks onto campus. Their sun-kissed heads whiplash, jaws fall open; equal parts confusion, fear and then... a weird, displaced joy? Complete strangers run up high fiving him unsolicited. Bron is bewildered. It's not the low-key loathing he was used to or the blatant neglect he was hoping for just to get through the day. To these kids he's an exotic creature from a savage land, his color recently canonized by the uprising in South Central. *Yeah, like I told you though, I'm from the desert,* he keeps reminding them after inquiring about the riots he wasn't involved in, but it's like a black kid can't exist anywhere else. They keep asking him if he raps. It's nothing he can't handle; with every ignorant quip, they're just potential customers. But first he needs their intel: Where those punkers at? They vie to be the first to help, taking his side sight unseen.

Kids keep tapping Tristan on the shoulder, smiling, saying someone's looking for you and Mikey. He asks who; they just laugh. And Mikey never showed to first period, so he's really, really freaking.

There's one! someone laugh-screams, every head turning

117

to Tristan, a path parting for Bron. Tristan's mind races faster than his feet, struggling without his morning line since Mikey was supposed to score more. His boots cement-heavy, his thighs jelly, he hobbles across the dew-sludgy grass of the football field.

Bron grabs the back of Tristan's neck, gripping like a cranking vice. He collapses; paralyzed by reverberating jeers roaring across the crowd, every student opting for a tardy to see this hard lesson unfold.

"Why the fuck you running? I haven't done shit to you?"

"What'd you do to Mikey, man?"

"Who the fuck is Mikey? Just stop struggling, let's talk—you're making this a fucking bust."

Running from Rico's drenched in sweat, Mikey approaches campus through the back way across the football field to sneak in undetected. Charging across the turf like he's running away from the train, only he's running towards it—some huge black guy choking out Tristan.

"Hey! Get the fuck off of 'em!"

"Man, sit your ass down," says Bron, releasing his grip to point. "You guys want a war—I'll give you one."

"Just sit down, Mikey," Tristan says, rubbing his neck.

"Listen, I just got back from Rico's—I know who you are, I know what's going on..."

"All right, good, 'cause I'm gonna make this really simple—you guys get to retire."

"What the fuck does that mean?"

"It means any shit you got in your pocket right this second came from me and my cousin. Like I told Rico, source gets priority here. So, you guys are done," he concludes, wipe-clapping his hands.

Tristan curses. Mikey tells him to fucking hush.

"Listen, I get it—Rico told me the whole deal. But we've got this whole school eating from the palms of our hands. We could join forces, you know, like, help you."

"Man, you think I need your help?" he says, a deep chuckle rising from his throat. "You think I'm gonna have a hard time here just because I'm black? I've just now walked on campus and these kids are already treating me like I'm the fucking Fresh Prince."

"So, you're really gonna just rob us of our job?"

"Ha—look at yourself. You don't gotta do this for a job! And rob you? I ain't gonna have to do shit—second I walked on this campus, your job was already gone."

16

It's noon, an hour past opening time, and Rico refuses to open the door. Outside lies weight of accumulation: if he even cracks it open, the dam will break. Every flood begins with a leak. His two front windows frame every passing eye outside. Every time one traverses the glass and breaches the boundary, another one enters the other side like Pac-Men chomping kernels of evidence, the way he's been combing the carpets for sustenance, listening to the walls for surveillance. In fact, the windows themselves watching me like two eyes, he thinks, reduced to an idling fish trapped in aquarium when all he ever wanted to be was ocean size.

Hearing himself tell Mikey it's over dropped his despair into a formless descent. Up all night running on vapors, counteracting it with one more line, streamlining his spirit into anvil plummet, spastic tentacles of cognizance reach in vain for any shard of shattered logic. Mikey left four hours ago yet Rico's still in discussion with him like he's in the next room.

A grand a week from The Vigil now Bron with the wind, rent past due and utilities looming, Rico ponders hitting up past Johns or turning fresh tricks on the beach. It was one thing to do upon first arriving on the scene but now they'd see how bad he's drowning. They'd give him some fucked up nickname, like they did with Sexual Pablo.

I'm supposed to be Rico, the neighborhood kingpin, he thinks.

Until then, he'll have to cut corners, be conservative.

He recalls the rig he got from the Blond Boy at the Boom: *You're still snorting? It's a total waste of product, not even close to the high of shooting*, he said, slipping Rico a clean needle. Rico thought it was sleazy, but he took the rig to appease his customer.

Seeing the spike there on his wardrobe, it suddenly makes sense: if he must buy less/make less, he'll have to stretch his own stash further. The good news: once he fires this needle into his vein, he knows it'll reveal all the greatest ideas any man has ever thought of.

Spying on Bron from afar, to see what makes him tick, Mikey deduces it's Bron's talk propelling him through suffocating Caucasian mediocrity. By fourth period, he's surrounded by giggling girls tweaking the air out of their own heads: *Oh my God, can I please touch your hair, please*? By lunchtime he's jumping in the truck-bed of the head quarterback's new Toyota pickup and forget food—they're going for a quick spin to get spun quick. After lunch, he returns with a blonde and brunette under each arm in justice-scale symmetry.

Suddenly every extrovert assumes just because they talk to the new black guy means he's now their best friend. Bron takes full advantage, turning up his charm and gift of gab, sizing up each kid, mentally logging tweaker symptoms from each student—grinding teeth with eyelids peeled past the point of excruciation—telling them that since he and his cousin are the source for the speed they've been getting from the Vigil, that him and his cousin's shit is uncut.

Upping their antsy, he gives them a taste of the really good crystal.

Within thirty seconds they're rejoicing this exclusive purity, taking their business to the black guy instead of the scowling, paranoid punkers.

Mikey convinces a kid to buy a bindle off Bron, then bring it back to him so he can sample his product. Opening the bindle, the difference in appearance glaringly obvious—this stuff a pristine white instead of the yellow shit they've been getting. His feet scraping pavement, he does a line:

In five seconds, he's past the fucking moon into vast heaven.

Revelation: If this stuff is coming straight from the cooker's kitchen, someone's been cutting their shit by the time it gets to them.

Rico is ripping them off.

His mind races. The first finish line: Rico's place. He doesn't want to rile the gang up quite yet, so he goes alone. The shop is closed at 4PM, no back in five sign or anything, only tin foil covering every inch of window.

The second finish line: deduce whether Rico is succumbing to stacked psychosis or avoiding The Vigil because he's been ripping them off.

But no Rico, no answers.

"Anyone know where the fuck Katrina is? Or Jasmine?" says Tristan, mumbling to himself in the living room as if someone is listening.

Rudy walks in on Tristan pacing in private panic.

"Hey Rudy, Jasmine been at your pad?"

"Nah man, I can't find her. Anywhere." Rudy plops on the couch, exhaling heavily. "If she's hurt, I'll fucking kill the motherfucker who hurt her."

Tristan changes the subject. "How's it been hanging out with her? Does she talk?"

"Only when we were kissing. It's weird... secrets... some bigger stuff I can't repeat. I don't know. Where she is now."

"What do you mean bigger stuff you can't repeat?"

"I can't say… Don't wanna get her in trouble with the law, you know?"

"No, I don't know," Tristan snaps. "Like you think we're narcs or something?"

"Nah man! Fuck, just shut up, okay? You're stressing me out." Rudy slaps his hands, hollering to Jerm and Dylan, signaling they better get to business. "Catch us up, Mikey."

Mikey dives right in, reiterating how bad Rico's crumbling, his observations with Bron throughout the day, demanding to know how they're supposed to navigate this new world with Bron at the center of it all.

"It was crazy. I've never seen a whole school take to a new kid like that, and this was before they knew he was the source," says Mikey.

"Yeah, it was a trip, like drugs weren't the main reason why everyone was all up in his shit," says Tristan.

"I don't have anything against 'em, but man, where I grew up you never really saw blacks and Mexicans associating," Rudy says. "But I wish I could have been there today when he jumped you."

"Man, he didn't jump me," Tristan says. "I'd say he fully restrained himself considering what he could've done to us. It might have looked bad from where Mikey saw it but man, I got off fucking easy."

"That's a good sign," says Mikey. "Maybe there's some potential there."

"What do you mean?"

"At least we know he's in control of his actions, knows consequence."

"True, true…."

"So, our only real choice to move forward is to find a way to join forces with him."

"Dude, you heard him this morning. Just 'cause he didn't fucking kill Mikey and I doesn't mean he wants anything to do with us."

Mikey scoffs. "Okay look—first, it's not the end of the world that Bron gets the high school—"

"The fuck it isn't. That's why we're here talking, right?"

"You're forgetting about us," Jerm says. "Dylan and I brought in $450 last week."

"And that's just from the D&D kids and the like, five kids wearing Nirvana shirts," Dylan adds eagerly. "They're buying more at one time so they don't have to come back so often— they're also buying for other kids too scared to approach us. If we had more, we could hustle more."

"Right, that's what I'm saying. I just really think we've gotta somehow convince Bron to come over here for a night and talk."

"Okay," says Tristan. "But let's wait until he's alone. I don't want to be in the middle of any those fucking honkeys pining for his attention."

17

Bron Todney is a goddamned politician. An octopus shaking every hand, accommodating every goofy kid patting his back who walks away in renewed confidence. Either they don't notice, or they just don't care he's annoyed with each encounter—he's just grinning smooth through it all; a rep to build, bindles to move, a game to play, a job to do.

"Fuck, we look like we're stalking him at this point," says Tristan. "Do they ever leave him alone?"

"Don't be jealous," says Mikey.

"Like, are they gonna offer to hold his dick to piss?"

"There's an idea—we'll follow him into the bathroom."

"He'll think we're gonna jump him or something."

"I think he knows no one in their right mind would jump him."

"Yeah but he's crazy enough to think we're crazy or something."

Obscured by his entourage, Tristan and Mikey creep like roaches, keeping Bron in their crosshairs. Finally, he waves his fans off. Severing himself from the gawking comet trail, he ducks into the boys room.

"Let me do the talking," says Mikey, swinging open the door.

Bron is alone, holding his own dick.

"Hey Bron!"

His head turns, eyes roll: *I'm taking a fucking leak here, fuck.*

"Hey man, sorry to bug you. Wondering if we could talk?"

Bron zips his pants, mulls it over. He pivots, shakes his head in disbelief, then smiles.

"You know what? Yeah, we sure can," he says. "Of all people, you motherfuckers are the first ones with manners to actually ask to talk to me—and I guess we've already been though some actual shit together. Just name the time and place and I'll be there," says Bron. "But long as we're at school, I don't fucking know you, right?"

Bron is repulsed he's joined a football team with the pansy -ass name *The Artists*. He throws down even harder to compensate and by the second day, the novelty of his pigment is overshadowed by his immense skill and agility, tarnishing the golden boys in comparison.

Exiting the gates of the field, he squints at Mikey's sloppy handwritten directions to his house, trying to decipher the address scrawled at the bottom, so he doesn't notice the cop car slowing to survey him.

Bron fucking Todney? Hackman whispers.

"Who?" says Sawyer.

"Right there. Do me a favor—pull up, go slow, don't be obvious."

"Wow, black guy. You know him?"

Hackman elbows Sawyer, then leans out the window for a closer look.

"*Bron Todney in da house!*" says Hackman, a mocking tone out the window.

Bron whips around—confirming the identity of Hackman's old archrival.

All Bron sees is the back of a cop car driving past him, containing some anonymous pig who somehow knew his name. Inhaling its exhaust, he coughs.

He's finally decoded Mikey's scribble: *DO NOT knock on front door. Go straight down driveway, enter gate on the right. Go to the weeds, south side of yard. Pull them back, you'll see cellar door. Open door, go downstairs, we'll be there.*

Damn, some paranoid suburban Narnia shit, he thinks. Opening the rust red cellar door, there's a string attached leading down the staircase, ringing a tiny teacher's bell. He descends, eyes slowly adjusting to dark—frantic voices behind another door—it opens before he can grab the knob.

"Bron, welcome to The All The Way House," says Mikey, beaming cordially. The Vigil make pitiful attempts at direct eye contact through their blinking.

"Damn, thanks for the invite to the sausage party. Where the girls at?"

"Man, that's a kind of a sore subject," says Rudy. "Haven't seen 'em in three days and one of 'em's my chick, so that's like, this whole other discussion we're not prepared for."

"That's cool, didn't mean to razz ya," says Bron. "Just as well we talk like men."

Scanning the room, Bron studies The Vigil in their insecure huddle.

"Hey, you know what y'all remind me of? That movie *Hook*. The pirate kids in *Hook*."

It's a blow to their stomachs. The embarrassment knocks them breathless. Feeling he fucked up, Bron scrambles for another ice breaker. "So, what's the deal? You guys all into heavy metal or something?"

"No, punk. Punk rock and like, other weird shit."

"Oh, so like Billy Idol and stuff?"

Tristan cringes. "Yeah, kinda. More like his first band, though."

Bron almost rolls his eyes but he's big on manners; catching himself before he appears rude. Mikey offers a folding chair that Bron pulls up to the card table. Crowding in half-circle, the big guy takes up one whole side.

"So, uh... man, I tried your crystal," says Mikey. "Fucking clean. Like doing it for the first time all over again."

"Ha, thanks. Wish I could take credit but that's my cousin's crew, picking up after the Peckerwoods." Bron dives into a whip-crack exposition how those two disparate worlds collided. It blows the Vigil's mind.

"Crazy. So, my next point—the stuff we've been getting from Rico has been... uh... different," says Mikey.

"Like, he cut it?"

"Yeah, like he cut it, yeah."

"Man, that's just what a dealer does," says Bron. "Don't ever think that just 'cause you see a dude every day to get drugs means he's your friend—he ain't. He's also not doing anything out of the ordinary. Only reason why my cousin ain't cuttin' his stuff—they can make as much as they want, it's cheap. Sure, they might get greedy and cut it one day. They wouldn't be doing anything wrong, it's just business. Still gets everyone high, right? Or else they wouldn't be fiending for more. It's better some people don't know how high they *could* get."

Tristan steps in. "Right. I think what we're all thinking is hypothetically what would it take to join forces with you? There are some interesting options."

Dylan speaks up. "What I, personally, would love to see, is that we don't deal with Rico anymore if we don't have to. He creeps me the fuck out."

Tristan is spun by Dylan's comment. He hasn't told anyone, but he's been seeing this, like, demon in his mind every time he tries falling asleep, like a stupid cartoon devil with a goatee. It was just annoying at first, but now he's convinced its Rico, caricatured like the murals in Rico's shop: Rico, the pants less Porky Pig demon in that red puffer vest and nothing else. *Fuck.*

"Ah, I think Rico's okay," says Bron. "He's just doing way too much of his product. He looked insane when I spoke with him. Personally, I don't even touch the shit."

"Really?" says Tristan. "How could you not?"

"What? Have you looked at yourselves? This is like crack all over again—I already seen this shit. Got my cousin and his crew back in the day. Then they kinda cleaned up when they started dealing. Kinda. Nah, they're still all fucked up, actually. That's why I'm vital to the operation because I don't do the shit. They do a lot of the heavy lifting but I'm their eyes, ears, muscle, and brain. To be honest, they're sampling their yields heavily. I mean, you sort of have to, to make sure it's legit. But who are they kidding, now they're tweaking balls just like you all."

A moment of introspection settles over the crew; of guilt and survival twisting within their constricted limitations. The Vigil are run-ragged and Bron feels comfy in their company. With the runaway train of speed in common, they're being pulled opposite directions, yet caught in the same finger trap.

"So, check it out—straight up, I'm a fucking Mama's Boy," says Bron. "I get good grades, play football, make her proud. Pay my single Mama back, you know? She moved me down here so I wouldn't be around my cousin so much—she saw which way the wind was blowing. So the more I think about unloading some of my responsibility onto you guys, the better it sounds. The less I gotta lie to my mom, the better."

Tristan, Mikey, and Rudy exhale, relieved.

"Dylan and I already got the junior high," says Jerm.

"No shit? Okay, okay. Yeah, I don't wanna mess with that shit, I got enough going on." Bron rubs his chin contemplatively. "You know, something weird happened on my way here."

They lean in closer.

"Let me ask you all a question—is there a reason why a cop would already know my name on my third day in town?"

As Bron relays the passing encounter, they freeze, paranoia choking the room, their hive mind darting a hundred directions then snapping back.

"I mean, I don't wanna wig the rest of you out if this was an isolated incident with me 'cause of my color or whatever...."

Tristan slurs with his own concerns. "I've been seeing

white vans. Every day a new one, or the same one. Like, so many white vans...."

"Here's something else," says Mikey. "One, the cops don't like us either. We make the town look bad for homeowners, which, let's face it, are who the cops are really serving and protecting. But, if we expand to Blackout Beach...."

"Black Out Beach?" asks Bron.

"Main Beach, sorry. Long story, man," says Mikey. "Down there, the little pockets where the freaks hang, we could get away with a lot more than the only black kid in high school might."

Bron calmly nods, the light going on in his head. "I dig you guys ain't sugarcoating any of this shit. Okay, let's do this."

The Vigil punch their palms, smiling wildly as they shake off their tension.

"One condition," cautions Bron. "Unless I'm walking down those steps—again, you guys don't fucking know me. That's the only way this is gonna work. Which reminds me— why am I coming down these backsteps instead of coming in the front door? Y'all better not be ashamed of me."

"Nah man, it ain't you we're hiding. It's my mom, man, she's on the shit too. Or she was, before we ran out. Now she's tearing the place apart upstairs thinking we're hiding it from her. I just didn't want to freak you out."

"Damn. I feel you," Bron reaches into his pocket for a bindle. "Here, this is for your mom so she can level out until I come by tomorrow with your first batch. And know what— fuck it, here's another bindle to get you guys through tonight and tomorrow morning, dog." He pauses, smiles. "Okay, *that's* what you guys remind me of. Like dogs. Not in a bad way, but like little Terriers acting all tough 'cause they're running with the big dogs now."

18

Needle in hand, Rico yanks opens his stash drawer.

A knock on the door—Rico freezes so fast he nearly shatters. It's always cops until it's someone else.

Muffled laughter from the other side, more knocks, now playful.

"Who is it?"

"It's your fucking bitches," Katrina giggles. "Quit jerking off in there, faggot!"

Running to the door, he swings it open like it's Christmas morning, desperately hugging his mascara-streaked teddy bears. "Oh my gosh, my little ladies. Save me from myself." His histrionics dilute his hellish internals brimming over.

"Oh, sweetheart, we gotchu." Katrina and Jasmine squeeze the hell out of him. Coddling, pressing their faces into his shoulder. Her eyes downcast, Katrina spots the needle in his hand. Gently, she unclasps his fist, rolling the rig into her palm.

"Honey, what were you going to do with this?" she says. She shows it to Jasmine, salivating.

"I was going to be a bad boy," he says. "Shoot the shit instead of snort the shit, to uh... you know, adjust."

Katrina eyes Jasmine, who nods back. "Rico, have you ever tried heroin before?"

"Ah, no?"

Katrina turns a red balloon inside out, revealing its brown contents. "Sweetheart, I promise this is what you need right now. Trust me. It pains me to see you like this. Let's have you come down, like, gently."

Rico stares at the earthy chunk. "Okay… where'd you get it?"

"This chick Dirty Anna at the beach. We've been going back and forth to Santa Ana with her to score, but she only had one needle for herself today. Yeah. So if we can use that needle, we'll get you high for free, yeah? We're like, basically never doing speed again. The boys are freaking us out, so we're doing this now, way better."

Rico nods, lips a pucker, relaying his recent woes: how everything's changed with Bron in town, how he doesn't know what to do since he's misbudgeted the shop and he's late on rent on top of his hustle swiped.

The girls say *okay* each time he pauses, their impatience unhidden. "So, we can use your needle then?"

"Okay. I would like to try, but it's not good we all share one needle, you know. How about I go last?"

The girls hyper-stomp and clap, totally stoked they're finally getting high after aimlessly walking the town, proud of the super ethical way they're all taking care of each other. Quick to fix, Katrina washes a spoon in Rico's sink. Negotiations: I'll do you and you do me; they carry their bond of hospitality into euphoric abyss.

Smirking, nodding, the tar traversing Rico's bloodstream... washing all the worry away... he giggles mystified how he could be so upset before the girls arrived... He's no longer sore at Bron Todney. *Everything is exactly how it's supposed to be*, he thinks. He looks at the girls: smiling pretty, heads dipping, then bobbing them back awake, their eyes thankful to be alive. Communal bliss. Not only is everything just fucking groovy now, but he can finally think straight. His entrepreneurial instincts kick in again.

"So... tell me about this Anna."

"Anna... she's great. Some call her Dirty Anna just 'cause she's a tough chick, just got outta jail. But she's totally trustworthy, been doing this stuff... fuuuuck... for like, a long time."

"Aha. So, you go with... Saint Anna to... Santa Ana to score... perfect. And no one is selling in Laguna, right?

"Yeah, otherwise she wouldn't go all the way to Santa Ana... to get it from the Mexicans on Minnie Street... Oh my God, Rico...they love us."

"Gangsters?"

"Yeah, gangsters. But they're cool, man…."

"So, I wonder if Saint Anna would introduce me so you won't have to go all the way to Santa Ana to score? I could buy in bulk, you know, change careers…"

The girls do another spazz-happy clap dance, this time in slow-motion. If they accelerate it's too much effort, a buzzkill. They already feel fantastic.

One eyebrow cocked, Rico hands Katrina the phone.

19

The clandestine partnership between The Vigil and Bron proves seamless. No territory dispute, clearer focus without risk of hinderance. And the whole *you don't know me, I don't know you* pact is effortless since Bron's with the football and cheerleader crowd. The entire school embraces their new star quarterback who can do no wrong. He's supplying something stronger than steroids to the team and more effective than iced lattes to the squad. Every customer, mistaking themselves for a friend, has learned Bron's slow, oozing three-part handshake: one sliding palm slap for the money, another for the bindle, then a finger gun.

Bron's got dibs on the AP and its outer membranes, radiating to the fiend majority, while The Vigil keep their crowd—primarily the poser punks who look up to them, the veteran delinquents. With the junior high on lock, Dylan's slings bindles at Main Beach after school while Jerm reports to The House to package, sample product with the gang; streamlining their efforts to support their own habits.

Minnie Street, Santa Ana—nearly comical how it all happens in broad daylight: Heroin, the neighborhood's main industry, with cocaine a close second.

Every five minutes another car turns onto Minnie Street, slowing to a crawl, cholos in khakis and wifebeaters run-skipping to their window. Everyone is either in on it or turns a blind eye to the assembly line exchange. A quick $20 for a balloon, the pass off less than five seconds—look both ways, done. Right behind him in this surging drive-through is their #1 Customer, being chauffeured by a pretty boy with a devilish goatee. Running up to their passenger window, the dealer holds up his finger, *one bag?*

Shaking her head no, much too slow for their patience, she alters her usual order.

"Actually… hey... so this is my friend Rico. We're gonna need, like... a lot," she laughs.

He tells them to pull over and get out of the car, frisking them, making sure they're not the cops or wired-up narcs. Rico gets twenty questions. He looks at Anna—three *bundles*, she reminds him, unable to hold in her excitement. Rico hands over the cash. Territorial lines are drawn. Rico is forbidden to sell north or east of Laguna. Minnie Street digs the arrangement—Rico taking the heat for the Laguna junkies, reducing the law of averages that might circle back to them. Another guy throws a bundled backpack through Anna's open window. Driving off, Anna does the spastic-happy-clapping dance, high heels kicking the floor of the car.

"What'd all they say?" she asks.

"Just if I ever sold outside of Laguna or if I'm late on a front, they'd kill me."

20

Dylan's stride is slowing, out of tandem with the gang. When him and Jerm deal at school, Jerm does most of the heavy lifting. Dylan just stands there: bored, lackadaisical, or guilty. Absent from The House after his posts at Blackout Beach.

Anxiety invigorated, The House weighs hypotheticals: he's getting steeped in Big Jim's civic history or he's coming down, trying to soothe himself in the postcard-perfect seaside scenery. Or, he met a girl— but Jerm would be the first one he'd tell about that, and Dylan hasn't told Jerm anything.

They hear familiar steps echoing down the basement stairs.

"Dylan, where have you been, mijo?" Rudy says, his impersonation of an overbearing mother. "You just come and go while we cook and clean, we should beat you with our chanklas." Snickering—it breaks the ice. Until they see Dylan isn't laughing.

"Hey guys, I need to talk. Everyone here listening?"

All hands abandon projects, all ears perk up.

"What's up man, you good?" says Mikey.

"I... man, I think I need to stop this shit."

What the fuck? Picking at their faces compulsively, the room erupts.

"Big Jim saw me selling at the beach."

"Who gives a shit?" says Tristan. "He deals weed, you deal speed."

"Nah, it's what he told me afterwards. He said everyone he's ever known who's done meth long enough has either turned gay or Christian."

Tristan and Mikey burst out laughing. Rudy just gets pissed.

"Fuck that, I ain't turning *any* of that shit," says Rudy. The only thing he's ever kept hidden from the gang is that he's still more or less Catholic, that he and Rico often discuss their

136

complex proximity to their faith. Not a secret—it's more that The Vigil would never understand. But now Rudy's self-conscious, because talking to a gay dude about Jesus is way too close to what Big Jim was insinuating.

"Don't Christians hate queers?" says Mikey. "It seems competitive, like they both assume they can persuade people their side." And right as he hears himself, now *he's* nervous— The Vigil assume they can convert anyone to meth and they're absolutely evangelical about it.

The anxiety viral, Tristan's hit next—some weeks he'll have a raging hard on for days with nowhere to put it, and one day he nearly justified asking Mikey to suck it even though in a perfect world that mouth would be Katrina's. But he's only made out with her once before she disappeared, that time he stopped kissing her to ask where Rudy was.

Fuck.

"Big Jim said after a while you'll fuck anything on this shit," says Dylan.

Now Rudy is cold sweating, recalling that sweet ass '63 Impala they saw parked in front of the theater the other day, the one he loved so much he pretended to fuck the tailpipe so they'd laugh, but long after they stopped laughing, he kept thrusting, forgetting they had walked on without him.

"Jim asked me if I've started seeing a demon yet... it freaked me out, like he was looking into my soul, because I've been seeing one every time I try falling asleep."

"Over here I just call that day three," says Tristan. "The day-three demon."

"So you've seen them too?" says Dylan.

"Yeah, I have... "says Tristan, yet he won't elaborate. When up for two-and-half, three days in a row, he's still seeing the cartoon devil with goatee like Rico's, only now instead of Rico's red puffer vest, this entity is wearing nothing but Mikey's green jacket. This cerebral superimposition appears so often he's long accepted he's losing his mind, in the privacy of his own head, so he never feels the urge to vocalize it. Until this very moment, where he sees Jerm, Mikey, and Rudy nodding gravely, and now Tristan is more terrified of their eye contact.

"Big Jim says it's something every tweaker eventually sees. The speed demon, he calls it. I'll close my eyes and it fills my whole periphery. But today, when I opened my eyes, it was still there." says Dylan, staring at Tristan.

"Why are you looking at me like that?"

"I think I should go," says Dylan.

"Wait, hold on. What does yours look like?" asks Jerm, attempting solidarity. "Mine's huge, a big face, very industrial, like every cell is a turning cog, with eyes made up of smaller, worker demons turning gears inside it. The gears are like, making fire, and the hotter it gets, it's like, it's burning itself into my brain."

"The one I see has like, big horns, muscular—this one, I can see its whole body," says Mikey. "And what its body is doing."

"What's its body doing?"

"Nothing good."

"You're probably just reading too many Faust comics," says Tristan. "What about you, Rudy?"

"I don't see shit."

"Why were you nodding your head with us earlier?" says Dylan.

"I was just agreeing with myself that you guys are fucking psychos," says Rudy, suppressing crystal-clear images of his crucified Jesus Demon communicating garbled gobbledygook through a fifth spike in its mouth. "Dylan—why do you keep staring at Tristan like that?"

Instead of answering, Dylan turns and walks way.

Sun setting at the end of an alleyway, Rudy walks home from work spun like a top, vulnerable and dangerous. Paranoia suffocates his psyche; the ocean breeze shivering him, like someone is shaking him. Avoiding Pacific Coast Highway, he strictly takes the alleys, convinced everyone's staring at him, spreading rumors, even when he's hidden in the city's back arteries. His right shoulder is stuck touching his ear from a kink in his neck, developed from whipping his head around trying to catch people trailing him, but all he ever sees is his own reflection in the dust-caked windows.

Hearing his name, he turns around, praying he's not imagining it.

Jasmine.

She stands there, lips quivering like she's gonna cry her eyes right out—a look of guilt, a searing stare of longing.

Running to his girl, he grabs her close, squeezes—fearing he's going to hurt her—furious she makes him this weak with worry, so he squeezes harder: relieved she's finally materialized.

"Where you been, baby?"

She looks both ways, bunching her red lips to one side, hesitates.

"What is it, baby? You look so sleepy. Don't tell me you lit another town on fire for me or something?"

Shaking her head, a decisive no. Looking up, she signals her hand for his ear. They crouch to the pavement, she whispers; her two hands curling around her mouth, a cave of secrets so he can't see her eyes.

He squints, listening intently, encouraging her to spill whatever she needs to.

"You what? You, the girls and Rico? Okay... who is Anna? So... what does that mean? Rico's selling dope now? Fuck, okay... and? Wait, look at me..."

One look at her and he knows—so pissed he could hit her.

Instead, he pushes her out of arm's reach.

"You know what? Fuck you. You and I—nah, we're over…" he says, turning around quickly so she won't see him tear up. Cursing her under his breath, the faster he walks, the faster her sobs will fade. He turns back to face her one more time to twist the knife:

"Hey, so what if you're working for Rico now—you go tell him we're working for Bron-*fucking*-Todney!"

Above a parking structure overlooking the alley, Hackman assumes he's merely eavesdropping on a tragicomical break-up between two random punks— fucking clowns, he spits—until he catches the guy's parting shot to the girl. Running alongside the ledge, he tries focusing on the guy's face, but he's already walking off in defined spite, a dip to his gait. That walk, those bleached jeans, suspenders— gotta be that fucking Mexican kid who jumped me with The Vigil, he thinks. Dashing to the other side to see the girl's face: she's crying, hands covering her eyes, then throws them down, regret renewing her vigor as she stomps down the alley.

Jasmine.

It's all making sense. After reports of high school kids on methamphetamines, then considering how insane the Vigil were to jump him for *their* missing speed, *then* considering Bron Todney is in town now and this Mexican kid claims they're *working* for him, one question remains:

"Hey Sawyer, ever heard of a guy named Rico?"

140

21

The front door swings open and slams shut, glitching their rabbit hearts. "Who forgot to lock the door? Why aren't we working?" says Rudy, pacing.

"What's the matter with you, fuck?" Tristan cringes, verging on stroke from Rudy's barge-in. Rudy's flushed red, a caged animal looking for somewhere to sit or someone to bark at. Eyes red, yet moist; he's been crying.

"Fuck, man, easy," says Mikey. "Moms passed out so we're up here doing... maintenance. We were like, hearing clicking and snapping... inside of the elec...tricities," he says, popping the top off the VCR. Around him, every music cassette they own is all the way unraveled, the magnetic spaghetti he's leading inexplicably around the video spools. "If the beings can see or hear us talking through the video machine, now they'll just hear Fear, Suicidal Tendencies, Discharge, Rudimentary Peni—"

"You fucking unraveled my Peni?" says Tristan.

"Sorry... sorry sorry. I saved your Fang and Pistols."

"Did you ever figure that riddle?"

"What am I supposed to do... call the operator?"

"Do not... call the operator. If you call her, she'll either know we know she's listening, or we'll be on her radar, then she'll start surveilling."

"The fuck, you guys," says Rudy.

"Shit, man. Have a seat what's up?" says Tristan, hesitant to find out.

"Well, I finally saw Jasmine."

"That's a relief. And?"

"I broke up with her—"

"Probably for the best then?"

"Yeah, she's dead to me. Like, her eyes were fucking rolling into the back of her head—"

"Wait, what'd you fucking do to her, Rudy?"

"Nah man, not like that! I mean Jasmine and Katrina on fucking heroin. That's why we haven't been able to find 'em."

"Ah fuck," Mikey groans, disappointed. "You know they're probably getting it from Dirty Anna. Big Jim told me she's out of jail hanging around the beach again. Fucking mess."

"She mentioned Anna. Rico is selling dope, they're all in on it."

Tristan sits fuming, constructing the theory Rico got the girls strung out and not the other way around.

"Fuck, we gotta go find 'em," says Tristan, standing from his brooding stupor.

"Man, fuck them, we got work to do—"

"I'm gonna go looking, that's my work to do. Anyone else coming?"

"I'm coming," says Jerm.

Run-skipping down PCH toward Blackout Beach, they pass the record store—closed, Blast—closed, circling back to rap on Rico's door, so hard The Vigil's fists are nearly bleeding. Scouring their haunts—Circle K, Coast Liquor, Reef Liquor, Broadway Liquor, the coffee shop—on the way to the Beach.

"What's with that white van?" says Tristan, head twitching, blinking rapidly, fooling himself he can disappear it. "You see that white van?"

"I see that white van," says Jerm.

"I've seen it six times on this walk, unless it's been six different white vans."

"What's worse, one white van, reoccurring, or six white vans, like an army of white vans?"

"I don't know what is worse, Jerm. Do I have to pick? I don't want to pick. What if it's the wrong answer?" says Tristan, his vision strobe-fluttering.

The hush of crashing waves hisses like a thousand snakes as the two approach Blackout Beach, its postcard details silhouetted against the Friday night traffic. The usual wastoid congregation exude a glaring lack of movement, not like their usual hyper-writhing. They spot Katrina and Jasmine—then, the shock of Dylan— *Fucking Dylan?* He looks fucked up, eyelids heavy on his elfin face, with a smirk Tristan wants to punch off his lips.

Dylan laughs, mocking the surprise encounter. The girls cackle, exhaling into toothy grins, their conjoined narcotic syrupy high an impenetrable wall. Arrogance has reframed them into vague acquaintances, brazen like they've always been this high. The girls coddle Dylan, hunching over him protectively. A coven with a new charm. Dirty Anna smirks under her shades, a cigarette dangling from her mouth that's nearly all ash.

Tristan points, the big case solved: "You guys are all on fucking heroin."

Dylan slobbers back: Yeah, real…like… adult drugs, not your like, shitty… nosy… baby powder."

"Baby powder?" says Tristan, about to remind him they've got the best glass in southern California, uncut straight from the source. But Dylan's comeback stings because they're spun, stunned at comet trails from every movement, like everyone's arms have fringy wings attached, every ripple of the ocean a jutting fanged sea serpent, blatant dread of the horizon erased, blackwater bled fully into the inky sky, a gaping hole they're all being vacuumed into by a wheezing, unholy inhale.

Drooling, Katrina and Dirty Anna spew hedonistic science on why heroin is the cooler drug. After every few words, they must slurp back up their saliva stalactites, and look around for their lost train of thought. Jasmine tunes them all out, nearly wholesome, picking flowers from the boardwalk's manicured landscaping, smelling each one, grinning, satisfied like she just ate a rich meal, though she's still constipated from this week's solitary cheeseburger.

Yet, Tristan and Jerm are almost jealous; the way they can all actually focus on their high, maybe stop and smell some fucking flowers while they're at it.

It's provocative.

"Nobody on this beach wants your fucking speed anymore, trust me," Katrina snaps at Tristan—he just wishes he could kiss her. He and Jerm are dwarfed by the enormous, suspiciously chill vibe. No need to put two and two together when they all got their $20 bags safe and accounted for in their veins. Scanning the perimeter, they see another—or the same—white van drive by again. Squeezing more vision from their sight, they see no other choice past doubling-down on Bron's pure glass. The town already caught fire—with the battle lines drawn it's about to blow up like bad chemistry.

First period, AP class. Filing in dutifully, the kids with the brightest futures who can't stop playing with their noses. Must be allergy season.

"Oh, Bron—I hate to say this, but you're actually wanted in the principal's office first thing," teacher says, or asks, like even he's surprised.

"Oh? You know what it's regarding?"

"No idea," he says, approaching Bron for confidentiality. "But so far you're at the top of the class here and I know you're kicking ass in the field, so I'm sure it's no big deal."

Grabbing his backpack, Bron exits the door, knowing this can only mean one thing.

Entering the administration office, they wave him through, expecting him.

He knocks.

"Who is it?"

"Bron Todney, sir."

"Hey there, Bron. Thanks for arriving so promptly. Have a seat."

"Sure, Principal Adams."

"First of all, I'm sure you're wondering why I called you in here. I'll get to that here really quick, but let me start by asking how your experience has been here so far?"

"It's been great. Mr. Lockey was just telling me I'm at the top of AP, coach says I'm doing really good in the field…"

"Good. What about at home, everything all right there?"

"Yeah, just me and my mom, keeping it real… simple."

"So Bron, the reason I ask is… Your name came up yesterday afternoon when Chris Jenson's parents called the school."

Bron gets that hot feeling in his forehead where no sweat pours. "Regarding what?"

"By law, I can't tell you everything, but Chris's parents had to rush him to the hospital where he tested positive for methamphetamines."

"Damn."

"Right? It doesn't sound like a kid like Chris, in AP and everything. And you're in Chris' AP class, right?"

"Correct."

"Have you ever talked to him? Any associations outside of school?"

"No, sir. Spoken to him briefly in passing, we know who each other are. Can I ask how my name came up?"

"Well, Bron, when Chris' parents asked him where he got it from, he said he got it from you."

Bron shakes his head. "C'mon, Mr. Adams…"

"I know, Bron. Believe me, it's uncomfortable for me to bring this up considering the uh… circumstances. For now, don't look at this as me accusing you, but passing on

145

information in a sensitive case..."

"Listen, for one— I'm shocked, but not surprised," says Bron, the authority of a lawyer out of thin air. "First of all— you know how competitive these AP kids can be. I didn't want to say anything at first, but I had a bad feeling Chris had it out for me the first day I walked onto campus. Beyond the competitive nature of AP, maybe he saw all the love I was getting, or maybe it's simply 'cause I'm the only black guy in school..."

Immediately ashamed, Principal Adams catches himself looking under his chair for a way out, like a neurotic tic.

"... but I guess the most important thing here is to look at the credibility of someone clearly not in his right mind. Anything he's gonna say will be the rantings of a madman, of course some racist shit is gonna come out."

Bron goes in for the kill.

"Mr. Adams, you know that racism is a mental illness, right?"

"Loud and clear, Bron. No further questions. Sorry to interrupt your studies. You will let us know if you hear anything, yes?"

"Sure. I mean, he probably got it from some guy at Main Beach or something..." he says, exiting the office.

Ugh, why did I fucking say that? he thinks, chiding himself for potentially throwing The Vigil under the bus since the beach is their territory. Remembering to smile, he walks down the hall back to class, pleased with his performance under pressure. It was like court, he fucking killed it. No further questions indeed, bitch.

He gets a page: Mikey. He looks around, ducks into the payphone under the archway.

"Yeah, what's up big dog? You want what? Nah, I must have a bad connection. You want what? Nah, you're crazy. Let me call you at lunch. Better yet, meet me at, nah... I'll call you,

146

how's that? Alright, fuck it—I'll come over and talk some fucking sense into you, bro."

Bron barely recognizes the basement. It's like a Halloween haunted house, sheets partitioning off different areas and—

"Wait, is this fucking blood?" he asks.

"Oh. Yeah," says Tristan, peeking from behind a curtain.

"Yeah, man," Mikey says, catching his breath. "Blood brothers—you know, razor blades... leftovers on the sheets, lets the demons know we aren't fucking around you know, like heads on stakes around our kingdom... but it's like... our own blood... I guess."

"Man, you guys are fucking psychos."

Rudy calls from behind his sheet in the corner. "Don't worry about it, man."

Bron jumps, purses his lips, annoyed.

"So, listen—I don't wanna tell you guys what to do but there's no way you need that much shit from me."

Mikey yells from behind his sheet in the other corner. "Listen, Bron—why do you care how much we're asking for if you're getting paid?"

"Because man, I know how this shit goes. It's a limited pond. You got that much shit on you, you're gonna get stupid trying to sell it. The law of averages will kick in, trust me. You guys take more than a kilo, you're never gonna see your parents again."

They go silent, then bust up laughing, unable to recall the last time they've seen their parents.

"Man, what?"

"Sorry, Bron. We're just in a goofy mood," Mikey's voice trails off, like it's falling down a pit.

Bron lifts another sheet open: Tristan shivering in nothing but tighty-whities, his right arm tendrilled in blood, exposed gristly muscle turned inside out. Tristan frozen, his ribs unpuff, indicating a sigh of relief seeing that it's only Bron horrified out of his mind—not the cartoon goateed speed demon he's trying to relinquish from his flesh, who's backstroking through his bloodstream, who's nesting in his brain.

"It's okay, man." Tristan says. "Not what it looks like, promise. Not like I'd kill myself or anything. Just trying to get him out of me, think I finally got 'em."

"Feel better?" Mikey asks, ignoring Bron's stuttering, pacing.

"Yeah, much better, just a little dizzy... I haven't had lunch yet?" Tristan lights up some brain-combusting shards in Mom's weed pipe, giggling at the vintage reference of "food."

"All right, you know what? I'll deliver your fucking kilos, then I don't want you guys contacting me again—for any reason—until it's all gone. But sell it—don't fucking do it."

Shaking his head, he turns the doorknob.

22

Standing on a tall dirt embankment, Bron peeps his yellow G-Shock, the "tough watch for tough jobs" indicating his cousin is 30-seconds late opening their reappropriated City of Riverside manhole cover from underneath. Exposed from every point of compass, Bron keeps turning circles, knowing anyone could see him disappear down this thing. *Just 'cause I can't see them doesn't mean they can't see me,* he thinks, unsure whether to continue slowly spinning or just open the damn thing himself.

Right when he starts to panic, the manhole cover moves like it's alive, belching from activity underneath. Cousin's ringed fingers from below, curling over, into a fist punching it aside into two come hither fingers. Bron hates climbing down into The Bunker; he just barely fits and he's bulking up more every week. Soon he won't fit at all, and he's stressing he won't realize that time came until he's stuck halfway down.

Similar to The Vigil, the buried Bunker is partitioned with cloth, but just one velvet curtain in crushed crimson, a decadent nod to the red phosphorus burning in the lab behind it, separating "work" from the "living room" where they can chill semi-civilized to conduct business.

Bron plops on the couch, pulls a wad from his shorts, then slams it on the "coffee" table before him.

"Damn. Going that good, huh?"

"Yeah, kinda," says Bron. "We'll see where it goes. Probably up their own noses."

"Sure they're not cops?"

"Bro, you should see these guys. When I left their place, three of the guys were cutting themselves behind these sheets hanging from the ceiling, saying they're letting demons escape or some shit. Like that bloodletting shit they used to do back in the day in Egypt."

"Bloodletting? Egypt? You lost me, cuz. You're in the desert but this ain't no Pharaoh shit."

"Sorry just a little freaked, bro."

Bro... Bro, his cousin mocks, emasculating his tone before hardening back. "Well, guess what—this shit *is* fucked up. No surprise motherfuckers get crazy on it. Long as you know they ain't cops I'll carve 'em open myself if it gets inside them faster. Here's your kilos for your vampire homies, homie..."

Cousin notices something, pursing his lips. "What the fuck is this shit?" he says, pulling a long pale hair from Bron's shoulder. "You into white meat now or what, blondie?"

Bron is silent; it's impossible to think when cousin is examining every inch of his body for cameras. "Blond bitch taking footage of this wildlife, I bet."

Vowing this will be the last time he walks down The Vigil's staircase, Bron brings the bundles with him to campus, leaving them in his trunk to drop at The House during lunch break, praying The Vigil will be somewhere else.

Descending, he grips his crucifix necklace for protection. Placing their product in the middle of the room, Bron is seized by a surprising moment of spiritual charity. Deciding these guys need God more than he does, he unclasps his necklace and drops it into Tristan's psycho sado-exorcist lair behind the stairs, stomping back up as fast as he can, back to fifth period clean, halo beaming.

150

23

Feeling floaty, Jerm roams the middle school campus during lunch. He hasn't slept in days, nor does he know what a day is anymore. He thinks it has something to do with that fucking sun, the piercing ball of fire that won't stop following him. Ducking behind buildings, bushes, dumpsters—there it persists, following him like a cop. A camera lens glitched in perpetual flash, or a magnifying glass of hell where souls go to burn.

Where we ascend to when we die, he thinks, so heaven is a lie, or else miles underground, the polarity flipped.

He digs a hole in the moist field with his bare hands, wide enough to fit his lanky body. Far from heaven, but the cold dirt cools the open wounds, all the scabs on his arms he can't stop scratching back open. Maybe the demons can just come and go as they please; the more confined they are, the more wrathful they become.

Cradled in the earth he starts tearing up. It has dawned on him, harshly, that Dylan isn't by his side. Mentally grasping for something more solid than the holes burned into his brain, he decides he feels floaty because he misses his best friend.

He opens his eyes, four kids standing over him, like mourners at his own funeral.

"Hey Jerm, can we get a couple bindles?"

When they're not tearing into their own flesh, The Vigil continue cutting corners, capitalizing on their uber-exclusive high-risk teen clique, writing a list of every kid wearing grunge band T-shirts, flannel, camouflage, third-wave tie-dye; vulnerable marks for the alternative rebellion mass-market, the unbeknownst participants the Bill Clinton Playing Sax Everything Is Groovy Neo-Liberal Three-Strikes Doc Martin Corporate Bootlicking Rock the Vote Psy-Op. The Vigil push their product hard—a race confined only to the tangled sausage of their potholed brains—before Rico and the girls can inform these kids the celebrities they idolize are actually doing heroin, not speed.

But the more they turn these kids into twitching lunatics, the faster they're taking over the upper level of their asylum, since the basement shackled Vigil have allowed them to use the front door. *Don't even think about coming downstairs, we'll come up to you,* The Vigil warn, pulling out their hair, losing parts of their mind with every strand, preoccupied with getting ripped off by the alternating cast embedding themselves upstairs, nesting in the corners.

Ascending from the basement, slaloming through furniture Mom's rearranged a dozen times over, Rudy takes their orders like a lurching subterranean car hop, returning thirty seconds later with the customer's danger dust, assuming they'll just leave. But some nights there's over twenty of them Mom thinks she's entertaining with her hyper-slurring '60s pontificating. Under her suffocating spell of circular nostalgia, they're terrified they'll upset her if they interrupt her by exiting.

The basement, now a dungeon of fire and dry-ice, smoke and abandoned mirrors. Since The Vigil have quit snorting, they're inhaling a glass pipe. The fumes of fuel swirling, clinging to the black, give the dark a grey matte. A zero-visibility fog, the illusion of buried light.

Sequestered behind their dirty hung sheets, each boy a spider waiting on their web to catch the invisible streams of unholy meth-summoned magnitude. Vaporous Speed Demons, ever ambient. Behind each sheet: Tristan, Mikey, Rudy, and Jerm engage in psychic battle after negotiations of psychobabble fails them, each boy part martyr part exorcist assigning their bodies into malleable vessels for shrieking tormentors, speed evaporating window frost separating them from this churning world. Unremorseful to opening the portal,

152

the boy's messages calcify into every teen's bloodstream, pumping translations of their inherent mission to fight these phantom comets beyond below. Every time a sale is made, it ignites the ammunition for this spiritual confrontation, distributed to adolescents brave enough to sacrifice their mind and body, cutting so deep into their flesh they're not sure what is gristle and bone anymore—anything solid: a barricade. The Vigil scream obscenely when the blade won't go further. Self-administered scars: war medals displayed proudly, oozing green from infection—any kind of topical treatment much less a hospital visit against the rules, now etching The Vigil into the same fanaticism as Christian Science, Jehovah's Witness, and Scientologists. The Vigil is living out a real-time Seppuku passion-play, the blade's intercourse to liberate/empower fear, the real disinfection coming from within, reveling in euphoric phosphorous blood red tides crashing, the acidic path of meth's chemical elements dissolving any synapse a foreign body could intercept. A single lightbulb burnt out in their sky of ceiling. Their lurching silhouettes are fallen soldiers zombified, suspended in negative image, shadowboxing in anguish. The Vigil cocky in their cowardice, this chimeric camaraderie. The demons undistinguished from benevolent allies, an architectural puzzle of agony overlapping, mind over flesh and matter of facts cackling, collecting all blood shed in Mom's expired prescription bottles, containing it for proof before drinking the spheroid circuitous fuel; a savage war tribe of cannibals harvesting skulls as trophies of their own bodies beheaded from the inside out.

24

"You got what you deserve, now go to Hell!"

Eyes slitting open, the four boys convulse-awake at Mom's triumphant condemnation, grabbing onto the other for dear life, like ants clasping together when drowning. Beef jerky scabbed over lacerations map their shirtless bodies, gouges too vivid a lesson into the depths of anatomy.

"I just wanted to let you guys know..." says Mom, stumbling down the stairs holding a mason jar of cash. *"Oh my God what the fuck is going on down here?"*

Mikey vibes she's spinning, oblivious to their homespun surgeries. "Sorry, ma, we'll clean the place up today..."

"Too cool," she chirps, oblivious. "I was just coming down here to let you guys know those nasty Menendez Brothers got convicted today. Lyle's prosecutor really hit the homerun—she told the judge: boys can't even be raped because they lack the necessary equipment to *actually be raped*. So it was all about money all along!" Mom parades around the room, taking handfuls of cash from the jar, throwing it in the air. Like green leaves falling premature, they land on each furrowed-brow boy. "Justice will *always* prevail, you know, in case you ever plan on murdering *me* for *this* shit," she says. Mom holds up the half-empty jar and it falls out of her hand, shattering on the ground. Both hands free now, she frantically wipes invisible crumbs off her Operation Desert Storm T-shirt.

"We'd never hurt you," promises Rudy.

"Too cool," she says, switching gears, "'Cause you're gonna do some construction down here for me."

Groaning, Rudy's eyes roll—Mom's been *encerrona*. He should have kept his mouth shut.

"Look at all you guys sprawled out here on the floor," she says. "No wonder—there's nowhere to sit down here! Here's what I'm thinking...." Burning on her morning line, she gesticulates to Rudy, her bony fingers drawing in thin air: a seamless bench built into the wall from one corner to the other, accessorized with cushions since they're losing their asses. "It would really make the place come alive," she concludes.

"Yeah... cushions. Sure. Cushions and fucking sandwiches are the answer to everything," says Rudy.

"Well, don't think I'm done pestering you, Rudy baby," she says, winking, and she ascends the stairs.

It's late afternoon at the LBPD. The sun-scorches its quaint adobe façade.

"Hey Hackman, you're gonna love this. Sounds like we got a reason to bust down the door of that black kid."

"Oh?"

"We just got a call from some parents whose kid freaked out on meth, had to be hospitalized due to some psychotic breakdown. They found him screaming in his bedroom. He had taken a hammer to his walls, completely destroyed them right down to the beams and insulation, saying he was looking for cameras, that he was being watched. Hilarious. Kid claimed he got the stuff from that black Todney guy, but the school didn't do anything when the parents called, so they put in a call to us instead and I want to plan a pounce."

Hackman's frozen. Now that he can legally bust his old rival, he's not sure he wants to. His skin crawls so bad he nearly forgets his lines. "Ah, sure. Maybe? Sounds like we'll need some more information."

"Man, you and all your need for *information.*" Sawyer air-quotes.

Hackman's nauseated, suffocating inside absolute power. The thought of raiding the house of a black family plays grotesque in his mind when he knows The Vigil and The All the Way House are the town's true blight. It'd only kickstart Sawyer's "spring cleaning," where they bust every other

155

ethnicity so white tourists can be comfy parading their vacation money.

"I don't think Todney's the guy."

"So what, do nothing? That kid's family is fucking livid and I want them off our backs."

"Give me an hour," Hackman says, slamming the door behind him.

"This is so fucking dumb," says Hackman, removing his uniform and stepping into jeans and combat boots, readorning himself in his leather jacket for the first time in forever. *Just another fucking uniform*, he thinks. Now that he's got Bron's address, he won't do this as a goddamn pig. Opting to wield nostalgia instead of his night stick, he wants Bron to see him for who he used to be, back when they fought like men even though they were just kids.

"So fucking dumb," he repeats, walking up to the Todney's just two blocks from his pad. "Fucking small town bullshit."

He knocks.

"Hello?"

"Mrs. Todney?"

"Yes, that's me. Can I help you?"

"I'm an old friend of your son's. He around?"

"Oh sure, sure. Broney, you got a visitor!"

Coming around the corner, Bron freezes, a silent *what the fuck*.

"Mind if we go outside for some privacy? And don't worry, man. You know you'd just kick my ass again."

"What the fuck. Hackman?" says Bron, opening the back door. His brain is obliterated, rectifying this specter to the present. "Yeah, let's go outside."

"*Bron Todney in the house*.' That sound familiar?"

"Oh, fuuuuck… you're a cop now? You're kidding me."

"I wish."

156

Catching up briefly, Hackman's nervous laughter keeps stalling business.

"So Bron, I need a favor and you'll need a way out of this."

"Way out of what?"

"We know you're dealing, and if you deny it, it doesn't even matter 'cause Chief wants to raid your house like, tomorrow—"

"What?"

"—and I'd be with him, and I'd prefer to avoid all of this shit."

Bron goes silent, defenseless.

"You're dealing with The Vigil, right?"

Still silent, now an admission.

"So I need you to make an anonymous call to the station. Give them their address, tell 'em that's where the shit is, done."

Bron can feel his skull compressing, his sweat freezing. Like his cousin, he's convinced there's cameras or wires picking up their every word and he's never even done the shit.

"Everything you just said, I ain't doing any of it."

"All right then, we'll see you bright n' early tomorrow? *Or*, we can come earlier, in the middle of the night…"

"Fuck. FUCK!"

"I know, I know," says Hackman, in disbelief at how tables turn.

25

Blast is going off the rails with an energy less frenetic from Rico's tenure selling the fast stuff; a cooler, invincible vibe. A glamorous teen haunt in hip contrast to The All The Way House. If you want to get high, like really untouchably high where someone could tell you your parents died and you wouldn't even care, all you have to do is ask. One free taste, then $20 a bag if you liked it.

Predominantly boys club, mainly a skater-kid contingent except for Katrina and Jasmine, plus whatever Dylan is now; the girl's diminutive male model mascot, craving their attention as much as his next bag.

But when he isn't looking, Rico is watching him, and tonight he watches him for a long time. "I can't believe I have not gotten a picture of you on my community wall yet. What kind of shopkeeper am I?" says Rico, scratching his face slowly, an itch never satiated. His other hand takes Dylan's fingers, rubbing his thumb around his palm, searching for a way to unlock him.

Dylan's skin crawls into ambiguous zones, raising goosebumps; he's ambivalent, because people you're scared of, you're also sort of fascinated by. Maybe you remain by their side because you're fascinated why you're so scared.

"Katrina, will you grab that fur coat for him? And Jas, wrap him in that pink feather boa?" Jasmine adorns him in layers of flair while Katrina does a quick makeup job. Dylan is all about it, even puckering a kiss when she finishes his lipstick.

"Very nice," says Rico, grabbing his Polaroid. "Okay, now a kiss to the camera, and hold it there please?" Dylan twists, pauses—Rico shoots. His femme-boy facsimile ejects. Rico grabs it eagerly. Shaking, it fades to life.

"Can I see?" asks Dylan.

Too high to hear him or just high enough to ignore him—

not a word spoken, he takes it to his bedroom, shutting the door.

"Uh, I'm sure he's just getting tape to put it up on the community wall," Katrina suggests.

Jasmine's eyes get big. *Yeah, he's probably getting it real sticky*, she thinks—her eyes rolling back, nodding off.

Locking the door behind him, Rico's eyes remain transfixed on his instant photograph of Dylan, a likeness he can actually take, keep, and own; his image finally safe to gaze upon for as long, for as hard, as he wants.

He wants.

He, once.

Whenever he stares at Dylan, the real one on the other side of that door, Rico senses everyone staring at *him*, making him uncomfortable just for admiring beauty, capturing purity before it goes bad. In a way, he reasons, he's protecting Dylan by burning him into his brain, where Dylan will be safe, so Rico can remain sane, because the longer and harder Dylan fills Rico's mind, the less room demons can come to real life.

The best part of staring at Photo Dylan is that Photo Dylan will always be staring back at Rico, never averting his eyes. We can just ignore our gap in age, the torture of time.

Then, a sudden quiet on the other side, and Rico feels a single presence through the void of a vanished crowd. Unlocking, then opening the door, in the middle of the showroom: its Real-Life Dylan, alone. Rico ponders if he is on Dylan's mind, and all other parts he is about to occupy.

Two figures stumble to the shore where the sun won't shine the naked eye deceived relying solely on varicose moonlight to illuminate the ocean against sky a horizon nonexistent if there's a crack to let more light in it must be plugged before it leaks advantage being taken a window of opportunity the perfect vantage you're squinting to see them right now no one is looking and the sand it leaves no footprints both silhouettes holding hands one taller shadow elongating if any eyes could see they'd assume the other is a child the way he can barely walk how the bigger one keeps lifting him back on his feet leading him to the rocks where shadows succeed the younger one's senses fading the other growing bigger the closer they approach the cliffs overhanging the unrelated adolescent must be gagged before he screams foreverveil eclipsing over agonized ecstasy of pain of apprehension and release I couldn't tell so I didn't ask what if he said no now I'll never tell so never ask me why we were just going with the flow the silent grunting of penetration filling the space of negation the friction the resistance confusion surrender and acceptance.

26

Both wardens and inmates inside the House, The Vigil's mental deterioration is nearly artistic the way its painting them into a corner. Poetic in their delusional recitals of impending doom. Elementals like sky and earth assume inexplicable displays of new gospel; their street a petrified river of bone, blackash and putrefied plasma of failures crossing over.

The expansive blue of day a mere trick from Heaven, a suspicious intermission before the nightwars. Their condensed red phosphorous aflame, sucked through glass pipes, chemically altered into exhaust. No more wondering what makes Laguna's tie-dyed sunset: The Vigil's billowing smoke, suspended by distance, their jaundiced eyes moisten to focus, curling plumes beckoning towards the sun—hell ever raging, protected behind the edge of the ocean waterfalling into misting humidity, collecting into cold sweat on goose bumping proudflesh, follicles rise through the scarring you're scratching, that green flash of the sun disappearing; like hitting a switch, now you're shivering.

Ushering summer, going harder, no construct of school interrupting their operations: teaching demons lessons in mutual detention, impaired beyond special education; devolved into cavemen, the guiding light only their eyes can see: superstition.

In the blindblack basement wondering if they're dead, cutting themselves again to make certain it still feels like pain, they regain confidence in the solidity of their existence. As far as liquid: blood flows best when contained.

A reanimating surge of adrenaline hits Mikey. Stomping the staircase, he's scolding twenty Converse and Doc Martins solemnly stomping out the front door, Mikey an Unholy

Moses condemning them to swim the River Styx of Cress Street. A weight lifted, The Vigil reclaim the upper level, out from their pit of contrarian atonement.

Each boy holds another's shoulder as they ascend the stairs; the weariest conga line. Circling the living room, Mikey takes Mom's throne, the rest rouletting in silence. The knock on the front door seems predestined. Calling on his last ounce of bravery, Mikey opens the door, calm and stately, a game-show host smile forming from his grinding teeth.

Mikey touches the visitor's shoulder, making sure he's seeing correctly, that it's no Speed Demon masquerading as Dylan.

Avoiding eye contact, Dylan takes mousey nibbles of the Hershey Bar he's just opened. Mikey notices his other fist holds the wrapper of another he's devoured.

"Wow, hungry huh?" Desperate small talk, the boys peeking around him.

"Not really, not anymore. Here, you finish it. Can I come in?"

Breaking Dylan's bar into five equal pieces, Mikey doles them out to all, parting a path for Dylan. Except Tristan: dead center, arms crossed, refusing the armistice of manufactured cocoa.

"I don't trust anything that's going on right now. How we know Dylan's not the cops?" says Tristan. "Empty your pockets before you take another step."

"Man, fuck you," says Dylan, reaching into his jeans. "Who's acting like the fucking cops right now?" Turning out both his pockets, he throws a red balloon, uninflated, into his face.

"There, you satisfied I'm not the fucking cops yet?"

Picking it off the ground, Tristan stretches it out. "What, am I blowing this up for your welcome back party?" He gives it two big puffs, ties it off, and uses static electricity to stick to the John Wayne Gacy clown poster rehomed above the fireplace. "There, 3D—Ugh what the fuck is that? Tastes like, vinegar. I dunno, like fucking Subway or some shit?"

"Chiva, stooopid," Rudy says, rolling his eyes.

Mikey looks at his watch. "Whataya say we move the furniture back, grab the gloves, blow off some steam?"

"Hell yeah," says Rudy, pushing the furniture flush against the walls. "Where the gloves at?"

Mikey smiles—the gloves haven't moved since the last time they used them.

"How about me and Tristan pick up where we fucking left off?" says Dylan.

Tristan is all exposed nerve from Dylan's surprise challenge, a mirror of his previous self. He hesitates. But Mikey is already putting on his gloves and Rudy is putting the other pair on Dylan—who's battling something tangibly internal, his new tough guy act transparent.

Slapping their fighter on the shoulder, they signal them to the middle of the room. Three steps forward, they stare each other down. Tristan sees some shit in Dylan's eyes—real animosity, a bona fide bitterness.

Before either of them can throw a blow, Dylan lets him have it, a lie he knows will hurt. "You know I fucked Katrina, right?"

Tristan throws an uppercut, falling into Dylan's collapse. Groaning, he's bit his own tongue, a sound so disgusting it fuels Tristan pummeling. Dylan's head hits the floor, a hollow boom rattling the hardwood. Straddling him for the kill, Tristan detects Dylan is crying, and instead, throws his gloves on the ground, Rudy lifting him from the armpits. Dylan rolls over, hiding his face.

Dylan grabs Jerm out to the porch, whispering in his ear between sobs. Jerm ducks his head back inside: "We'll be right back. We're going to the park."

The Vigil befuddled. To pick up the pace of their pacing, they suck and blow from the glass pipe, as if it will accelerate the longest hour they've ever waited.

Jerm swings open the door, grim-faced.

"Sorry, Jerm. Where's Dylan? He okay? I really didn't mean to get him like that."

"It wasn't you who got him, Tristan. It was Rico."

"What do you mean?"

"What do you think I mean?" Jerm says, clenching his teeth.

THREE

"In every wolf is a punk looking for revenge."

–prison aphorism, source unknown

1

Jerm's eyes remain stationary; an ominous head nod.

"Wait, this is real? Like, everyone's thinking the same thing?" says Mikey.

Tristan punches the wall. Rudy's head downcast, receiving/processing.

Jerm clenches his teeth. "Rico took him, sounds like he drugged him...

"Just fucking say it so we're all on the same page," says Tristan.

"Fine— Rico fucked Dylan. Against his will. Rape," says Jerm. "There, I said it. You on the page now?"

"This is fucking insane," says Mikey. "Did he tell you the details?"

"He barely remembers it," says Jerm.

"What more details do we need?" yells Tristan. "He got fucked by a 27-year-old who stole our chicks and our customers and now Dylan's virginity."

"Didn't Katrina take his virginity?"

"Fuck off, man, that's not the point."

Pulled by a riptide into unchartered coves, every comment makes them feel worse, further from resolution, their silence slow boiling to rage.

"Where did he go?" says Rudy, his heel hyper-tapping.

"I told him to go to his parent's. He needs to see a doctor." A deeper silence chokes the room. "Dylan told the girls and they refused to believe him. They said Rico would never do anything like that, that Dylan should probably come out of the closet already 'cause he was leading Rico on if anything did happen. That's why he broke down and came to us."

Tristan exits the living room into the kitchen. Visibly afraid, he's pacing from one end to the other, compelled to sequester his naked reaction. Every time he passes in view of the others, he targets sharp eye contact to remind them he's still listening.

"Fuck. It's not like we can go to the cops for this," says Mikey. "What are we supposed to do, call fucking Hackman?"

Every girl they've ever known had been sexually assaulted at some point. "Is it, like, a morbid existence being female?" Tristan once tried asking Jasmine, long before he tried removing her teeth. Yet nothing could prepare him for this.

Spit balling ways to confront Rico, they're leaning towards beating him senseless when Tristan returns to the room.

"Everyone, stop. Just fucking stop for a second and listen."
They stop.

"Let me present a vital point right now that will make us all feel a little better," he says, holding pause with pageantry.
"What?"

"Would anyone care if Rico died? Think about it."

"What are you saying?" says Jerm.

"What do you *think* I'm saying?"

Tristan cuts up five rails, their consumption magnetic, immediate.

"You see—times are different now," he says, knowing everything there is to possibly know about *time*. "Remember when we all saw *Sleepers*, *Natural Born Killers*, even fucking *Thelma* and fucking *Louise*? Those are the feel-good flicks, man. Remember how good we felt after coming out of the theater—why do you think that is?"

Rudy mumbles, "It's not real life, bro."

"But it is! It is fucking real life. They're getting us ready to revolt against our oppressors, whether they're the cops, fucking rapists, or our own fucking parents. The fucking Menendez Brothers, Lorena Bobbit—I mean, she just castrated her rapist husband, but you get what I'm saying... he *could* have died. The good guys are the murderers now.

Don't you get it?"

Three out of the four boys are pacing, getting it. Rudy remains seated.

A mounting energy is coalescing inside Tristan, honing itself into an arrowhead destined to pierce a beating heart. "It's up to us to cleanse our generation," says Tristan. "If the cops can kill innocent people, if the government can send troops to annihilate whole countries of innocent people, then guess what—we, are allowed to kill actual guilty people. Take matters into our own hands. Responsibility. Murder is perfect...ly... righteous and justified if it's born of trauma... abuse.... Revenge— its own natural law nobody can argue with. How can you argue with eliminating evil?"

Three out of four boys ramp up their pacing, can't argue with it.

Like a train gaining momentum while the passengers simultaneously lay down its tracks, The Vigil riff on ways to execute Rico.

"Fucking hold on, you fucking psychos!" Rudy's objection slices through the thick chatter. "I'm not doing this, and the rest of you ain't either."

They're shocked—a traitor.

"Oh? What are you then, a rapist sympathizer?" says Tristan.

Rudy looks like he could kill him right there.

"Man, fuck you. You realize I've already taken someone's life, right? I've gotta pay for it every *fucking* day. You *don't* wanna do this, man. Trust me."

Living with Rudy's past for so long, they've suppressed it. Burying obstacles to keep moving forward. It's like hearing it for the first time all over again.

Only Tristan's anger is unphased, infernal, untamed, propelled by righteousness. The declaration of tweaker fatwah brings him a decisive, treacherous calm.

"Listen, Rudy... I respect your stance, everything you've been through. But this is happening, with or without you."

"Fuck, you guys have no idea what you're doing. On top of you wanting to snuff someone out, you'd be killing a gay man, and you'd be white guys killing a brown guy."

Rudy feels his blood brothers dripping though his fingers.

"I don't give a shit what color he is or his sex stuff," says Tristan. "None of that has anything to do with the fact that he's fucked Dylan up for life. Someone we were supposed to be looking after. This is how and why every chick we know... you know, like Jasmine... got so fucking nuts. That alone should be enough for you to get behind this."

"How are you gonna do it then, gangster?" Rudy says.

"It'll be safe, clean, leave zero fingerprints. But if you're not going to be involved, you think I'm gonna tell you?"

"*Safe*," he scoffs. "Even if you do pull this off, what are you gonna do then?"

"Be fucking proud we did the right thing."

"Yeah, fucking right. You'll never sleep again if you pull this off."

"Rudy, I'm doing this so I *can* sleep again."

2

The more Katrina thinks about it, the more she just wants to ask him, just casually. Not a confrontation: *What did you do last night?* Something more like *hey whatcha do last night?* Wondering if she should pull him aside, less of an audience, but Jasmine's presence might encourage honesty, or something like it. And Jasmine keeps staring at her, like *when the fuck are you going to ask him?*

"Hey Rico, can I ask you something?"

"Sure, honey. Anything."

"Did you and Dylan hang out last night?"

His eyes widen, trying to swallow the floor.

"Ah, yes? Why you ask?"

"Can I ask what you guys did?"

"Um... why?"

"Just curious."

"We fixed here, then went down to the beach, talked."

"Just talked?"

"Yes, just talked. Why do I get the feeling you're interrogating me?"

"Did you guys have anything to drink?"

"Yes. People get thirsty, you know. Where is this going, Katrina?"

"Okay, listen... I'm just gonna tell you. Dylan said you made him a cocktail and doesn't remember anything after that. Like, he got drugged or something."

Rico looks furious enough to cry. "What? Like *I* drugged him?"

"Uh, yeah."

Rico is trembling. "That's insane. I mean, we fixed, like every night. Not my fucking fault if he can't handle his drugs."

"So, nothing happened?"

"What do you mean, 'happened?' If he can't remember what

171

happened, what did he claim *happened*?" Rico pauses. "Listen... I was comforting him. He's losing his mind. He says back when he was spun and would try to sleep, he'd see a demon who looks exactly like Tristan, and now when he nods off, he dreams of same demonic Tristan, only he's older, decaying, an elderly devil devoured by flames, screaming for help."

"Uh, never mind. It's cool..."

"No, it's not cool." Rico throws down the lighter and spoon. "Is he claiming I took advantage of him?"

"Uh, I didn't say that."

"What did he tell you?

"Ugh, listen, I'm sorry. I shouldn't have even said anything."

"No, fuck this—that little shit isn't allowed here anymore. No more drugs for him. And if I see any of you talking to him ever again, I'm cutting all three of you off."

"Dude, it's cool. Don't worry about it."

"You know what, I'm not worried about it. But I don't need little closet faggots like that starting rumors about me. I'll fucking kill that little kid."

"Jesus, settle down, Rico. Are we gonna fix or what?"

3

At first The Vigil is vaguely concerned by how readily Tristan has it all figured out, like maybe he's been thinking about it long before this incident. Like he had this whole plan waiting for someone—anyone—to fuck up.

Fear metabolizing with adrenaline, Tristan is elevated to leader, undisputed. They're only following orders, leaning in with focused scrutiny, as if any word they miss might cause the plan to leak and sink.

Tristan reminds Mikey and Jerm about that bottle of Thallium he swiped from the whale painter house after the fires, a morbid souvenir—the scentless, mostly tasteless but caustic substance, a lesser-known poison to arsenic.

"What's perfect about Thallium is if... sorry, *when* we slip it to Rico, it'll take him two to three days to die, giving us a wide-open alibi, says Tristan. "Since Rico sells dope now, there'll be countless suspects—Bron, his cousin's crew, the Santa Ana gangsters... even the Nazi Lowriders could technically put a hit out from jail. All that would come up first, far before we're suspects.

"Under the guise of a truce, one of us will call Rico, invite him to Bluebird Park for a harmless night of forties, maybe even flirt with him over the phone to assure he shows up....All St. Ides except one Mickey's for him, his brand, which will be pre-opened, the Thallium salts dissolved. Whoever hands it to him will reopen the cap so it looks like they're breaking the seal.

"I'm more than happy to do that particular honor, so you guys don't have to worry about being anything other than accomplices," concludes Tristan, diluting murderer into martyr.

Shocked at how easy it sounds, they go over it all again, forgetting another person is in the room hearing every word, staring at them in disgust.

"What's it gonna be, Rudy?"

"What do you mean what's it gonna be? I ain't doing shit. You might think this plan is tight, but you're not considering the aftermath, which makes me positive you guys have no fucking idea what you're doing, like you didn't listen to a word when I told you my story. Like you guys don't give a shit about me, or yourselves. Or your fucking families."

"The Vigil is our family, Rudy—we're taking care of our own here."

"Nah, fuck that," he says. "You guys all got fucking real families to go back to once you're all done playing pretend gangster. Some of us don't have that option. Once you go through with it though—"

"It's already happening, Rudy," says Tristan. "How can we trust you're gonna keep your mouth shut if you're not gonna be involved?"

"Man, if there's one other thing I know I'm not—besides a *two*-time killer—is a fucking snitch. Keeping my mouth shut kept me out of trouble, there's no way I'm gonna tell anyone shit. So knock yourselves out. Anyone else you're gonna take with you but I'm fucking gone."

Mom's voice chides from the other room, something about a project for Rudy. They freeze—proof they're already being sloppy.

Mikey mutters *fuck*, cursing them for yelling indoors about shit they shouldn't even be whispering about. He walks toward her room, calling out to her. "Hey Ma? Did you have something to add to our conversation? We didn't mean to wake you."

"I need to talk to Rudy. He still there?"

Mikey checks the living room; the front door slamming behind Rudy.

Loaded with their vigorous plan, The Vigil muster the guts to walk outside. Tapping the asphalt with their boots, they're reassured it's merely a street and not a petrified stream of bone, ash, brimstone, or coagulated flesh. They cock their brows, chuckle—delusions from mere hours ago now seem silly, ancient. They feel smarter now; the lines they just did off the kitchen table propelling them into commitment with no room for error.

Tristan urges they walk to Bluebird Park because, "Okay, one. It will be safer to talk about this stuff there with no one listening in, you know, we'll look just like four kids hanging out talking about kid stuff. Two. Did I mention that this is where it's actually gonna happen? Might as well start mapping it out."

On the way there, Tristan elbows Mikey. "There, do you see that white van? Hey Jerm, there's the white van again."

"I see that white van," says Mikey. "That's the third time I've seen that white van on our walk already, unless…."

"Unless it's three different white vans?"

"Yes."

"Either way, don't look into the white van, Mikey."

"How can I, there's no windows?"

"Just keep walking and be glad there are no windows on the white van."

Arriving to the park with so many questions:

"What about the girls? Should we tell the girls?"

"Why would we tell the fucking girls—they've chosen their side."

"When are we going to tell Dylan what we are planning?"

"Maybe he wants the honor of handing the bottle to Rico?"

"No, I want to do it," insists Tristan.

"Okay, fine but Dylan should be there, it might help get

Rico over to the park, unless Rico is suspicious of all of us now."

"He's suspicious of us anyway—we're working with Bron."

"Oh fuck," says Jerm.

"What—what?"

"Remember when we first met Rico outside of the Boom, he said one day when we least expect it, he'd take something from us? Well, looks like he took it."

4

Tristan holds a paper bag; neither beer, nor wine, nor whiskey.

Like a striptease he slowly reveals the bottle of Thallium Standard Solution (T-100) 1000mL, made by Fuji Film. All the caution symbols on the back of the label; under DANGER: a silhouette, an explosion in the throat, a skull and crossbones Tristan points to with a prideful grin, assuring they all see it.

"*For Laboratory Use Only* it says, only this ain't gonna be no fucking experiment, right?"

Unnerved by his glee, they nod and force giggles.

"Jerm, call Dylan. Find out if he's home and if not, make sure he knows what we're doing for him."

"I… think we need to leave him alone, let him put himself back together instead of rubbing his face in the humiliation of this," says Jerm.

"We're *eliminating* humiliation, filtering it out through blood osmosis," says Tristan.

But Jerm is too preoccupied to with Dylan's well-being to focus.

"Dude, pay attention," says Tristan. "There's nothing we can do about where Dylan is right this second."

"Sorry, sorry…We're cool with Rudy knowing, right?" says Jerm.

"He's already in denial mode. His conscience won't let him rat."

"Okay, and no one's in contact with the girls, right?" checks Mikey.

"Nope."

"Nope."

"Okay, good," says Tristan. "You know what, fuck it—I'll just call Rico myself."

"Nah, let me do it," says Mikey. "You're doing enough. I want to feel useful."

Jerm almost speaks but clips it.

"What's up, Jerm?"

"Nothing. I mean, okay… don't take this the wrong way, but do we all need to actually be there for it?"

"What? What do you mean? Of course we do. And now that you said that you have no choice. Don't tell me you're getting cold feet," says Tristan.

"Jerm, at this point if you're not there, you're another liability."

"No, I was just playing Devil's advocate, the less people there, the less chance of error, you know…"

"You're *gonna* be there, cause if you're not, *that* leaves room for error, mentally. Your presence will help us focus because there won't be a loose end out there to keep track of."

"You calling me a fucking loose end? Fuck you, man."

"I'm not calling you a fucking loose end until you get loose, dog. Don't make me put a leash and muzzle on you, bitch."

Mikey steps between them. "Shhhh, your voices are echoing through the trees… they can hear what we are saying, they can hear what we're thinking…"

The next morning, they all awake paralyzed yet electrified with the same thought: the liquor store, an idea fresh as their first invigorating sips years ago. A thinning of the blood, a gladdening of the heart; just what the hangman ordered.

Tonight's the night.

If Tristan is off the deep end, it no longer matters—they're flying off it with him. Striding gallantly ahead, he leads the way as if the rest of them don't know where they're going.

Jerm whispers to Mikey, "How is it that we're going to kill someone tonight, yet it feels like our own execution?"

5

Rico is up early, hyper-blinking, repelled from sleep—all night stressing about his conversation with Katrina. *Can I trust these sleeping angels, curled up fetal, peaceful on their claimed corners of my bed?* he thinks. He misses the brotherhood of The Vigil, the camaraderie of young men not quite as fucked up as he is, yet. Longing to repossess that innocent spirit—maybe that's why he plunged into points of no return with Dylan the other night. He's cringes at his behavior; certain parts he can't seem to trick himself into forgetting.

Grabbing his works, he cooks a fix, the next best thing to facing his transgressions. Weighing his options: how long could he leave town without both his businesses going awry. At least for a while he should get the fuck out, clear his head until the accusations blow over.

The phone rings.

No, we are not open yet, he thinks, grabbing the receiver.

"Yes?"

"Hey man, it's Mikey."

Rico's stomach drops a mile down. He's suspicious. Of what, he isn't really sure.

"Oh! Hello, Mikey!"

"How you doing, Rico?"

"Oh! Well, I'm okay, you know, crazy as usual."

"Ha ha, yeah, same here. Listen, the boys and I have been talking and we're just really... I don't know, man... You've been gone forever. We miss you, I guess is what I'm trying to say?"

"Ah, man. I figured there was tension since, you know... since everything got all fucked up when Bron came to town."

"Ah, not even man, this town's too small to waste time on petty shit. It's just drugs, you know. Shit comes and goes, like money comes and goes, right?" says Mikey, forcing a polite laugh. "Well, you wanna meet up tonight, just the guys?"

Rico pauses hard enough to burst a vein.

"Yes, possibly... Now, let me ask you Mikey, is Dylan with you? Have you spoken to him this week?"

"No? We figured he was with you and the girls? We were going to invite him too."

"No, I have no idea where he is. I think it would be best if it was just us anyway."

Mikey winks to the boys: Rico is nearly admitting guilt.

"Well, that sounds good enough to me, Rico. What do you say, Bluebird Park, around ten? We'll buy the forties?"

"Oh, why not your house?"

"Ah well, my Mom's kind of on a bad one. Kind of a big reason why we need to get out. You know, just the guys."

"Oh, okay. Got it. Okay then, Mikey, see you at the park at ten. Grab me a Mickey's, I'll owe you."

6

Jerm feels a swell of déjà vu watching Tristan lead the three of them back to the liquor store. Remembering Mikey calling Rico as they eavesdropped into the receiver, muffling flatulent laughter. Then, time snaps like a rubber band—after finishing their first round of forties, they're heading back to the store and it's not even noon yet.

Entering the liquor store's dusty threshold, Tristan turns his head, he says it again, like earlier today, "What'll it be, guys?"

Mikey beelines to the coolers. Frantically grabbing more 40s than they can hold, like their last day on Earth.

"We'll take all this and a fifth of Kesler there," says Mikey.

The clerk smiles, "All of this for your mother again, huh? Thirsty woman."

"Hot outside—I heard there's a heat wave coming," says Mikey. "One fifth of Popov for her too."

Swaying playfully from their buzz, the pendulum of the bulging plastic bags. "Just a thought, guys," says Jerm. "Maybe after we drink this we should crash out for the afternoon? Like, we shouldn't get too fucked up before nightfall, you know…."

"I appreciate that, Jerm," Tristan interrupts. "Doesn't matter though. All we're doing is having a drink with our buddy Rico tonight, right? We gotta just keep on telling ourselves we're just giving our buddy a beer. Don't keep telling yourself what you're doing, 'cause the more you think about what you're doing the longer it'll take to do what you're doing."

Taking over The House for the afternoon, it feels like old times—Tristan blasting his Fang *Landshark/Where the Wild Things Are* cassette, drinking tough, committing genocide on the third world of their brain cells still developing. *And I'll just sit and grin/the money will roll right in,* they sing along, losing their minds; how prophetic those lyrics were for The Vigil before they even had a specific title for their intent. Blurred tracers trailing their movements, double vision and double dialogues: just as you close one eye to see straight again, every time they think "Why are we celebrating when we are going to kill a man?" they just take a bigger sip than the last one. There, one dialogue again: encoded tough-guy chatter inflaming their adrenaline, back to chanting with Fang: *They called me a murderer! / They called me a junkie! / They said I did not belong in this world...*

"No passing out, Jerm. Off the couch, bitch," says Mikey, slapping him across the face. Jumping off the couch to recirculate, Jerm tries walking to the kitchen but lean-runs sideways, crashing into the fireplace, like the whole world is tipping over. Tristan high steps so he won't repeat the stumble, assisting Jerm from the ash.

Mom claps her hands, "You guys are just the best, helping each other out, no matter what."

Mikey stumbles down the basement and emerges with a quarter ball. "No one is falling asleep— I'm gonna leave this right here on the kitchen table if anyone needs a bump."

"We need a bump," they say.

7

"Well, there goes the sun," says Tristan, a benign comment encrypted: they have two hours left.

"Very astute, Tristan," Mom jabs. "You gonna let us know when the sun comes up, too, cock-a-doodle-doo?"

"Juuuust sayin...'" he says, like Nicholson's *Here's Johnny.*

The living room littered in empties, Tristan sails into the kitchen to calculate the swirling inventory. Ten 40s: four King Cobras, five Schlitz, and one stigmatized Mickey's hidden behind so no one will drink it by mistake. One eye peeking into the living room; the two boys have just cracked a fresh one.

He twists the cap off The Mickey's. He removes the Thallium from his trench coat's inner pocket. He pours it into the gaping brim. He caps it back up, extra tight. Watching the clock on the wall, he stops twisting, realizing he's been revolving his fingers around it for five whole minutes, almost admitting he's nervous. Turning the cap counter-clockwise, his dipso-instinct kicks in, a thirst he can't ignore. His cognizance snaps back, shocked that he was about to drink it. Hand tremoring, he shoves the befouled bottle into the fridge behind the others.

The phone rings. Mikey hollers: *Quiet, please!*

He picks up the phone: "Hey! Sounds good to me!" then hangs up.

"Rico is leaving Blast on foot. We got him his Mickey's, right?" Code for: *has that stuff been poured in?*

"Yeah, got it." Tristan returns to the kitchen, a racket of glass from the fridge.

"Well, shall we walk?" Mikey asks, scanning the room for agreement.

"Let's do it to it," Tristan says, hoisting the trash bag full of 40s over his shoulders.

Jerm exhales heavily, picking himself off the couch.

"Okay, you guys be safe," chirps Mom.

"We'll be safe, but we'll be late," Mikey assures her. Mom counts them as they stumble out the door, "One, two, three... wait, who's missing?" she asks herself. "Oh, fucking Rudy. Where's that little rascal been?"

8

Three figures struggling to stand fall into the chain-link of Bluebird Park. Unlatching the gate, they forget what they're doing halfway through, dogpiling as it opens. Flat on their backs, they gasp between guffaws. Vision swirling, Tristan inspects the bag's contents: all intact, yet he continues knocking them over. Other hands assist, only making it worse, until they take a deep breath, fondling each 40 oz, tumbling them back in.

Talking chainsaw spastic, brash and elastic, their thoughts in syrupy fluctuations often dissolving before reaching the insides of their arid lips. On the cement picnic table at the park's deep end, they remove the bottles from the bag again. Isolating The Mickey's as the table's centerpiece: a moonlight dial, its shadow pointing to Tristan. They crack their 40s. Rico will arrive any minute, but don't look like you're waiting. The moon doesn't move, nor does it go dim, yet the night darkens, accumulating weight of burden. Their speech indecipherable, slurred non sequiturs and fizzling oral motor skills—it's all the goddamned funniest shit they've ever heard until—they hear the gate unlatch in the distance and
they
suddenly
forget
what
funny is.

9

Rotating like slow-cooking rotisserie, Tristan wakes up, winces—the rancid smell of punk-house couch fabric under his nose, his Vigil brothers sprawled across the hardwood. He takes a breath, exhaling staccato; convinced they drank the Mickey's and they're dead.

But in his mind, events replay forward, backwards; every angle incomplete—infuriating, like torn pornography. Yet, he can still see Rico entering the park.

"Do either of you remember what happened last night?" he whispers, kicking them in the ribs.

Squinting, struggling to recollect.

"Yeah, we had forties in the park with Rico," Jerm says.

"And did Rico drink the Mickeys?"

"We were having a hell of a time opening it for him, but then he got it opened."

"And he drank it?"

"Yeah, pretty sure he drank it."

"We'll just say he drank it," decides Mikey.

"Neither of you sound sure that he fucking drank it," says Tristan, unsure himself which he prefers: that he drank it, and don't have to worry anymore, or that he didn't drink it and don't have to worry anymore.

Either way, they're worrying.

"Fuck. Well, where is he?" says Tristan.

Mikey grumbles. He calls Blast. No answer.

"Fuck, I just want this over with."

"Should we do a line about it?"

Mikey scrapes, chops.

They do a line about it.

"Should we... should we call Dylan?"

"And tell him what? That we aren't sure, but pretty… pretty sure Rico is dead, even though he might not be dead yet?"

"Should we check the park?"

"Scene of the crime, you're fucking crazy."

Whining sirens rising to crescendo—three cop cars converge in the driveway, the last onto the lawn, blocking traffic. Officers jump out, guns drawn, wide stepping to the front door. An officer bangs three times with his fist: *POLICE, OPEN THE DOOR!* flanked by two others; one salivating to use the battering ram.

Oh fuck, oh fuck… The boys drop to the ground. They just killed someone—now they want to cease to exist. Maybe not die but just disappear. No, they'd settle for dying. Instead, the terror is paused; time has stopped so their panic can expand. *Why are we so fucking scared now but not when we were actually going to kill a man?* thinks Jerm, watching Tristan and Mikey on the verge of tears, army crawling to the couch.

Mikey peeks through the blinds, isolating the shortest cop in the back of the formation. "Fucking Hackman," he whispers.

Seconds go by like minutes. In three heaves, the termite-infested front door unhinged, barging in guns pulled, their own infestation.

"ALL OF YOU, AGAINST THE FUCKING WALL!"

The Vigil clumsy: eyes bloodblurry, bladders full, knees jelly. The cops scream at every move—even when they obey, it's the wrong thing to do. They line them to the wall, hands clasped behind their heads. More cops barge in through the kitchen, more guns pulled at the ready.

Two aim at Mom's door—locked. In comes the battering ram.

"That's my mom in there, please be gentle —"

"OPEN THE FUCKING DOOR NOW!"

Splintering wood, they start coughing—her room hotboxed in toxic haze, Mom blows it—a thick mist, the stench of burnt celery from her glass pipe. Dropping it, her bone-thin talons grab a ladder to heaven.

"Please be careful with her," says Mikey.

"You—shut up! Where are the drugs? Where you keep the drugs?!?" demands Sawyer.

The boys look at each other, paralyzed but slightly relieved—drugs, not homicide.

The cops overturn the couch, open the basement door no one locked.

Two cops go downstairs, Sawyer cuffs Mom's boney wrists. Two more cuff the boys, their Miranda's read by the intertwining swine. Mikey eyes Tristan, chin motioning outside to Hackman.

"Who's gonna ride with that fucking guy?" Tristan says.

"Looky here!" The cops emerge from the basement with what little is left of The Vigil's meth bundle; the flattened, wrinkled manila envelope, a small miracle they hadn't replenished their supply.

Led out to the glaring sunlight, Jerm sees Mom in a car by herself, Jerm shoved inside another, Tristan and Mikey riding together in Sawyer's, Hackman in the passenger seat.

"What, too much of a fucking pussy to get your hands dirty?" Mikey spits.

Hackman sinks in his seat. "It's called a fucking ride-along," he whispers. "I had no fucking clue we were ending up here."

"Fuck you, Hackman. This is all you, man," Tristan says.

"Hey—shut the fuck up!" Sawyer eye-daggers Hackman's hands visoring his face. Pulling out in a swift procession, they turn on PCH, hitting a red light; a lengthy pause, everything in slow motion.

Huddled up in front of Blast; Katrina, Jasmine, and Dirty Anna await their friend who will never come. Staring ahead, the line of Laguna's finest enter their view just long enough to lock eyes with Mom and their estranged boys; every cuffed hand struggling, wishing they could wave back.

10

"Has anyone been booked here in the last five minutes, like three or four boys with an older woman?" Katrina asks, wheezing for breath. Nodding smugly, the receptionist peers over her shoulder. Her eyes roll back into place.

"Yes, convenient timing," she says, deadpan suspicious. "I don't know what you ladies are going to do about it, unless you intend to bail?"

"How much is bail?"

Looking the girls left to right, then right to left, she shakes her badly permed bobblehead. "More than you can afford, I'm sure..." she says.

Concerned with the fading look in her eye, Mikey begs to cell with Mom. His request is curtly denied. Sawyer assumes it's a mother/son helmed operation, until the other boys ask to share a cell with her too. She can't make eye contact with them, or she'll cry. Instead, she stares at the ground, explaining loudly: "That's not how it works when you go to jail; it's not a party. If it was a party, we would all tell them the same innocent story."

She starts moaning *This is the end, beautiful friends, the end...* accepting the bust as a tardy penance for a lifetime of derailment; the naked guilt of not being a better parent. Exhausted, she looks forward to whatever they throw at her— even the nightmare of detox would be a life-preserver, her entire life a turbulent ocean. Not a sober day for as long as she can remember and now it's better she didn't recall.

The boys: suffocating under avalanche of bewilderment, uncertainty, remorse; unsure exactly what to feel remorseful for. Maybe somewhere out there Rico's only paralytic, nauseated, the Thallium taking its time. Maybe Tristan put too much in and maybe they ran home after the poison worked quicker than anticipated. They pair off into staring contests through the bars, fearing their mutual gaze, urging each other's eyes to tell a story none can. Is memory suppression the guardian angel for murderers, rendering the act a false memory altogether? To see if he can return to the party, Tristan closes his eyes, to tell himself an innocent story.

This time, when he sees his demon, the demon is crying.

Running back to Blast to get bail cash, the girls pray Rico has surfaced, but it's 2PM and the closed sign is still up.

Circling back, upstairs to his backroom—locked, curtain closed. *You're only allowed here when I'm here* was Rico's only stipulation for sharing his dope treasury as their crash pad, and a safe place to stash their money so they wouldn't be walking town with bulging wads.

Banging on the door until their knuckles ache. Katrina speculates: money versus time. "Should we break in—maybe he's just passed out?

Jasmine shrugs. Anna removes her shades, squinting. "I swear I talked him out of leaving town so we wouldn't run out of dope, I don't think there's much left."

"That's why we should just break in, see if his stuff's still here," says Katrina. "We know what he'd take with him. And whatever—we'll pay for the window when we get inside to get the money to pay for the window we're about to break, right?"

Rummaging through their purses, Jasmine excitedly— then, sadly—pulls out Rudy's brass knuckles she forgot she had. Slowly inserting her fingers through the holes, her eyes heavy, closing, lights fading amber to black, a brief dream from the blue; her hand gripping the crescent moon hanging over the ocean. She pulls her arm back, envisioning breaking the impenetrable horizon. With one punch she shatters the window, startling herself awake, smirking. Anna and Katrina squeal silently, gently clapping.

Anna reaches in and unlocks the door. The three enter the room. Empty of Rico, full of things he would've taken with him if he fled: his antique gold pill box where he'd measure out his Klonopin, his wallet filled with four balloons, eight crumpled twenties, and his contact lens solution. While his room is usually an eye-tearing minty-smoke gas chamber, now only a faint lingering of his menthols remains.

"He probably got lucky in some hot dude's bed," Katrina says, but she doesn't really believe it. She writes a quick note, apologizing for the window, explaining how they're worried of his whereabouts. Pooling their stash together, they're surprised to have $2,080 to work towards The Vigil's bail, even if some of it is from Rico's wallet.

The condescending receptionist is shocked when they return to the station by 3:30, then sort of charmed when they pull out cash rolled up in wads, frantically unfolding, counting on her desk. "There. What does that get us?"

"Ladies, that's very, very sweet of you but it wouldn't have freed up one of livers. The good news—they were all released about fifteen minutes ago."

11

Walking with his parents to their car, Jerm gives Tristan and Mikey a goofy wave goodbye like its nothing more than school letting out.

Tristan sees his parents roll up in their beat-up sky-blue Volvo.

Tristan mumbles to Mikey: "If they ask us anything, just say the speed was a slip up and not, like, a career move like it is. Like it was. Whatever."

Tristan's parents are already cracking jokes, how their son is no worse than Big Jim was in the '60s, how Big Jim turned out fine; unaware, at this very moment, he's collapsing over his metal detector, his heart slowly stopping, the crowd at Blackout Beach presuming he is merely nodding out.

With no idea what to expect withdrawing from meth, they can only imagine they'll be puking. Tristan has grabbed a communal bucket; so far, it's collected nothing but dry heaves. Mikey has pimped a bottle of Kesler to settle their frayed nerves.

Tristan pops a minty green Tic Tac to brave the walk into the living room.

"So, how's our little fugitives doing?" his dad says, in attempt to break ice he doesn't realize shattered long ago.

Fugitives? thinks Tristan. *We're not running from anything?*

"Fugitives?" Tristan asks in a goofy, animated fashion. "Seems to me like we got good and captured, Dad."

"Petty criminals, I mean."

Unplugging the landline, Tristan carries it into his room.

Side by side on the bed, Tristan and Mikey mumble back and forth, despising the sound of their own voices. Passing the bottle, they're dead set on passing out, anything to fast-forward this nightmare of living. All they receive are falling dreams, precarious whiplash-brief teases. Losing balance of their subconscious, their eyes pop back open, blinking, twitching, gasping. Out of time with their own insomnia, one keeps waking the other, every little seizure squeaking the bedsprings.

Tristan's memory continues its weak recall, every scene cut abruptly. Until it goes all the way back to the beach, the night he and Jerm found Dylan with the girls. How happy they looked, not a care in the world. He stops there; his envy of how high they were makes it the memory vivid, buoyant. Complete.

"Let's call the girls, tell them we wanna score some dope," he says, popping out of bed.

"We could ask them if they've seen Rico," Mikey adds.

"Okay. Do you want to call?" asks Tristan.

"Don't act like you're not creaming your jeans to call Katrina. Just call her," says Mikey. He takes the phone off the hook, hands it to Tristan.

He dials her pager. She calls him back thirty seconds later.

"Hey… Katrina," he says breathily, pseudo-humble; he wants something. Dope, missing info, her hot body, her hand in marriage, eternal forgiveness—he'll take anything from her right now.

"Tristan, oh my God—what's going on?"

He offers selected details of the last twelve hours. She tells him they tried bailing them out. His heart soars, then plummets. He forces himself to change the subject.

"Katrina, listen... This is sort of hard to ask, but I know you girls are working for Rico. Heroin, right?"

"Yeah, I'm sorry... we're like, in pretty deep."

"Are you with him right now?

"Dude, he's like, gone."

Tristan's stomach twists. "Gone, what do you mean?"

"Fuck, I don't know. No one has seen him in almost two days. He mentioned something about leaving town 'cause he thinks he's in trouble, he was really vague about it. We're think we talked him out of it, but he's gone and... but like... all his stuff is here."

Tristan's eyes dart to Mikey like they'll never ever shut again, his acting remaining flawless. "Wow, okay. You mentioned trouble, what kind of trouble?"

"That's the thing—he wouldn't tell us. But he was acting really strange, really somber but like, panicked."

"Do you know if he had... *has* any enemies?" asks Tristen, cringing at his slip of tense.

"Not reeeeally." She thinks for a second. "The only thing I can think of, which I really don't want to think of—"

"Yeah?"

"Okay, so when Anna took him to Minnie Street the first time to buy big, those guys said if he sold dope anywhere outside of Laguna, they'd kill him."

"Oh, good, that's good."

"What do you mean that's good?"

Tristan curses himself, silent—he shouldn't have made this call drunk.

"No, I mean... that's a good place to start. Can someone talk to those guys in Santa Ana?"

"Fuck. I don't know. I don't really know them. I guess I could talk to Anna?"

"Yeah, let's do that. Wanna call her and see?"

"Yeah, I'll call her right now, check in with you tomorrow?"

"Okay, thanks." He pauses. "Hey—I love you, okay?"

"Uh, okay! Bye!"

Tristan hangs up the phone. He stares at the carpet.

"Well?" asks Mikey.

"Well, what? You heard everything," says Tristan, passing him the bottle.

"I mean, I don't know... now what are you thinking?"

"Mikey, please don't ask me what I'm thinking ever again."

In silence, they gulp the rest of the Kesler, surrendering to some estranged cousin of sleep paralysis, jerking like marionettes, remaining distracted by someone else, lying very still, somewhere out there.

The next morning, when Tristan opens his eyes, he has no idea where he is.

Right, parents' house.

He looks to his left—Mikey's wide-eyed, already awaiting his direction.

"What now?"

"I dunno, wanna go for a walk or something?"

Cautiously, they make small steps down Pacific Coast Highway. Young and senile. Slow and aimless. They gain distance, block by block, not really speaking. Unaware they're heading towards Blast until they arrive, right as Jasmine is turning the closed sign to open.

12

Dizzy, windblown, teetering; the thought of entering Rico's store nauseates Mikey and Tristan. Startled behind its glass, Jasmine waves, motioning to Katrina.

Jasmine opens the door, smiling; her rot-mouth displayed bravely. Katrina rushes over, tackling Tristan and Mikey—ha, ha, ha—hollow, forced laughter from the boys. Tristan squeezes Katrina hard as his weakened state allows, unwilling to let go; the warm feel of a woman's body, someone who's alive.

He searches for anchor in her and Jasmine's eyes, finding only a shimmer, the glassiness of a junkie's gaze. "Wow, you girls look like you're... feeling good. Any word from Rico?"

"No, nothing," they say, pouty-lipped.

"What about Anna?"

"She borrowed a car this morning, headed to Santa Ana to talk to those dudes, see if they know anything."

"Fuck, she went alone?"

"Yeah, but she's one of their best customers."

Browsing the store to distract themselves, Tristan notices Mikey thumbing frantically through every rack. "Mikey, the green jacket's long gone, man."

"Oh? No, it should be here," Katrina says, shuffling through the coat rack. "Shit, guess not? It was totally here two days ago. I saw Rico staring at it." Folding clothes while they chat, like they own the place.

"Wait, you girls are opening the shop today?" says Tristan.

Katrina shrugs. "We figured why not, you know? If Rico's gonna be gone for a while, we may as well help him out so he doesn't lose the place."

"I wouldn't do that," says Tristan.

"Uh, why not?"

"'Cause you don't know where he is or what's going on. I feel like we should all leave."

"What's the problem? What's *your* problem?"

"I just think it's safe to assume the worst here," says Tristan. "What if something happened to him? You might look suspicious if you just open the shop like it's yours."

"That doesn't make any sense."

"It does though—like those old movies where the girl knocks off a dude so she can take over his life? Only this is like, real life."

"What? Are you saying we like, killed Rico?"

"That is *not* what I'm saying." Short of breath, Tristan strides outside for fresh air. His stomach twists—Rudy across the highway, speedwalking down the beat.

Tristan screams his name, waving his hands. Direct eye contact, Rudy's finger over his lips. Tristan screams louder. Rudy double-swipes his hands like *you don't fucking know me,* running down the block.

Tristan gets he's still upset but it stings to be snubbed in public.

Anna pulls up in front of Tristan. Exiting the vehicle, she brushes past him, hoisting her purse over her shoulder, stomping into the store.

"Girls! Out, out! You gotta get out of here!"

"What? Why?"

"I talked to those guys. Rico owes them money. They fronted him an extra bundle two weeks ago with two weeks to pay it back."

"Fuck—"

"See, that's the kind of shit I was talking about!" Tristan says.

"They know about the shop?"

"I kind of fucked up," says Anna, ashamed. "They tricked me into telling them about Blast. They seemed concerned of his whereabouts like they actually cared about something other than their money. Their eyes kept darting to each other as I was talking."

Katrina locks the front door, flipping around the closed sign. Scrambling to the backroom, the girls collect their belongings, piling it on the backsteps. *Leave the dope, no, take the dope—we'll sell it to pay those guys back, no, we can't have that much on us, okay, we'll keep coming back only in the middle of the night, yes.*

13

Sequestered in Tristan's old bedroom, he and Mikey fight for shut eye; sleeping off the last two years might take the rest of their lives. Every moment sleep evades them, they try calling Rudy. Exhausted, they search for the will to walk to his house.

Every idea is the wrong idea.

Alternating with more unsuccessful calls to Dylan, whose parents say he's "unavailable" and "he's away for a while," in a resigned, icy tone. Eventually when they hear his parent's answer, they hang up.

From jail to detox, Mom collect calls her only son every night; her phone privilege at 8PM, offering semblance of family routine.

Days pass, unlearning the difference between dead, disappearing, grounded, or Mom being locked away to purge her own poison. It's all the same kind of gone. Even in Tristan's bedroom, he and Mikey feel they're still in a cell, cut off from their gang they assumed would last forever.

Tristan's Dad wakes them with a knock on the door. "Hey, uh... Mikey. Phones for you. It's your mother."

It's 8AM, not PM. A call out of routine suggests urgency. Mikey grabs the phone, greeting Mom like she's the child.

He says, "Oh, okay," a hundred times.

He hangs up.

"What is it, man?"

His eyes glaze over, shocked, his will to react drained. "Mom's got cancer. Bad kind. Might only have a couple weeks."

Not including trips to the emergency room for alcohol poisoning, Mom hadn't been to the doctor for a full check-up since her late teens. Her stubborn negligence was as bad a habit as the bottle. In her wet brain, as long as she could "see" Mikey, she was being a good parent. And when she saw two or more of him in her blurred vision, even if they were other children, she was Supermom, against all odds.

Now returning to The House for in-home hospice, Mom is at the mercy of Mikey; her caretaker when her nurse goes home every evening.

Tristan alerts every severed member, calling Jerm first.

"Hey, you okay?"

"I don't even know what that means anymore," says Jerm.

"Well, Mom is sick, not long to live, I guess."

"Then, I guess I'm doing better than her, I guess…"

"You guess? Jerm—Mom is dying, don't you fucking care?"

"Yes, of course I care *Mikey's* Mom is dying…" says Jerm. "Just… one thing at a time." He takes a deep breath. "Listen, I just got back from the Bluebird Park—"

"Why, in the fucking world, did you go there?"

"Because maybe I wanted some fucking proof of what we actually did."

"Fine. What did you see?"

"I got close enough to the table to see all the 40s were empty."

"The Mickey's?"

"Like I said, empty."

"Don't tell me you touched any of them."

"I'm not an idiot. I left as soon as the park maintenance guy showed up. I watched him throw them in a garbage can. Done."

Since Rudy won't pick up, Tristan shows up at Rudy's door on a Saturday morning, knocking on wood. His uncle answers the door, "Rudy moved to San Francisco to live with his Tia." A weak closure, Tristan remains unnerved from his last sight of him, running away from cries of his name.

Jerm tells Dylan's parents it's a time-sensitive emergency; they give him a new number where he's staying. Jerm calls Dylan, who sounds distant in tone and location.

"Where are you?" asks Jerm

"Somewhere safe," is all Dylan says.

Jerm explains that Mom's illness is terminal, how they're gathering nightly to keep vigil like their namesake, in solidarity with their fate family.

"I no longer feel any solidarity with The Vigil, the girls, the house, all of it, all of you."

"What, why?"

"It all just swirls down into the same drain. If we hadn't fell into that whole crowd, none of that would have happened to me."

Jerm's stomach writhes; Dylan sounds like his parents now. Jerm wants to tell him they didn't "fall" into any "bad" crowd, that they made mistakes together as they learned, like an open-air classroom, no rules and no boundaries. He hesitates; imagining Dylan asking him what it was, exactly, that they learned, so he drops it. *We killed Rico*, he's dying to tell him, *the worry is over*, but he doesn't dare utter it, unsure whether he even believes it or whether he'd rather not even conceive it, the glaring embarrassment of zero proof to give him. Nothing to receive, even through a receiver, so he hangs up, ashamed for disrupting Dylan's private recovery.

14

The remaining evenings at The House stretch and linger into one long night. The Vigil heralded confrontation, climax; how much apocalypse could they fit into a day. Now, to preserve the gravity of their matriarch, they must haunt her orbit, spun-weary moons refusing to move. At happy hour, when the hospice nurse completes her shift, The Vigil arrive to assure Mom lives her last days the way she prefers: like nothing has changed. A never-ending pre-wake party resisting Mom's demise. A last-ditch ritual. They arrive wearing suits and party dresses, ceremonial Old Fashioneds from a cocktail book; 40 ouncers now forbidden. Voices delicate until Mom triggers laughter, her irreverence intact. As if she's wearing a clown nose staring down death, hidden deep in her audience.

Sitting upright in her bed, a negated saint in exile, adorned with flowers, a ventilator, medications. With an IV drip of morphine, she's high as a kite, anticipating her release to the wind. A static-channel euphoria morphing her into mist above the mortal riptide. It'd be beautiful if this installation wasn't so temporary, this boiled-down essence of the gang's courtship with death, the present never romantic as they remember. Now forced to rub their faces in a dream they can't look away from; something inside them demands to feel every aspect if they ever expect to evolve.

Forever embedded in the walls, her scent remains—vodka and Virginia Slims, now with a medicinal tinge. "Mom, what would make you like really happy right now?" asks Tristan. "Want a bottle of Popov, a pack of smokes?"

"Oh, me? Oh no, I'm happy, sweetie. I've got all you around me, a great nurse, beautiful flowers." She pauses, smiles. "I'm going to die, but I know I did this to myself, so I feel I'm actually in control of this—no one else killed me but my damned self, damnit."

Only the girls laugh with her. The boys shiver, like it's too cold in there. They file out of the room, staggering for air a ventilator can't facilitate. A good thinning of the blood. Straight to the kitchen to make more drinks, Mikey mixes their medicine.

"Why aren't the girls drinking?" says Jerm.

No one answers because they haven't learned: dope makes booze lose its allure. Mom refused vodka because she's on morphine, the girls on street tar, so they're bonding, between them a secret language where everything is groovy.

"The girls are hogging Mom," says Tristan.

"Ah, let 'em have their time, man," Mikey says. "We'll get our time with her."

"I'm just antsy. No one should look as hot as Katrina when someone is dying, its obscene. I need something to do. Let's, like, clean the basement or something."

"Nah, man. I've sealed it off again," says Mikey. "Going down there is starting to scare the shit out of me." Rolling up their sleeves, they assess their gouged-up flesh, comparing bulging relief maps of scar tissue; a miracle they escaped infection or amputation. The proud flesh keeping those tortures confined, the blood underneath still itchy, and the fact they can't scratch is cruelty.

Holding tight to fresh drinks, they return to Mom's room. She's elated, like they're visiting her for the first time, like they weren't just in there ten minutes ago, high as the heavens.

"Horray, the boys are here." Announcing each one by name as they enter, opening credits of their own variety show. "Now, wait a second, where's Rudy?"

"Rudy moved to San Francisco last week. His uncle said he just up and left."

"Goddamnit—right before he was gonna start that project for me," she laments. The project: her odd mortal tether. "There's no way I could see him?"

"We've been calling him all week. He won't answer."

She reflects for a moment, reminiscing in melancholy. "Well, if we can't have Rudy—

(Oh God, don't say it.)

"—I'd love to see Dylan. Where's your sidekick, Jerm?" " Ah, I'm working on it. He's caught up with family stuff...."

(Please don't say Rico.)

"Oh, okay. Well then where's Rico, that sexy man?"

The room goes cold. Tristan downs his drink, excusing himself to make another.

"Rico is missing, actually," says Katrina. "We think he may be out of town, we're really not sure."

"Missing? Don't you think we should file a missing person's report?"

"I think we will in another couple days."

"Good, 'cause the third person I really want to see is Hackman, maybe he can help?"

Trapping their reactions to their roiling guts: "Hackman? After what happened here, Mom?"

"Yes, I'd like to thank him," she says, "If it wasn't for the raid, I wouldn't have seen a doctor. I may be on my deathbed here, but it's the best damn deathbed a gal could hope for— otherwise, I may have died in my room alone while the rest of you were doing God knows what. Now we all live it up a bit," she says, signaling to her litter, proud of her house where they're no longer hiding anything.

15

The boys gather in the garage.

"If we get Hackman over here, the girls will tell him Rico's missing. If Mom doesn't bring it up first," says Tristan.

"Well, I hate to say it but we gotta just let that happen or it'll look weird—denying a woman's dying wish?'" says Jerm, keeping watch from the backdoor.

"Okay—what's the most incriminating thing he could ask us? No one's asked us where we were that night yet," says Tristan.

"Why would they? We weren't even friends with him anymore."

"You mean we're *not* friends with him anymore. All it's gonna take is one slip like that to make shit suspicious. Just... keep acting like everyone is gonna live forever or whatever."

Mired in guilt for discussing alibis when they should be spending time with Mom, they reenter her room to find her alone.

"The ladies stepped out for a moment, guys."

The boys fluff her pillow, refill her water, make sure she's comfortable, and burn her fading image into their minds.

Securing a spoonful to tide them over, it's almost midnight when the girls enter Rico's back alley.

Approaching the stairs, they gasp—a light on in Rico's apartment. Hollering his name, they tear open the unlocked door to a scream.

"Oh my God! I'm so sorry," says Anna, catching her breath. "I thought you guys were Rico or like, the cops or something."

"What are you doing here?"

"You think it's okay I'm crashing here for a bit?"

"Sounds like you're already doing it."

"Yeah, I'm just starting to feel really... I don't know...

206

bad. It was weird letting myself in through the broken window, I just don't have anywhere else to go." She retrieves the lighter and full spoon. "I mean, someone's gotta keep the fires burning here, right?"

Sick at the thought of keeping watch for Rico by doing dope in his apartment, they fix up, get over it.

Katrina notices Rico's ID on the dresser—the fact he doesn't have it on him adds further worry. She knows this old Mexican ID with his parent's address is his only one, after leaving his California Driver's License in the Boom Boom boy's room, lost and never found. She sighs, unsure why she's grabbing it—perhaps preemptively sentimental— and crams it into her purse before they leave.

Hackman couldn't reconcile why he hoped The Vigil would eventually call him, the way he was so reluctant when Mikey finally rang him to break the news about Mom. "Well, if it's true, that sucks," he said. "But if I come over there and you guys lay one fucking hand on me, just know that I carry a gun now and could literally get away with murder if I wanted to." Hackman promised himself he'd act tough, nonchalant about the whole thing, but ten minutes later he's at the front door in leather jacket, jeans, and combat boots, like nothing ever changed.

Mikey's eyes swollen from intermittent weeping. "Really good to see you, Hackman."

"You too, fat boy," he says.

"What the fuck is this?" says Mikey, lifting his pin laden lapel—a police radio.

"Oh, sorry," he says, rolling his eyes. "I'm technically on the clock, just didn't want to show up in uniform. I'm not gonna stay long, I just wanted to pay my respects to the old lady."

Hackman enters, waving shyly. He hugs the girls extra

hard—his stint at the station like a chauvinist monastery.

Unprompted, he overexplains. "Okay, for the record—I had nothing to do with the raid. I was just riding around with Sawyer. We got this anonymous call. Once I heard the address, I just wanted to fucking disappear. The lights were already flashing, man."

No one had asked, so they just shrug. Leading him into Mom's room, her eyes light up crying his name. Hackman dives into her, a little too rough, forgetting he's squeezing a delicate woman. The gang encircling the bed, Hackman lies next to her, bursting into an avalanche of apology.

"I know, I know..." she says. "But I want to thank you. It's strange, but really. I do." She kisses him on the forehead.

"Can I get you anything?" he asks.

"Hmmm... let's see, what could you do for scaring the living crap out of us that morning..."

The boys brace themselves.

"Oh! How would we go about filing a missing person's report—"

She's interrupted by a cacophony static on Hackman's radio.

"Shit, sorry. I gotta take this."

Something about a fire.

Something about a car and suspects.

Something about the 7000 block on PCH.

The girls cry Anna's name.

"What, you know about this?" he asks them.

"Just let us come with you."

Expecting the worst, they get it.

Blast From the Past is engulfed in vengeful, unrelenting flame, spreading to the adjoining businesses. The shattered front window indicates it's no accident. Fire engines and two cop cars barricade the street, more coming. All the gang can do is watch. Hackman jumps the lines showing his badge.

Two minutes later the hoses are out.

Twenty minutes later the flames are out.

Thirty minutes later, the charred lifeless body of Anna is carried out.

Rushing over to her gurney in hysterics, the girls can't comprehend why medics are pushing them away when they just want to see their friend who they insist is still alive because denial is insidious.

The cops divulge to Hackman: Witnesses saw a white van pull up in front of the shop, the passenger lobbing a sealed bucket of combustible material through the front window, immediately engulfing the interior, then turned North on PCH.

Jasmine stands transfixed by the smoke and last tendrils of flame, remembering the one she started when the whole town went up.

She taps each one on the shoulder; for once, she'll lead the gang back to The House. "But first we go to the beach," she whispers.

The beach: the end of civilization, where you go when nothing feels civilized. And right now, its high tide, its reach aggressive, oversaturated, leaving no grain of sand dry. Its foams reach for the feet of The Vigil; their legs dangling off the boardwalk. Every time the ocean roars like a firing squad echoing in the great open wide, there's something pushing, pulling from beneath its red tide.

Jasmine points, and everyone looks, as a brilliant blue flashes across the shore. Every time a wave crashes, it flashes again, sometimes multiple flashes in one crash like visual Morse code. Like the ocean is screaming, from behind a wall. Or winking, like it knows it all.

Why do they call it red tide when it flashes blue, she wonders. Opening her eyes wider despite the sting of tears, she spots a crimson presence only she can see, focusing behind her retina. It forces her lens convex, pulling it to the foreground as she resists, a tug of war, a battle of wills, an argument between spirit and body where there is no right and there is no wrong; merely elements borrowed when operating at a loss.

Allowing herself an extended blink, when her eyelids return open, the curtains somehow stay drawn.

16

"Guys, I think Mom's fading," says Mikey.

Mom stares at them all, mouth agape, overwhelmed by what she's seeing.

"Just, be good to yourself, okay?" she creaks, squeezing every hand. "If people aren't good to you, don't forget to be good to yourself because...."

"Hold tight, Mom."

"You interrupted me, Michael. Now come over here, all over you, while I finish what I was trying to say."

Gathering around, they stroke her arms, heads nestling into every inch of her.

"I was just going to say, if people aren't good to you, don't forget to be good to yourself because..."

Pausing, she feels their collective weight.

"... you can't learn a goddamned lesson when you're dead."

And with that, she goes.

Gone for an hour now, The House is promptly overrun by the nurse, her assistant, a medical team removing Mom's body. The Vigil pair up, consoling one another in private. When Mikey isn't dealing with questions and paperwork, he's crying into Tristan's shoulder. Jerm and Hackman weep grotesquely next to one another, staring off into space. Still mourning from Anna, Katrina lays on top of Jasmine, who hasn't said a word beyond sobs since the beach; she won't even open her eyes despite Katrina squeezing her bawling like they'd float away too if she let go.

Tristan approaches Katrina. She sees him extend his hand and allows him to pull her in close. In paralyzed silence, exchanging extended glances, communicating absolute surrender, they're frightened it's the end. Not just of Mom, but of everything. Yearning to find some kind of beginning in each other's eyes, they close them instead, falling asleep in each other's arms.

To give Mikey space, everyone says goodbye, but even after Mikey shuts off the living room light, they can't bring themselves to leave the property.

Tristan takes Katrina's hand, leading her into the garage for privacy.

Curling into his arm, she says, "I promise I never had sex with Dylan, just so you know."

"Yeah, that's what they all say."

Melting into the bottom bed of the bunk, they resume their places in each other's arms until they're writhing, working it all out through the physical ciphers of love, slowly, surely becoming the same body, disappearing into one.

They jerk awake at the creak of the door.

Jasmine, her palmed face peeking from the crack.

"Katrina... I can't see... Do I still have pretty eyes?"

FOUR

A Decayed Past

1

Tristan is staring at Katrina, who now goes by Kat, and her eyes are closed.

Lying in bed together in their Hollywood apartment on Sunset and Western, she's still asleep. Now that she's conquered the false prophet of preservation, she needs all the rest she can get. After five years of spurious attempts to kick, she's tried it all: methadone, Suboxone, therapy; valerian and kava they'd steal from the health food store when money was tight. She'd invariably slip by scoring cheap pharmaceuticals like Valium or Xanax to ease the anxiety of withdrawal, another numbing gateway to relapse. Before she knew it, she'd be nodding on the real stuff, praying to phantoms again.

Breathing heavy, he covers his mouth so she doesn't stir. Knowing he's next to clean up, one to nurse the other, finally ridding themselves of their respective poisons, aiming to live the luxury of maybe not dying.

He grabs the Jameson for his sun salutation, the daily morning shot to kill the guilt long enough to reach his "proper" breakfast shot he must mix with milk, his motivation to get out of bed. Tiptoeing to the fridge before she wakes up, he's pouring three fingers of J since it's his day off, topping it with a fistful of white, innocent, wholesome milk to wash his golden shame into something less blinding. Sipping slowly, he stares at her, in awe she may have reached sobriety, searching for a reason she could possibly be proud of him.

Ten years ago, after Mom's memorial, the gang knew they had to scatter. How further things could escalate if they maintained their self-destructive organism. The memorial felt crueler having to look after Jasmine, who, while present, couldn't bear witness to the ceremony, having gone blind the same night Mom passed. One moment, she was all eyes; the next, two empty lenses of darkness.

Ever inseparable, Jasmine and Katrina always held hands out of security and affection. But with the death of her sight, Jasmine leaned on Katrina with all her weight: her caretaker, cook, cleaner, stealer, drug runner, her guiding light until that light went out too.

"I'm tired of holding your hand," Katrina said to her one night at the beach before she walked away, leaving Jasmine to stare into milky black through her cataracts, only looking back to assure herself that Jasmine was getting smaller.

She knew it was cruel, but somebody had to make the first move.

Grabbing Tristan's hand instead, they escaped to the closest big city—Los Angeles, where their bad habits could limp along in anonymity instead of the echoing co-dependence of an insular, suffocating faction.

Tristan recalls how lucky he felt when they signed that first-year lease. Until it all came crashing back through the front page of the L.A. Times the next morning: The Columbine Shooting, where two trench- coated youths killed twelve students and a teacher on that blood-soaked April day in 1999. Spending that whole morning staring at the paper, he read the article five times through. After The Vigil set their campus on fire, a more massive event of carnage was something they entertained, so tangible they could taste it, like a universal instinct being shared through a grand unconscious network of America's nihilistic youth. They too, made hit lists for kids they didn't like, teachers who had crossed them. It was the next logical step, an ultimate climax.

Those two kids really fucking did it, he thought.

Seeing this bloodbath on international news exhumed "the whole Rico thing" from Tristan's cornered conscience. The Rico thing was a big reason—maybe *the* reason—why Mikey insisted the boys disband, to ensure it'd never be brought up again. Inevitably someone would slip up and spill it,

216

especially after the girls filed the missing person report. Hackman obliged, begrudgingly; convinced the fire was all awash in a hole-ridden heroin deal, that those Santa Ana dealers either had him killed before they torched the joint or Rico fled back to Mexico. Either way, the dealers got away clean, even after the LBPD urged SAPD to raid Minnie Street, to "do their fucking job."

But Katrina would pursue it, daily, in her conscience—Rico's disappearance impossible for her to let go of, making it harder to let go of the needle.

Which made it harder for Tristan to get through the day unless he started with those two shots every morning and just kept right on going (some days it was easy not to think about Rico; since he never saw proof, it just seemed abstract. But he *saw* Anna's dead body, with the rest of the gang as witness. All this time he privately blamed himself for her death, since she wouldn't have been squatting in his shop if he was actually "living" there, nor had he ever forgiven himself for annihilating Jasmine's mouth "looking for cameras," her pain the direct catalyst for her and Katrina meeting Anna, then promptly becoming junkies), which made it harder for him to stop drinking until he blacked out every night, which made it harder to remember half his life anymore—which was sort of the point; to wash it away in some ambiguous blur that no one, including him, could ever get to the bottom of.

Because time doesn't heal all wounds as much as it distorts and disorients the source from which the pain came.

And in Tristan's perpetual spiral of self-disgust, he often toyed with this idea: the length his own precarious life is the statute of limitations for the murder he can't deny he committed. All it accomplished was more roguish notoriety in Los Angeles where he'd sought to escape attention. Everyone glommed onto him—Tristan: that fucking crazy guy who'd fight someone twice his size, get 86'd from one bar only to close out the next, who would drink, eat, snort anything (with the exception of heroin, a hypocritical moral superiority to hold over Katrina) thinking *maybe tonight's the night* because somehow every evening had to end in some dramatic climax he hoped was his own fateful death: redemption! Everyone wanted to be friends with him because they feared him, maybe even fascinated why they were scared, preferring to be on his good side, because if it really was his last night on Earth, close proximity might earn them a shortcut to their own legend status by association.

Tristan sips his morning elixir, like butterscotch cream with a kick, then nearly chokes, startled by their landline ringing. He dives for it before it can wake her up—*Hello? No, please quit calling!* The first of many calls they receive daily from Kat's junkie friends buzzing around again, convinced she's fallen off by now. Junkies are like maggots: crawling from decay, before becoming flies, circling around the next rotting body. Always in a group to normalize their sickness until they find themselves alone, together; sufficient euphoria always out of reach.

She stirs. Breathing heavier, he prays she'll just go back to sleep. Committed to the roll of her nurse the whole week, he took a leave of absence from work so they can just get this done, once and for all. The rolls set in stone—Kat, the patient; Tristan, her caretaker, her cook, her cleaner, her guiding light who is already slurring at 8AM because those are just the rules for now until it's his turn to give it up.

When the phone rings again, his arm darts out, chokes it, but the phone slamming on the receiver wakes her up.

"Who was it?" she asks.

"Don't worry about it, sweetheart. Please, just go back to sleep."

Her upper body flings upward like a horror flick jump cut, mouth open, breath labored. Gazing into an uncertain future, her glassy eyes threaten tears at the wrong thought or word, so he treads carefully.

"You okay?"

"No. I'm not okay. I feel like the last ten years is just repeating everything we tried to get away from by moving here, but worse."

"Yeah, how?" He knows exactly what she means but plays dumb, to allow her to articulate herself.

"How many times has the phone rang this morning? These people aren't our friends—they just need to be convinced they're not... I don't know... slowly killing themselves."

He nods, afraid to speak—he might slur his words again, which would upset her further.

"Our friends don't give a shit that I might be doing better, Tristan. There's not going to be any congratulations, no 'we're proud of you'... They're just waiting for me to fall again so things will just stay the way they are. But we're fucking adults now, shit."

It took one of them to achieve sound mind to find the guts to say it out loud.

"You're right, Kat. If you could do anything, what would you do?"

Overwhelmed with the thought until it's hard to deny.

"I mean, I'm a week sober. That's huge. So as of now, maybe, *maybe* I've escaped heroin. A fucking miracle, right? But Tristan..." She pauses, making sure he's looking her in the eyes.

"Do you think we'll ever be able to escape our friends?"

The look in her eyes is too much—he immediately turns away. It's so true he takes another sip, stomps to the window, looks across the street: there's all four of them, trading off calling from the payphone. He looks to Kat—a healthy blush of color has returned to her face. Turning his eyes back to the window, he curses their cagey pacing.

The phone rings again—Kat grabs it before Tristan can, wanting her own chance to tell these fuckers off. Unloading her silver tongue to whomever is on the other line, she gasps:

"Mikey? Oh my God!"

She looks up at Tristan, eyes wide. Confused, he downs his special milk for courage, and yanks the phone from her hand.

"Mikey? This really you, man?"

Laughter, a disarming sincerity.

"Yeah, sure is. It has to be me considering the proposition I have for you, if you're interested?"

He gets flushed: *what-could-it-be-this time*.

"Uh, okay... Do we need to discuss this in private?" he asks, triggering a glare from Kat.

Mikey laughs again. "No, not at all, man. In fact, is there a way to get Kat on another line? This concerns both of you. But shit man, let's catch up first."

Curling up on the bed, they share the earpiece, urging Mikey to fill in the gaps of the last decade. For the kid voted "most doomed" or "least likely to succeed," they're humbled by his positive life path:

Not long after the funeral, his estranged grandparents passed away in quick succession, leaving Mikey a small inheritance. Tristan and Kat are amazed he didn't just blow it all, the way they would have, but being the only child of an alcoholic gave him enough accumulated knowledge of what *not* to do.

"Looking back, it's like we made every mistake we possibly could," says Mikey.

Tristan and Kat laugh because it's true.

"So, I enrolled in cooking school, knowing that if I fucked up, it'd be a fast track to bad habits. Not to brag, but I breezed that shit. I duked it out at some South County restaurants, then partnered with an investor, and then I opened my own bistro here in Dana Point, trying to keep out of the shadows."

"Did you keep living at The House?" asks Tristan.

"Oh God, no. Are you kidding? In that house all alone with nothing but fucked memories for company? No. In fact, I considered tracking down Jasmine to burn the place down."

They crack up, relieved to hear Mikey's dark humor intact. "I don't think I ever told you, but my grandparents actually owned The House. They gave it to Mom out of guilt, for basically disowning her. So I ended up inheriting it once they passed. I've been renting it out to a decent family for the last five years, although this is going to be their last month in there. Which... brings me to my proposition."

Their faces push closer into the earpiece, exchanging a quick glance.

"Would you... guys like to buy it?"

"Us? Buy a house?" It sounds like a joke.

"I know it sounds crazy, and I don't know what your financial situation is like, but hear me out..." The more he speaks, the more it makes sense. Mikey wants the house to stay in the extended family, to those of its origin. He was never able to relax knowing some square, vulnerable family was living there, their wholesome vibe desecrating The Vigil's contrarian temple; a place so much a part of them, so fucking alive he was surprised the walls hadn't bled. He felt bad, dishonest, with such nice people living in a place where such crazy shit occurred.

"They're sweet, but man, they complain about everything—like the black mold in the basement," Mikey explains. "It's such cheap rent. I knew the basement was a mess, I sealed it off for a reason. 'Just pretend like it's not there,' I told them. we didn't even know the basement was there for years, right?"

Mikey, the wheeler-dealer side of him blossoming with age, inquiries about their financial state. Tristan must come clean first, no bullshit.

"So, listen... We've uh, been better, but we're on the up and up," he says, squeezing Kat's hand. "Kat is a week sober off dope. Next, we're gonna focus on me, which isn't going to be fun, but I know it's gotta happen."

"Damn. Well, maybe this is a sign to get out of the city," Mikey says. "I couldn't imagine trying to get sober in Los Angeles."

"Yeah, I mean, it's gonna be fucking tough no matter where I do it."

"Any savings?"

"Uh, yes and no. Not a lot. We've held jobs but we very much, uh, live for the day, I guess.... So, what's the scene like in Laguna, as far as temptation goes?"

"Oh, it's completely changed. They finally repaired the electric grid at Main Beach, so no one calls it Blackout Beach anymore. They installed LED lights on the boardwalk, so it feels like a helicopter spotlight on anyone walking down it. Not to mention the cameras they attached to the lights. Remember, cameras?" Mikey giggles. "They're actually *there* now, actually watching people." Mikey and Tristan laugh together, humbled. "No one even hangs at Main Beach now except tourists, all year round. All the old faces dead, in jail, or just moved on. You couldn't find drugs here if your life depended on it. Most street corners you'd barely recognize— all the old shops now high-end chain stores. Zero affordable housing...."

He pauses.

"Except for mine. So, what would it take to get you two in there?"

On the verge of panic, Kat and Tristan both feel he's hard selling it to the point of suspicion. Tristan takes a deep breath, disappointed it sounds too god to be true.

"Man, this is really sweet of you, Mikey. And a lot, I mean... all of this makes sense and I get it, but the money just isn't there for us to make this kind of jump."

"Okay, listen—I move you guys in, no money down. The restaurant scene down here is like the mafia, so if you guys commit to staying clean, I can get you both jobs, like fucking *that*. You give me a grand a month for mortgage until you can afford the down payment and the house is yours—your name on the deed."

They're blown away.

They'd be idiots not to take it.

They've been idiots for years.

Idiocy was going to stop, right now, at this very phone call.

Tristan looks at Kat. A tear rolls down her face, she nods.

"All right, fat kid, we'll take it."

2

A month later, Mikey sits on the porch of The House, staring past the lawn. He wonders whether the term "living fast" really means that you accelerate your lifespan, speeding past all your destinations. And now that he's back here, he wants to run the other direction.

A U-Haul pulls up ass end into the driveway, their white Toyota Camry in tow. The more they inch towards him, the lighter he feels. If he is being honest, this 'gift' is more a favor to calm Mikey's neurosis than it is to help his friends. He just can't let the house go completely. He'll be comforted, or at least accustomed, to know it's still there, with people he knows occupying a space he's terrified to see empty. He's lost trust in himself and all the other things he's filled it with.

Tristan waves at Mikey. He jumps out, hop-skips straight to him, embracing his large frame, since thinned out. Kat's lips go right to Mikey's cheeks, mushy with freshly applied lipstick. "Oh my God, please don't do that," he says, chuckling yet oddly self-conscious. "My wife will get... weird."

"Man, we barely recognized the place—I imagined a new paint job, but a white-picket fence? Hilarious," Tristan says, punching his palm.

"Yeah... had to make it market worthy, make it blend in" says Mikey, rolling his eyes. "Now it's nice and inconspicuous in case we ever wanna start selling drugs again."

Laughing, he punches Tristan in the back.

Kat yelps outrageously. "Ugh, such a non-option. Next order of business after settling in is getting *this* guy off the sauce," she says, tapping Tristan's chest a little too hard. Five weeks clean and sober, Kat is committed to her new healthy lifestyle—she'll be damned if Tristan isn't going to follow her. Letting him slide during the emotional extraction of severing ties from his L.A. friends, she demands his future begins today.

"Well, shit, I'd offer to give you guys a tour, but I have a feeling you already know your way around," says Mikey.

Unloading the last box of Tristan's records into the house, they deflate on the couch, exhausted.

"So, I don't want to be a dick, but you're gonna have to get handy with this place," says Mikey. "This is your place now. I'm like, the bank, not your landlord. So, no random calls if the sink doesn't work or whatever."

"Of course. I'm looking forward to man-up like that," Tristan says. "You mentioned the previous family kept complaining about stuff though?"

"Man, the only thing wrong with this place, I'd say, is purely cosmetic. There's a patch of black mold in the basement that keeps coming back, ever since it flooded during El Nino."

Mikey digresses, illustrating the '97-'98 storm as "biblical" when the ocean wiped out the boardwalk, causing its waves to break on the movie theater, the streets becoming rivers for two months.

"Man, we thought the fires were bad... water fuuuucked this place up," he says, laughing. "Anyway, so the basement flooded, and I just never completely dealt with it. The family claimed it was giving them respiratory problems, but I'm positive they were overreacting. That stuff ain't as bad as people make it out to be."

Kat's eyes pierce with doubt; before she can counteract, Tristan swoops in. "Yeah, no biggie. Maybe I'll end up tackling it, if we do decide we want to open the basement up to possibilities."

"Knock yourself out, man. But seriously, if you don't feel like fucking with it, just pretend it's not even there."

After settling in, it's like Mikey is pretending Kat and Tristan aren't even there. Foolishly, they assumed him selling them—giving them—the house, would eventually reunite them, now older and wiser, shackled by real responsibilities. But Mikey immediately makes himself distant. When he said not to call him for repairs he meant: no, really, don't call me for anything.

They can't complain, after he got Kat a waitressing gig at a new craft cocktail bar across from Main Beach. "It'd be best if we didn't work under the same roof," he told her, explaining he'd been in and out of therapy, committed to the tools he was given.

"The Vigil was the worst case of psychotic codependence a person could ever encounter," he told her as if *he* had the PhD suddenly. "Like if obsession, detachment, denial, and sociopathy were all mixed into the same napalm." She couldn't disagree, but treating Mikey like a stranger after their long history and his enormous gift to them was hard to swallow. Especially after failing to introduce them to his wife and two kids, which they were shocked to find out he had when Kat's manager casually mentioned it. *Is he ashamed of us?* they wondered.

Growing resentful of his stable life—which they know is childish of them—soon, they are too hurt to even try to call him. Left without any friend at all in their old town, it no longer feels new; it feels foreign in ways they can't reconcile.

And now Tristan has nothing but time on his hands and it's his turn to sober up. Kat agreed to be the sole-provider for the first month he dries out, so he can hit a new job clean when he's ready to.

But after a few days… or hours… he's already stir crazy, annoyed by his own existence. Without alcohol, his pleasure receptors are confused, out of alignment; he's forgotten what fun, happiness, or relaxation is. He can actually feel the weight of every anxious moment he ever drowned in alcohol, because all those moments he only suspended, never actually dealt with. And now he feels their accumulation, crashing back with a vengeance.

Best to stay busy, maybe I'll start fixing the place up, he thinks, looking behind a new couch flushed against the neglected door to the basement, deciding to see about this alleged black mold situation down there....

After pulling the couch from the wall, he spends a fumbling minute seeing which of the three smallest keys from The House's jangling ring fit into which of the triple padlocks; the same staples and hasps installed by a teenage Rudy. Coughing, he chokes on the dead air, a wafting stench of dampness, neglect. Vivid memories invade his mind, thoughts he hasn't allowed since the last time he was down there almost eleven years ago. Thoughts he can't trust even now in real time, in real life; looking back, they feel mythic because they *felt* unreal.

Reaching the bottom stair, he pulls the chain on the exposed bulb. The room illuminates, and he shivers. Assuming he'd see something shocking, forgotten—drugs, their bloody sheets of self-mutilation—instead, there lies before him a basically clean, normal basement, empty except for his own projected torments. Part of him is disappointed, let down by his rising adrenaline revealing nothing but unreliable memories.

Scanning the room, he stops at the corner. Something that wasn't there before: an newly constructed add-on bench, a "sitting area" built into the wall. It strikes him odd, considering the previous tenants never inhabited this space.

Walking closer, a dizziness overtakes him; black mold taking residence all over the addition.

It is bad.

Sniffing closer, he coughs, fresh air a sudden luxury. He assesses; he'll have to tear the whole bench out to get to the bottom of where the black fuzz is coming from. He recalls seeing a container of bleach upstairs under the kitchen sink. He'll also need to find a hammer to tear it apart, though some of the boards are warping, nails already rising from their embeds. Piece of cake, he thinks.

Returning upstairs, he notes the wholesome Technicolor contrast, smiling with homeowner gratitude. He's already getting handy, both Captain and Swabber of his ship, a one-man navy. Grabbing the Clorox from under the sink, he opens the toolbox for the hammer, and marches back downstairs armed with tools for resolve.

He drops to his knees for quick demolition of what appears a rushed, careless job by an amateur contractor. Shaking from his skipped morning shot, he's beginning to panic how bad the rest of the day will unfold; he makes a secret deal to allow himself one beer, maybe two, when he's done down here. He tells himself he must earn it.

He eases the claw of the hammer into the first nail head, pushing the handle at an angle. Up it goes, out it comes. Another one, like butter. The nail extraction repeated on the other side of the plank, he lifts the 2x4 up off the bench, releasing a cloud of suffocating pungency into his nostrils, a stench he can taste. He gags. Five more planks to uproot. He starts on the next one, struggling with the smell he can't get used to. This one comes up even easier, the mold eaten away the bottom.

He looks down.

Adrenaline choking every pore of his being, he vomits.

A human skull stares up at him from underneath the lapels of a green '60s Teddy Boy jacket; it's brilliance once verdant, now obnoxious.

He jumps back, choking out an obscenity-speckled scream.

Hyperventilating, he tries rising to his feet, but muscle reflex lost, his body slumps back to the cement floor. Subtly convulsing, he prays it's all a DT hallucination as he crawls back to the job, peering tentatively over the half-demolished bench.

Rico.

Wearing the jacket he repossessed from Mikey, over a pair of navy-blue Dickey's. He looks down at his shoes—a pair of red Nikes he can't deny belonged to a man they vowed to kill. Accelerating roulette wheels of all the ways he could spin this: If this is Rico, where is his red puffer vest? The rest of his clothing was popular fashion back in those days, this could be anybody.

(*You're running out of bullshit*)

The smell is demurred by the sight. Whoever it is (*there you go again*), they've decomposed down to the bone, the petrified muscle remaining intact. *If you had the guts to kill a man, Tristan, don't you have the guts to look at the man you killed? I mean, he's dead. What does it matter anymore? It's not like he can be offended.*

Exercising the muscle of denial so frequently over the years, he has almost convinced himself none of this ever happened at all. Forcing himself to stare at this corpse, to rub his face in reality, he tries hating this once-person, the soul who inhabited this body. But smiles, laughs are recollected instead, instant time-travel to suppressed good times, criminal fellowship, the adrenaline of danger: pure adventure.

Looking at his watch: Katrina will be home in six hours. He could give him a proper burial, scoop what's left of a person into a trash bag and dig a hole in the backyard, maybe the garden, and... but he doesn't have the courage. *First you kill him,* then *you decide not to treat him like trash,* he reprimands himself, before he reminds himself *no one would ever know.*

Quarantine this to the buried compartments of your mind, so only you, just you, will be tormented for the rest of your life.

If he tells Kat, she'll leave him immediately, maybe even call the cops. Suddenly he doesn't trust his own girlfriend of eleven years, glossing over the fact that he's the fucking devil here.

But this wasn't just me, he thinks.

He told you not to call him, but this isn't some leaky faucet.

3

Pulling up to The House, Mikey is cursing, annoyed with Tristan, the eternal drama queen. The nerve to call his restaurant during lunch rush, then to demand he just drops everything to come over... If this was some sentimental bullshit, like *Hey, look what I found—remember this?* he's going to be pissed.

Tristan's catatonic on the porch, a thousand-mile stare.

"This better be good, Tristan."

"I'll tell you right away it's not good, just please keep your fucking voice down..." he says.

"*Oh* my fucking God."

Locking eyes to assure they both see it, down at the corpse, back to each other. Mikey begins to dissociate; Tristan snaps him back. "Don't tell me you didn't know this was down here. Your fucking hot potato house."

"Tristan, I swear to fucking God... I'm driving over here all pissed that you were gonna make me fix something—"

"—Yeah, fucking fix it."

"Dude, I have no idea what is going on."

"Where did this whole add-on come from? Is this a bench or a fucking casket?"

"No idea, man. I haven't been down here since right after Mom's memorial. I only took a quick look to make sure nothing was left behind."

"Well, as you can see, something fucking was.'"

"Man, fuck you. You were the one leading the whole campaign to snuff him."

"It was all of us, man. Someone just needed to be in charge."

Mikey's head rolls back then lurches forward; he vomits his lunch onto the cement, exacerbating the basement's stench. Oddly cathartic; now he can think a little clearer.

"Okay, first thing, that jacket. One thing I know for sure—he was not wearing this jacket that night. He was wearing shorts and a tank top. We were in the middle of a heat wave, remember? It was the one time I ever saw him without his red vest."

"Yeah it was fucking hot, but honestly... I barely recall leaving your house to meet him. I'm not even sure he came to the park!" He pauses. "What else do you remember from that night? Like, anything else, even if it seems inconsequential?"

Mikey's silent. He closes his eyes; it only reveals more darkness to his recall.

"Man, all I know is that he showed up to the park, and he was not wearing this jacket. Do you think we did this?"

"Yes, I mean... I know we did this. We planned it out, we fucking did this to a human fucking being. I mean, he's right here. It's all here."

"I just... I have this feeling there was an accident—"

"This is no accident."

"But an accident in the plan—do you remember an argument breaking out at the park that night?" says Mikey.

"You're just making shit up 'cause you're fucking scared. We need to deal with this. This is real fucking life." Tristan paces around the room, exactly like he did on the night he demanded they kill a human being. Only now he's so scared his iron will is disintegrating, rising from his own body, trapped in the dream of a ghost, banished behind stars, forbidden to return... until the cloying stench of their shared vomit pulls him all the way back. He gags, then recomposes himself to talk. "What always left me unsettled, is the way Rudy snubbed me the next day across from Blast. I feel like we have to find him, talk to him. It was a weird way to exit our lives."

"Tristan, you're clutching your fucking pearls about someone refusing to be an accomplice to murder. Again. *You* made someone exit their life!"

"Mikey, just because you're on the straight and narrow now doesn't mean you can paint me the psycho. We were all involved, man."

"If we were all involved, should we track down Jerm?"

"No, absolutely not. I felt bad enough calling you. The less people have this on their conscience, the better. This is between you and I." He pauses. "And Rudy. I'm convinced he knows something about this."

4

Replacing the planks on the bench, they reseal the homespun catacomb. Clock ticking until Kat gets off work, Mikey drives them to Rudy's uncle's place, praying he still lives there.

They spot his construction truck parked in the driveway. Running up the porch, they knock calmly.

Jorge is cordial at first, then slightly apprehensive once they identify themselves. "You know he left town because of you guys, right?"

Tristan and Mikey do the whole *everything is different now* song and dance so well that he offers up his nephew's phone number and San Francisco address. "You can try, but I don't think he wants to talk to you guys."

"What now?" asks Mikey.

"Back to The House. Rico needs a proper burial. That's one area where we can give closure." Tristan instantly regrets his wording; closure would have been a conversation, not killing somebody.

"Do you want to keep the coat, Mikey?" Shaking the remains from the other frayed clothing, the green coat has retained its integrity, a testament to vintage tailor ship, the commitment to quality materials from yesteryear.

"What am I gonna do, take it to the fucking dry-cleaners?"

"Sorry, I'm not thinking straight. I just know you loved it. We should burn the clothes, right?"

"Not here. I'll take the clothes somewhere else to torch."

Piling the remains into the black trash bag, they counteract their fear by pondering every human, not just this one, as nothing more than something that will one day rot away, regardless of morality. *We all become... earth*, thinks Tristan, feeling like dirt as he stabs the shovel into the garden's soft, fertile soil. Slow and solemn. By the third strike he picks up his pace, frantically excavating.

"I guess, when you have a conscience, you never really get away with anything," says Mikey.

"If that's the case, I would have preferred to be callous sociopath."

"Are you saying, 'preferred to be,' like you're claiming you weren't?"

Tristan, silent.

Mikey keeps watch over the fence, assuring there's no eyes beyond the neighbor's hedges. Five feet deep, only Tristan's head above ground when he calls it quits. On their knees, they lower the bag into the hole, arching all the way over so they don't drop it, a last-ditch attempt to show respect.

"Should we say anything before we cover it all up, a prayer or something?"

"Fuck, I don't know. I don't really believe in God. If I did, the last thing I'd to tell him is that we did this."

"He already knows. It's God, you idiot."

They find no footing in ruminating a Higher Power, but it prompts a philosophical verdict that's vaguely comforting: if this happened a decade ago, and if there is a God, he's already forgiven us. The battle they'll wage with their own conscience is the atonement.

The crime is the punishment.

Patting down the last batch of dirt, Tristan feels no closure; rather, the vast terror of his oncoming lifespan.

5

Mikey volunteers to drive them to San Francisco. "My wife will think I'm up to no good, but it's gotta be done." He tries convincing himself he'll be an even better man when he returns, yet it doesn't quite stick.

Tristan hates the fact he's writing Kat a note instead of telling her, or even asking her, if she minds that he'll be gone for a couple days. "Something time sensitive," he writes. "I'll explain when I get home. Don't worry." He tells himself he's not really lying since he can't be completely honest with her until he knows the whole truth.

The pair are silent for the first hour until they pass the winding hills of the Grapevine, where the stark horizon of the wide agricultural landscape settles their nerves. Catching up on books they've read, bands they're into, they attempt to keep it light, yet they're helpless against nostalgia's crashing gravity. "Hey, Fang was from the Bay Area, right?" says Mikey. "I never wanted to tell you this, but I always thought they kind of sucked. Or not as good as you claimed they were. Honestly, I was always surprised Fang and the Sex Pistols were your favorite bands—especially the Pistols, who are just like, cool I guess, but pedestrian. Beginner stuff. So I never bothered trying to figure out your weird riddle about them—"

"Sammy and Sid were murderers. Can we change the subject?"

The fresh breeze of the Bay is a brisk slap to their face. The directions lead them to Polk St. where there's a light on in the apartment. Hesitating, they call first on Mikey's Nokia cell. No answer. They speculate: Rudy wouldn't dare answer a 949 number. A payphone at the corner, they try again.

"Hello?"

"Rudy?"

236

"Rudy, this is Tristan. I'm with Mikey out here..."

CLICK!

Tristan cringes, feeling like one of Kat's old L.A. junkie friends trying to disturb someone's recovery. *This is stalking, I'm a fucking stalker*, he thinks, fixated on Rudy's apartment so he doesn't leave or turn off his lights to hide.

The window remains illuminated, a signal for them to proceed, as if he's saying, "Well, I'm right fucking here, come and get it."

Walking up the stairs. Apartment 3A, to the left of the top.

The door swings open. Still clad in denim, Rudy's hair grown out into an explosion of jet-black Johnny Thunders rocker locks, a Dead Moon patch on his jean jacket pocket. For a second they think they have wrong guy until he speaks, his animosity familiar.

"What!" says Rudy, holding a baseball bat.

"We need to talk to you, man."

"There's nothing to talk about."

"Just give us a half-hour, you'll never hear from us again. What are you gonna do, call the cops?"

Rudy takes the bat off his shoulders, resting its head on the ground like a cane.

"All right, you guys got me for a half-hour, then if I see you again, it'll only be to pull this bat from your head. Cool?"

To accelerate their exit, Rudy dives right in. "So, what— you wanna know why I stopped talking to you?"

They nod sheepishly.

"It shouldn't be that mysterious. What I tell you guys? I didn't want to be involved with any of that shit with Rico, right?"

"And you weren't, right?"

"You fucking idiots." Rudy paces for something to punch. "You guys are the sloppiest motherfuckers I've ever met. All

I was trying to do was a job for Mom and I end up doing all your fucking dirty work. The fucking beaner of the gang the whole time, huh?"

Mikey and Tristan open their mouths, no words exit.

"You killed a guy and I saved your fucking lives."

Rudy's recall is crystal clear. "Mom was pestering me to build that stoopid add-on in the basement. It was her weird-ass way of caring about us, giving us a place to sit down there, when she could have been... I dunno, maybe not doing drugs with us, for starters? She kept it between the two of us—she wanted it to be a surprise. I mean shit, it's not like I was building us a fucking swing set or some shit, you know? It just got into her head, she wouldn't let it go.

"So, when you guys were planning to do the whole thing with Rico, that's when I planned to build it. Maybe to distract me from what was going on. Or maybe to keep an eye on you guys. I was going to start that morning after. Like, hey I'm just the fucking carpenter here, right? So, I show up and no one's fucking there. You're all gone, like evacuated.

"So, I didn't notice at first when I go down there with my tools, but on my second trip down with the wood, then I see Rico, all curled up. Yeah, he was fucking dead. Head in a puddle of vomit. Whatever you gave him, it worked quick. I felt his pulse. He was out. And you motherfuckers were gone."

"Hold on, man. For one, we didn't bail," says Mikey. "The house got raided and we all got taken in. Mom, all of us. For possession."

"We dealt with him at the park," Tristan interjects. "Why would he be at the fucking house? Rico couldn't have been there, or the cops would have found him."

"Did you guys go downstairs at all?"

"No, but the cops did—that's where they found the drugs. This makes no sense."

"Well, when I showed up at noon that motherfucker was

238

down there dead as fuck. What was I supposed to think? I wanted no fucking part of killing our friend and what happens? Now, I gotta dispose of him because I'm thinking you guys just ran when you saw he was dying, like suddenly you couldn't handle it. Just like I thought. So, what did I do? I went to work, fast I could, before who fucking knows who would come down the stairs thinking I killed the guy.

"The least the guy deserved was a proper casket, some privacy to carry him into the afterlife where God could judge him. Him and I were both raised Catholic—we had an immediate bond like that, and he shared a lot of secrets with me."

He pauses.

"Do you guys even know why Rico's parents were so broke? Why he insisted on sending them money every month?"

Tristan and Mikey upturn their palms. "I mean, I think we all just assumed everyone in Mexico is broke?"

"Something happened between him and their pastor, so bad they went broke hiring lawyers. Thing is, everyone down there is Catholic—even the lawyers—so they weren't as thorough as they could've been, and they botched the case.

"Obviously, Rico got bitter. His family got desperate, so he said fuck it, started selling coke to support them, from a last resort to a way of life, all because he felt responsible for their hardships.

"Anyway, I knew I had to act quick because... well, Rico was fucking dead, but I could still maybe save you guys. I felt an obligation, maybe to atone for my own shit. Like face a copy of my own crime to make peace with it, so I could move on. But here you are, making that impossible all over again."

Mikey and Tristan listen without interjecting; the subject of murder obsoleting opinion.

"I'm gonna take a wild guess here—you guys haven't even talked to Dylan since?"

"He disappeared around the same time you did. He blamed the whole gang for what happened to him."

"For one—he should have grown a pair and immediately taken it up with Rico himself," says Rudy. "If he would have found the guts to beat the shit out of him, or at least cause his own scene, that would be all the proof anyone needed, then we all could have moved on. You should have encouraged him to stand up for himself. What'd you do instead? You made it all about you.

"So no wonder Dylan disappeared. You were gonna blow the whole thing up. You think someone who just got raped is gonna put all his friends in danger because of it? Have it turn into front page news because somebody fucking died? When you get raped, you already think it's your fault…"

Pivoting, Rudy punches a hole in his wall.

"You realize if it wasn't for me, you guys would still be in fucking prison? You made it so a rapist would never learn. What did I tell you back in '93—you can't teach someone a lesson when they're fucking dead."

He whips to the window, punching it twice until it shatters the third time.

A woman cries Rudy's name from the bedroom, a rare voice that sounds a lot like…

"Is that Jasmine?" Mikey asks.

Rudy glares, an eye reserved for each of them.

"I think you guys should leave now…"

The silence amplifies a fumbling of their bedroom doorknob. When it opens, a woman materializes from the dark room. Pushing her long amber hair aside, she fumbles to put on dark glasses; to prove she still exists, even if she'll never see herself again. "Who is here, Rudy? Was that glass?"

Jasmine has grown taller, sleeker; her hair grown past her waist, undyed to her natural auburn never seen by Tristan and Mikey. It's a pleasant shock, seeing her in such elevated attire, heightened past yesterday's threadbare slips, now in a glaringly expensive and intricate black lace evening gown trailing behind her. Like a French Morticia Adams, she is pure class eclipsing camp. Her neck is adorned with three silver chains: a large cross, the other a heart locket, the last one a brilliant turquoise broach she's compulsively rubbing with her thumb and forefinger, a source of security. Once they focus on her dark glasses, Tristan deflates, reminded she can't even witness her own beauty. Then, he recalls—even with her sight intact, she was never really able to see it.

And when Mikey says, "Jasmine?" she shrieks "Mikey!" back, smiling fearlessly, revealing two rows of golden teeth, an eccentricity loaded with more logic than mystery yet still bolsters spellbound wonder in Tristan, watching how hard she's hugging Mikey, hoping maybe there's a chance everything will be forgiven.

"Hey, Jasmine!" says Tristan.

Recoiling from Mikey, she freezes, growling through her gilded bridges. *"Get him out of here, Rudy,"* she says, pointing in Tristan's direction.

"I... I'm sorry, I'll just..." Before he can say he'll wait outside, Rudy's pushing his shoulder gently out the front door.

Feeling guilty for the sudden privilege, Mikey isn't sure where to start. "How are you doing, Jasmine? It's... really good to see you," he says.

"So good to see... uh... its good, good to have you. Anyway, I'm good," she says. "Rudy takes good care of me, so it's all good," she says, nodding her head. "I mean, I'm fucking blind but at least I can speak like a normal person now, I'm not afraid to talk anymore. I made a little... trade with myself, I guess. Or someone else did, or something else..."

Triggered by nostalgic company, Jasmine's speech trails off again.

"How'd you guys reconnect?" asks Mikey.

"Man, so my uncle found her on the boardwalk… You wanna tell the story, Jas?"

She sighs, annoyed to revisit it. "After Katrina abandoned me on the beach, I couldn't stop crying. I couldn't tell if it was day or night, but I felt safe on the sand, afraid to go beyond the boardwalk. It was pathetic—all I could do was cry Rudy's name, and luckily his uncle was walking by…"

"Listen, I'm really sorry things ended the way it did, Jasmine. I wasn't thinking straight," says Mikey. "I don't think anyone was."

"It's fine. You're fine. I just don't want to be around Tristan—or Katrina—ever again."

"Yeah, I get that. So, you've been to the doctor, obviously."

"Her doctor had a couple theories," says Rudy. "Blood infection traveling from her abscessed teeth, or something called Giant Cell Arteritis from shaving the sides of her head all the time, like it could've happened from scalp inflammation. But Jasmine wasn't really hearing any of it— she's still got her own idea."

"Which is?"

"Talk to the blind gal," says Rudy, shaking his head.

"Jasmine?"

"I mean, the last thing I saw was that flashing in the ocean, the red tide. I was so fucking high, just bawling my brains out, I know… but there was something out there… the more I stared, the more my eyes were bulging out. And since I was so high, pain wouldn't even register, so I just kept staring at this… feeling, until it was too late."

"A feeling?"

"It was communicating with me, yes. *A fucking feeling.* You know, like, I have these feelings, they don't have to make sense to tell a story… especially about the mean times…and in the meantime—*this* mean time—I think I'm done talking," she says.

Sensing her stress, Rudy wraps his arms around her from behind, giving her the confidence to speak again: "Mikey, the thing about the last thing you ever see, is that even after you go blind, you can't stop seeing it. I hate to say it, but you've made me see too much tonight," she says.

"I'm... really sorry."

"It's fine, you're fine. Honestly, compared to everything we've seen, being blind isn't so bad. It's sort of comforting," she says, walking cautiously backwards, shutting off the bedroom light.

"Sorry about that, Mikey," whispers Rudy, leading him to the front door. "She's convinced she can communicate with Rico, that's what all that *feeling* shit was all about. She's thinks she's even 'writing a book' about it," he says, air quotes matching his eye roll. "And I think you can guess who's doing all her typing while she just talks and talks and fucking *talks*...." Rudy shakes his head, smirks. "Hey, for real though—take care." Gently, he closes the door.

"We should just get a hotel tonight," says Mikey.

"Why, so we can pay to not sleep?" says Tristan. "I'll drive us home right now. I need something to focus on, distract myself."

Mikey decides not to tell his wife; to be honest about something she had nothing to do with would do more damage than good. She only knows one side of him, and he prefers to keep it that way.

In the spirit of getting clean, Tristan knows he must tell Kat about everything, even if she never sees him the same again. Even if she never wants to see him again.

Hitting the endless black ribbon of the 5 freeway by ten, it's like they're the only ones on the road, like the weight of their guilt cleared the whole highway. Even with no traffic, it's becoming the longest road trip of their lives. Tristan would have preferred white noise, congestion, something to inspire road rage—all he gets is pure regret, suffocating his heart and mind. He imagines piercing his flesh to drain it, the way they used to bleed out the speed demons; impossible, now that knows he was the demon all along.

Mikey is passed out, snoring in the passenger seat. Tristan prays sincerely for the first time in his life. His psychic dialogue overlapping and scrambled, he begs for redemption without clear focus who might judge him.

Who is judging him now?

His own standards:

A good place to start, the acknowledgment of his present values, his vow to never kill a human being ever again. Searching for his seventeen-year-old self somewhere under all those layers of armor, self-delusion, what he believed necessary to simply survive and keep moving.

That teenage version of himself finally materializes, fronting with tough guy posturing. It's instantly transparent: he was the most cowardly one, proving his small-town street-prowess by removing a man from the earth, by manipulating Mikey and the rest into believing they couldn't be men unless they killed another man. Finally, once the final veil fades and Tristan has a clear vision of himself at seventeen, he's not sure whether to hug him or kill him.

6

Pulling up to The House just before dawn, Tristan hands over the keys. Mikey grabs his hand, pulling him close, the tightest embrace they've shared since Mom's memorial.

"Good luck with Kat, man. Call me and let me know how it goes?"

"You sure I'm allowed to? I don't want to intrude on your life, man."

"Hey, you are my life. It wasn't doing anyone any good pretending like you weren't just right down the street."

They squeeze once more. It's difficult to let go. Standing in the middle of the street, he watches Mikey drive off, then looks at the house—once a house of secrets, now a parlor in front of a one-man cemetery.

It's all on him what it becomes next.

Walking up the porch, he sits, staring at the street. Knowing she's fast asleep inside, he doesn't want to disturb her. He'll disturb her plenty once she wakes up.

Waking up alone on the couch, it takes Tristan a second to realize this wasn't his doghouse yet. He remembers being woken on the porch by Kat, who then tucked him in on the sofa when he refused to sleep in their bedroom. Vowing to tell her everything before allowing himself the privilege of sharing the bed with her again, he required that extra pressure of discomfort to ensure he'd follow through.

He cringes at the sweet note she left him, considering he just disappeared for twenty-four hours. *I'm at work until 8pm, but when I get home I wanna hear all about your trip! Love, Kat*

Reading it only reminds him how bad he was about to destroy her.

Rushing in the door, Kat gives Tristan the biggest hug he does not deserve, culminating in a certain grinding of her waist, suggesting an impending fuck—which, for once, is the last thing on his mind. It's cruel to see her in this loving of mood, a dread polarity to what will soon follow. Tonight might be the last time she touches him, and he can't even savor the affection, knowing he's about to sever their union.

It's nearly ballet the way she's twirling around the table, arranging forks, knives, and plates for their first new home-cooked meal. *Maybe I should tell her after dinner?* he thinks. *If I tell her during dinner, she might lose her appetite. If I wait until after dinner, she might throw it all up.*

Tristan serves up the pasta, his hands shaking, the sauce sanguine. "Let me know when you want me to stop," he says, instead of *say when.*

"So, what were you guys doing in S.F.?"

"Rudy invited us up," Tristan says, in disbelief that he is already lying.

"Oh, Rudy? Wow, that's awesome!"

"He didn't exactly invite us up, truth be told. But we found out where he lives, decided to surprise him. You know how I always felt uneasy about the way he skipped town without telling anyone."

"Sure, I can imagine, honey."

No, you can't imagine, he thinks; it's strange being called "honey" before he turns her forever bitter.

7

With ten minutes left of his shift, Mikey runs to the parking lot to stare at his car, cursing at himself for leaving Rico's clothes in the trunk this whole time. "Fuck. Parade it all around California, why don't you?" he mumbles.

He walks out, hesitates, then reminds himself he's the boss—he can do whatever he wants. Confirming he's the only one out there, he approaches the car, acting natural. *Why wouldn't I decide to clean out my car with the last ten minutes of my shift,* he overthinks.

Fatefully, he's parked next to the dumpster. A lot of trouble to burn the clothes when he can just throw it in the trash. He reminds himself: he and Tristan are the only ones who know about this. He recalls the irony, when Tristan claimed *no one would care if Rico died,* no idea a decade later he and Mikey would be the ones who cared the most.

Opening the trunk, one eye on the kitchen's backdoor until the hatch obscures the view. Focusing on the clothes, a deep breath fills his lungs with unwanted nostalgia. Staring at the jacket, marveling how this whole mess, the whole downfall of his youth and someone's actual living, breathing life all started with what was inside this pocket. His hand darts into the same fateful spot, where that ball of meth was behind the lapel, some unseen force making him mime the past.

He feels a piece of paper. *Money or a stray bindle, heroin or speed?* he wonders. He yanks out an old flyer for a Stitches show they all went to, the same one they sloppily hung up in the basement before it turned into an abattoir.

Flipping it over, there's Rico's distinct tiny handwriting. An inch from his face, he reads it feverishly, skipping lines before starting over again, re-reading the scrawl three times. Like going backwards through a wind-tunnel, the pressure of a decade-long guilt finally dissipates.

A suicide note.

Hands trembling like he's holding the most cursed, sorrow-laced winning lottery ticket, he rips out his phone to call Tristan, praying it's not too late.

8

"What are you trying to tell me, baby? Why are you crying?"

"I'm sorry... Just give me a second." He doesn't want to hear himself say it any more than he wants her to hear him say it.

He grabs the ringing phone for one last stall—Mikey repeats Tristan's name frantically over the line so he takes it into the bedroom.

Thirty seconds later, an alarming exclamation, a confused orgasm straddling agony and ecstasy, trailing into spent relief.

"Read it to me!" he says.

Opening the door, Kat sees Tristan laying on the ground, collapsed. "I'm okay," he mouths to her, raising his finger up to say, "Just give me a second here."

I came here this morning for redemption from you all but maybe it is better no one is here. I see now how I must finally stop seeking redemption from a congregation. I'm sorry you had to find me like this, but those who take their own lives aren't allowed a proper burial.

I know what you guys were trying to do last night. I may be careless, but I'm not fucking stupid. You can treat me like a monster, but I refuse to be treated like an idiot.

Maybe next time use guns you fucking pussies.

I stayed up all night, thinking about what I did to Dylan. Yes, this is a confession, but one I don't know how to fit an apology into, because when it happened to me, no sorry could ever make it better. In fact, I wanted to kill Pastor Juan.

When I realized what you guys were going to do to me, the way you all stopped talking when I opened my beer, I started swinging at you, because when I was your age, I made a promise to myself that no one would overpower me ever again. But now Santa Ana is after me too, and they have guns.

In Catholicism to kill yourself is the greatest sin. I will finally remove myself from its hands in the most defiant way I can, on my own terms, and if I awake in the fires of Hell, it won't be God punishing me for what I stole since he never punished anyone for what was stolen from me.

With love and mercy, Rico

Mikey arrives at the house twenty minutes later. He hands it to Tristan—he reads it one more time so he can see it with his own eyes.

"Mikey, I think Rico was trying to give you the jacket the morning after," says Tristan, staring at the letter.

"Just give me the fucking letter already," Katrina says, grabbing it from Tristan. Covering her mouth as she reads, she breaks into tears. "What... the fuck?" she repeats.

They tell her everything—from displaced adolescent revenge to years of disembodied denial to the discovery in the basement two days ago.

"Kat, there's no easy way to say this, but he's in the garden now," says Tristan, watching her walk down the hall to the backyard, her hands covering her face.

"I found his prescription of Klonopin in the other pocket," Mikey tells Tristan. "It was empty, so I'm guessing that's how he did it."

"I need a fucking drink," says Kat, returning to the living room. "I'm going to have a drink, Tristan. But not here. I need to be... not here. Like, anonymous. Is there anywhere we could go?"

"We could go to the Boom Boom Room," says Mikey. "It's changed owners—called Victor Victoria now."

"Okay, but I just want it to be the three of us," she says. "The gay bar is good—we won't know anyone there."

Mikey buys a round of boilermakers to their table in the corner, away from the bustle of the Friday night crowd. Raising their cheap blended whiskeys, releasing the spirits from their eternal thirst. The booze opens the floodgates, letting it all out; dissecting the past, relating it to the present and their uncertain futures. Noticing how fast Kat is drinking, Tristan fades from her and Mikey's conversation, to where a buried truth pummels him: he wonders why, exactly, they're so relieved now, pondering the narcissism it takes to celebrate evading a life sentence in prison; when, if it wasn't for them, Rico would still be alive. The tightening on his chest puts pressure on his mind, searching for a way to escape all over again.

Then, across the room:

"Is that... Dylan?"

The three of them zero in on their estranged friend; now a pretty blonde, and from the looks of his packed table, quite popular. He's holding court, talking the loudest, communicating something wild with his hands, triggering his friends to hysterics.

Kat is already up, heading to his table. Sneaking up on him from behind, she wraps her arms around his ribs, her head on his shoulder. He whips around: a *no-fucking-way* smile beams across his face. She points to Mikey and Tristan—they see him smile and wave; he starts to walk over, stops. They see her mouth the words *trust me* as she takes him by the arm. He runs up tackling them, suddenly fearless. They return the embrace with equal fervor. He sits down. "Holy shit," they all repeat, exhaling. Kat whispers in Dylan's ear, then turns to Mikey. "Can I see that note?" She grabs Dylan. "I'm gonna take him for a walk on the beach, okay?"

Tristan nods, looks at Mikey; they down the rest of their pints, a race to forget.

When she wakes up with the bed to herself at noon, Katrina's realizes it'll be her first day alone since they moved back to Laguna. Recalling the night before: how on their fourth pint, Mikey got a call from his bistro, informing him one of his servers walked out mid-shift. Mikey immediately offered Tristan the position. "The only thing is—you must start training first thing tomorrow. And to make matters worse: you're going to be very, very hungover," he said, before Tristan graciously accepted, slurring thank you, again and again.

By the time she's woken up, Tristan is at work; a miracle he made it there on time after she had to use all her strength to hold him up on the walk home last night, then made sure he made it to the toilet in time to vomit. It felt powerful, symbolic—like they were finally flushing everything away.

But here she is, alone, on the couch under the front window, sipping her morning coffee. It should be a comforting moment of awakening, of new beginnings, but the caffeine makes her fixate on the backyard she's in direct view of, a straight shot at the end of the hallway.

Taking a sip, it's gone cold. She finishes it in one reluctant gulp. A jolt to her brain reanimates her from the couch, to walk down the hall, down the couple of steps to the lawn out back. It's painfully obvious, the mound by the garden, where the remains of her friend lay. They didn't even bother to hide the shovel.

Maybe it's the caffeine making her mind race, and she knows it's masochistic, but she feels an urge to see what's left of Rico; unsettled, or even selfishly left out, from the boy's final viewing, even if it's not really him anymore. Suddenly, she feels she hasn't been through enough—a need to rub her face in the cold, soiled reality of it, to make it that much more tangible to process.

Checking her watch, she sees Tristan won't be home for six hours. Wondering if she's projecting reverse deja vu, like when Tristan kept checking the time, calculating digging a hole versus what time she would be home, because the shovel is already in her hand stabbing the warm Earth. She's so nervous she misses the mound, just to the right of where she meant to dig, making a metallic scrape when it should have been an easy slide into dirt. A resistance instead of envelopment.

Something clicks in her mind, making her forget about her dead friend, if just for a second. She plunges the shovel into the same spot.

Knowing exactly what it is, she keeps digging until she can see it with her own eyes. Finally exposed, she falls to her knees to unearth the mason jar packed with cash. She nearly faints with excitement—she knows there's tons more where this came from, buried all over the yard from back when they didn't have back accounts, only paranoia.

Unscrewing the lid, she grabs the tufts of green bills from the jar. She starts counting, careful to organize for immediate deposit, in their responsible adult bank account.

She counts $3,900 in this one and resumes exhuming.

In an hour, she's recovered nineteen jars, counting the total at $60,320. She immediately wants to call Tristan at work but thinks it would be even better if she told him to look up their balance. A nice surprise; Tristan wouldn't have to see all the dirty money.

She gets it all tightened up, organized by size of bill to make it easier on the cashier. It's making her incredibly anxious having all this money, especially since she'll have to walk to the bank with all of this naked cash in her backpack.

She starts walking, tries to keep a peripheral sight, assuring no one is following her, but she caves when she grabs Rico's old ID out of her wallet. It's something she did often throughout the years, looking at me for reassurance when she was nervous about something, but now she's looking at my parent's address, igniting a crazy idea that just seems like the right thing to do even if it's a gamble and she'd be gone for 24 hours into another country, and she's arguing with me, body against spirit, neither can tell what is right or wrong or even sane until she leaps from faith, falling from grace, and she's turning around, walking back home, getting in the car, and starting the engine.

You just fucking do it.

Thank you:

Jeff Schneider at Pig Roast Publishing.

Lisa Carver for editing. I've never had that much fun with an editor in my life.

Ruby Wells for copyediting.

Elle Nash for assistance ax-hacking/reimagining. I'm truly grateful that her extensive editorial notes and unorthodox approach helped me realign the course of this novel.

Corinne Halbert for the cover art—a true honor.

James Nulick for last minute recommendations.

William Duryea, Rudy Johnson, and the regulars at Misery Loves Company for facilitating/listening to developing drafts.

Early beta-readers: Seth Miller, Jack Chandelier, Stephen J. Golds, and Anthony Todaro.

Special thanks to Scott Miller at Trident Media Group who spent a year hustling an earlier 450-page version of this novel, formerly *The Devils of Blackout Beach*. It was a thrill while it lasted.

Dedicated to 461.

Gabriel Hart lives in California's high desert. He's the author of *Fallout from Our Asphalt Hell, Virgins in Reverse/The Intrusion,* and two volumes of poetry: *Unsongs* and *Hymns from The Whipping Post.* He's written countless short stories, including "Crossing Alvarado," nominated for *Best American Mystery and Suspense* in 2022. Other works can be found at *Expat Press, Hobart Pulp, Apocalypse Confidential,* and *Rock and A Hard Place.*

Hart is the Editor-in-Chief at *Beyond the Last Estate,* a literature/arts magazine launched in 2024. His literary journalism has appeared in *Lit Reactor, Los Angeles Review of Books, Cemetery Dance,* and *3am.*

www.gabrielhart.net